monsoonbooks

Stephen Leather is one of the UK's most successful thriller writers with twenty-seven books to his name. including the bestselling Thailand novel *Private Dancer*. Before becoming a novelist he was a journalist for more than ten years on newspapers such as *The Times* and the *Daily Mail* in the UK and the *South China Morning Post* in Hong Kong. Before that, he was employed as a biochemist for ICI, shovelled limestone in a quarry, worked as a baker, a petrol pump attendant, a barman and worked for the Inland Revenue. He began writing full time in 1992. Stephen Leather's bestsellers have been translated into more than ten languages. You can find out more from his website, *www.stephenleather.com*.

T0167956

BANGKOK BOB
AND THE
MISSING MORMON

STEPHEN LEATHER

monsoon

monsoonbooks

Published in 2011
by Monsoon Books Pte Ltd
71 Ayer Rajah Crescent #01-01
Mediapolis Phase Ø, Singapore 139951
www.monsoonbooks.com.sg

First published in Thailand in 2011 by Three Elephants.
www.threeelephants.com

ISBN: 978-981-08-7776-7

National Library Board, Singapore Cataloguing-in-Publication Data
Leather, Stephen.
Bangkok Bob and the missing Mormon / Stephen Leather. – Singapore :
Monsoon Books, 2011.
p. cm.
ISBN : 978-981-08-7776-7 (pbk.)

1. Private investigators – Thailand – Bangkok – Fiction. I. Title.

PR6062.E27
823.914 -- dc22   OCN693786042

Printed in Singapore
15 14 13 12 11   1 2 3 4 5

1

She was wearing a lurid Versace silk shirt, had a diamond-studded Rolex watch on her wrist, diamante Gucci sunglasses perched on top of her head and a Louis Vuitton handbag on her lap. She pretty much had all brand name bases covered but she still looked like a sixty-year-old woman with more money than taste. She had brought her large Mercedes to a stop next to a fruit stall and she wound down the passenger side window and waved a ring-encrusted hand at the fruit vendor. I was sitting behind her in a taxi that had only just managed to avoid slamming into her trunk.

The fruit vendor was also in her sixties but had clearly had a much harder life than the woman in the Mercedes. Her face was pockmarked with old acne scars and her stomach bulged against her stained apron as she weighed out mangoes for a young housewife. The fruit vendor pocketed the housewife's money and waddled over to the car and bent down to listen to the woman, then nodded and hurried back to her stall. The driver tapped out a number on her cellphone and began an animated conversation.

'Hi-so,' said my taxi driver, pulling a face. He wound down his window, cleared his throat, and spat a stream of greenish phlegm into the street.

Hi-so.

High society.

From a good family. But in Thailand being from a good family didn't necessarily equate to good manners. The woman in the Mercedes almost certainly wasn't aware of the dozen or so cars waiting patiently for her to get out of the way. And even if she was aware, she wouldn't have cared. After all, she had the Mercedes and the diamond-encrusted Rolex and we didn't so it really didn't matter that she was holding us up. It was the natural order of things.

There was no point in getting upset. She would move when she was ready, and not before and there was nothing that I or the taxi driver could say or do that would change that. Acceptance was the only option.

The Thais have an expression for it.

Jai yen.

Cool heart.

Don't worry.

Be happy.

Sometimes, for emphasis, they say jai yen yen.

Real cool heart.

I settled back in my seat and turned to the letters page of the *Bangkok Post*. A reader in Chiang Mai was complaining about the air quality. The farmers around the city were carrying out their annual field burnings and the mayor had warned the population to stay indoors with their windows closed. A Manchester City fan was complaining that he could only get a Thai commentary for his team's last match. A reader in Bangkok was complaining about his erratic cable wi-fi service. For many people Thailand was the Land Of Smiles, but the average *Bangkok Post* reader seemed to spend most of his time complaining about the state of the country.

The fruit vendor hurried over to the Mercedes with a bag of mangoes. She handed them through the window. The woman put her cellphone on the dashboard and then took the mangoes out of the bag one by one, sniffing them and squeezing them to check their ripeness. She rejected one, and the fruit vendor went back to her stall to replace it. The woman picked up her cellphone and resumed her conversation.

I twisted around in my seat. There were now two dozen cars behind us, and a bus. The air was shimmering with exhaust fumes.

Jai yen.

I went back to my paper. A tourist from Norway was complaining of the double pricing for foreigners at the Lumpini Boxing Stadium. Tourists paid up to ten times what locals were charged, she said, and that wasn't fair. I smiled. Fairness wasn't a concept that necessarily applied to Thailand, especially where foreigners were concerned.

The fruit vendor returned with a replacement mango. The woman smelled it, squeezed it, then put it into the carrier bag. She opened her Louis Vuitton handbag and took out a Prada purse and handed the vendor a red hundred baht note. The vendor zipped open the bag around her waist, slipped in the banknote and took out the woman's change. The woman took the change, checked it, put the money into the Prada purse, put the purse into her handbag, placed it on the passenger seat and closed the window. I didn't see her thank the fruit vendor, but that was par for the course for Thailand. Women who drove expensive imported cars did not generally say 'please' or 'thank you', at least not to fruit vendors. The window wound up, the woman checked her make-up in her driving mirror, then put the Mercedes into gear.

We were off.

Finally.

Jai yen.

The taxi moved forward. The Mercedes lady was talking on her cellphone again. She indicated a right turn but then turned left on to

Sukhumvit Road, oblivious to the motorcycle that narrowly missed slamming into her offside wing.

The traffic light turned red and the taxi jerked to a halt. There were two policemen sitting in the booth across the road from us. It was getting close to the end of the month which meant that the police were looking for any excuse to pull over motorists and either issue a ticket to meet their quota or collect some tea money to pay their minor wife's rent. Bangkok's traffic light system was perfectly capable of being co-ordinated by a multi-million-pound computer system but more often than not the police would override it and do the changes manually, using walkie-talkies to liaise with their colleagues down the road. That meant that when a light turned red, you had no idea how long it would stay that way. Your fate lay in the hands of a man in a tight-fitting brown uniform with a gun on his hip.

Jai yen.

I went back to my paper. My taxi driver wound down his window and spat throatily into the street again.

Just another day in Paradise.

Not.

2

YING IS A STUNNER. A little over five feet tall with waist-length glossy black hair and cheekbones you could cut steel plate with, a trim waist and breasts that are, frankly, spectacular.

Whoa, hoss.

Stop right there.

I'm married and old enough to be her father.

And I'm her boss, hoss.

She looked over her shoulder and flashed her perfect white teeth at me as I walked into the shop.

My shop.

Dao-Nok Antiques. It's sort of a pun on my name. Dao-Nok is Thai for turtle-bird and my name's Turtledove. I'm not sure if anyone else gets it but it makes me smile.

Ying was carefully rolling bubble wrap around a wooden Chinese screen that we were shipping to Belgium. 'Good morning Khun Bob,' she said.

Khun. It means mister, but it's also a sign of respect. She respects me because I'm older than her and because I'm her boss.

'You are late,' she added, still smiling.

Not much respect there. But she wasn't being critical, she was just stating a fact. I was normally in the shop by nine and it was now nine-thirty.

'There was a mango queue,' I said.

'I see,' she said, even though she didn't.

'All the way down Soi Thonglor.'

'I told them you wouldn't be long.'

'I see,' I said, even though I didn't.

'They're waiting, in your office.'

I frowned. 'And they would be ...?'

'An American couple. They need your help.'

There was a coffee maker by the cash register and I poured myself a cup and took it upstairs. The door to my office was open and my two visitors looked up, smiling hesitantly. He was a big man run to fat, in his mid to late forties. His wife was half his size , with wispy blonde hair, and probably five years younger. He pushed himself up out of his chair and offered me his hand. It was a big hand, almost square with the fingernails neatly-clipped, but it had no strength in it when we shook. 'Jonathon Clare,' he said in a Midwestern accent. 'This is my wife Isabelle.'

'Nice to meet you, Mr Clare,' I said. Mrs Clare smiled and offered me her hand. It was a child's hand, milk-white skin with delicate fingers as brittle as porcelain. 'Mrs Clare,' I said, shaking her hand as carefully as possible. I went and sat behind my desk and flashed them a reassuring smile. 'So how can I help you?' I asked.

'Matt Richards at the embassy said that you might be able to find our son,' said Mr Clare, dropping back into his chair. It creaked under his weight.

I nodded. Matt Richards was an attaché at the US Embassy. He was an acquaintance rather than a friend, someone I bumped into from time to time on the cocktail party circuit. He was an affable enough guy but hard to get close to. I kind of figured he was a spook, CIA or maybe DEA. Whatever, he was cagey enough never to let his guard down with me and I never really cared enough to do any serious probing. It wasn't the first time he'd sent along people who needed help that the embassy couldn't – or wouldn't – provide.

I picked up a pen and reached for a yellow legal pad. There were a whole host of questions that I'd need answering, but from experience I'd found that it was often better just to let them get it off their chests as quickly as possible. 'I'm listening,' I said.

Mr Clare looked across at his wife and she nodded at him with raised eyebrows. He was twice her size but I got the feeling that she was the one who ruled the roost in the Clare household. 'We're Mormons,' he said, slowly. 'From Salt Lake City. Utah. I'm telling you that because I want you to know that Jon Junior is a God-fearing boy who has honoured his mother and father since the day he was born. He's not a boy to go wandering off without telling us where he's going and what he's doing.'

Mr Clare reached inside his suit jacket and slid a colour photograph across the desk. I picked it up. It was a graduation photograph, Jon Junior grinning at the camera with an all-American smile, his wheat-coloured hair sticking out from under a mortarboard, his blue eyes gleaming with triumph, a diploma in his hand.

'Second in his class,' said Mr Clare proudly. 'Scholarships all the way. A man couldn't ask for a better son.'

'The apple of our eye,' said Mrs Clare, nodding in agreement.

'How old is he?' I asked.

'Twenty-one,' said Mr Clare.

'Twenty-two next month,' added his wife.

Mr Clare handed me a sheet of paper. 'We have a photocopy of Jon Junior's passport. We also told him to photocopy all his important documents. You can never be too careful.'

'Indeed,' I said.

'We've already got his birthday present,' said Mr Clare. 'A digital camera. State of the art.'

Mrs Clare reached over and held her husband's hand. He smiled at her with tight lips.

'And he's in Thailand?' I asked.

'He came two months ago,' said Mr Clare. 'He wanted to take some time off before joining me in the family business. Janitorial supplies. Cleaning equipment. We're one of the biggest in the state. There's barely a hospital or school in Utah that doesn't have our soap in its dispensers.'

I decided it was time to cut to the chase before I got the complete Clare family history. 'And when was the last time you heard from Jon Junior?' I asked.

'Three weeks ago,' said Mr Clare. 'He phoned us every week. And wrote. Letters. Postcards.'

'Do you remember when exactly he phoned?'

Mr Clare looked over at his wife. 'March the seventh,' she said. 'It was a Sunday. He always phoned on a Sunday.'

'And when did he fly in?'

Mr Clare looked over at his wife again. 'January the sixteenth,' she said.

'Did he apply for a visa in the States?' I asked.

'Why does that matter?' asked Mr Clare.

'If you apply for a tourist visa overseas then you get sixty days, which can be extended for a further thirty days,' I explained. 'If you arrive without a visa, immigration will give you thirty days in which case Jon Junior will have overstayed.'

'Is that bad?' asked Mrs Clare.

'It's not too serious,' I said.

And in the grand scheme of things, it wasn't.

Mr Clare was nodding. 'He applied to the Thai Consulate in

Chicago. He had a visa.'

I made a note. 'And which airline did he use?'

'Delta,' said Mr Clare. 'He flew through Seattle.'

I made another note, then looked up, smiling reassuringly. They seemed less worried now that I was asking for specific information. 'The letters that Jon Junior sent, do you have them?'

Mr Clare nodded and looked across at his wife. She clicked open a small black handbag and handed me half a dozen airmail envelopes. I put them down next to the photograph.

'And since the phone call, you haven't heard from him?'

The Clares shook their heads. 'Not a word,' said the father. 'And we've spoken to our bank in Salt Lake City and he hasn't used his credit card since he spoke to us.'

'What sort of phone did he have? Did he use a local Sim card? With a Thai number?'

Mr Clare nodded. 'He bought it soon after he arrived. We've called it several times. The first time it was answered by a Thai man but since then it's been switched off.'

I pushed a notepad towards him and asked him to write down the number.

'What about emails?' I asked. 'Did he email you?'

'We're not big fans of emails,' said Mrs Clare. 'I also say that if it's important enough to write, then it's important enough to put down on paper.'

'He did have an email account, but that was just for friends,' said Mr Clare. 'With his mother and I, he wrote or phoned.'

I asked him to write down the email address. 'He came here as a tourist, right? He was just here on vacation?'

'He was a tourist, but he said he was going to get a job teaching English,' said Mr Clare.

I sat back in my chair. 'I thought you said he was just taking a break before joining you in the family firm.'

'He changed his mind. He said he'd fallen in love with the place.'

'With the place? Or with someone?'

Mr Clare frowned. 'What are getting at?'

'He might have met a girl. Or a boy.'

'Our son is not gay, Mr Turtledove,' said Mrs Clare, icily.

'I bet he could have teamed up with a guy he'd met. Maybe gone up country, trekking with the hilltribes. It's easy to lose track of time when you're in the jungle. Or maybe he met a girl. Thailand is full of beautiful women.'

'Our son is a virgin,' Mrs Clare said. 'He is a virgin and will be on his wedding day. He has promised us that.'

I tried not to smile but I figured that any red blooded twenty-one-year-old male would have a hard time clinging on to his virginity in Thailand.

'I am serious, Mr Turtledove,' said Mrs Clare. 'Our son believes in the Bible as the word of our Lord. Besides, if he had met a girl, he would have told us. Our son tells us everything.'

'How many children do you have?' I asked.

'Six,' said Mr Clare. 'Three girls. Three boys. Jon Junior is the oldest.'

'And has he been in touch with any of his siblings?'

Mr Clare's brow furrowed. 'I told you, he hasn't been in touch since the last phone call.'

'You said you hadn't heard from him. That doesn't mean he hasn't been in contact with his brothers and sisters.'

'They would have told us,' said Mr Clare. He folded his arms and sat back in his chair and glared at me as if daring me to contradict him.

I doodled on the notepad. 'How was your last conversation with Jon Junior?' I asked.

His glare darkened. 'Now what are you suggesting?'

I kept looking at the pad. The doodle was turning into an angel with spreading wings. 'Jon Junior came out here on a holiday, then he calls you to say he wants to work here. He's your eldest boy and you were expecting him to work in the family firm, so it must have come as a shock.'

'A surprise, yes.'

'So did you argue with him?'

'We had an exchange of views.'

'And you weren't happy about his career change?'

Mr Clare tutted. 'He wanted to throw away his education to live in the Third World, in a country which hasn't even opened itself up to the Lord.'

'It's a Buddhist country, but there are Christians here. And churches.'

'That's not the point,' said Mr Clare. 'I didn't want him throwing away the opportunities he had worked for.'

'So you did argue?'

'I don't like what you're suggesting,' said Mr Clare. 'You're making it sound as if I chased him away. I didn't, Mr Turtledove. We discussed his plans, and we agreed that he should give it a go. If he wanted to be a teacher, that was up to him. But yes, I made my feelings clear on the subject, of course I did.'

Mrs Clare patted her husband on the shoulder. 'Teaching is noble occupation, and we told him so,' she said. 'We suggested that if he wanted to teach, he should come back to Utah. He said he wanted to teach in Thailand, for a while at least, and we gave him our blessing. We said that he should try teaching in Thailand for a year.'

'Then he would come back to Utah,' said Mr Clare. 'That's how we left it.'

'We have also taught our children to follow their own path, but to use the Lord as their guide,' said Mrs Clare.

'When he said goodbye, he said he loved us and that he'd call again in a week,' said Mr Clare. 'That was the last we heard from him.'

I looked down at the doodle again. I'd drawn horns on the angel and I flipped over the page before the Clares could see what I'd done. 'Do you have an address for him?'

'He was staying at a hotel in Sukhumvit Road but when we spoke he told us that he was checking out and moving into an apartment. He said he'd write to us with the address.'

I asked him for the address of the hotel and wrote it down.

'We've already been there,' said Mrs Clare. 'So have the police. He checked out, just as he said he did.'

'You've spoken to the police?'

Mr Clare shook his head. 'The embassy said they'd spoken to them. And they said that they had checked all the hospitals.'

I nodded and smiled but didn't tell them that in Thailand what people said they had done didn't always match up with what had actually happened. More often than not you were told what you wanted to hear.

'Did he tell you where he was going to be teaching?'

'A small school, not far from his new apartment,' said Mr Clare. 'I don't remember if he told me the name.'

'Did Jon Junior have any teaching qualifications?' I asked.

Mrs Clare shook her head. 'Not specifically,' she said. 'But he did help tutor at a local school some weekends.'

'Did he mention anyone he'd met here? Any friends?'

'No one specifically,' said Mr Clare.

'Do you think you can find our son, Mr Turtledove?' asked Mrs Clare, her hands fiddling in her lap.

'I'll do my best,' I said, and I meant it.

She looked at me earnestly, hoping for more information and I smiled as reassuringly as I could. I wanted to tell her that doing my best was all I could promise, that whether or not I found him would be as much down to luck and fate as to the amount of effort I put into it. I wanted to explain what it was like in Thailand, but there was no easy way to put it into words and if I did try to explain then they'd think that I was a few cards short of a full deck.

When a crime takes place in the West, more often than not it's solved by meat and potatoes police work. The police gather evidence, speak to witnesses, identify a suspect and, hopefully, arrest him. In Thailand, the police generally have a pretty good idea of who has committed a crime and then they work backwards to get the evidence to convict him. Or if the perpetrator has enough money or connections to buy himself out of trouble, then they look for evidence to convict someone else. The end result is the same, but the approach is totally different. What I really wanted to tell Mr and Mrs Clare that the best way of finding where Jon Junior had gone would be to find out where he was and if that sounds a bit like Alice in Wonderland, then welcome to Thailand. But I didn't. I just kept on smiling reassuringly.

'Do you think we should stay in Bangkok?' asked Mr Clare.

I shrugged. 'That's up to you. But I can't offer any guarantees of how long it could take. I might be lucky and find him after a couple of phone calls. Or I might still be looking for him in two months.'

'It's just that my cousin Jeb is minding the shop, and when the good Lord was handing out business acumen, Jeb was standing at the back of the queue playing with his Gameboy.' He held up his hands. 'Not that money's an issue, it's not. But Mr Richards said there wasn't much that Mrs Clare and I could do ourselves, not being able to speak the language and all.'

I nodded sympathetically. 'He's probably right. You'd only be a day away if you were back in Utah. As soon as I found anything, I'd call you.'

'God bless you, Mr Turtledove,' said Mrs Clare, and she reached over and patted the back of my hand. She looked into my eyes with such intensity that for a moment I believed that a blessing from her might actually count for something.

'I would say one thing, just to put your minds at rest,' I said. 'If anything really bad had happened, the police would probably know about it and the embassy would have been informed. And if he'd been robbed, his credit card would have been used, here or elsewhere in the world. If it had been theft, they wouldn't have thrown the card away.'

'You're saying you don't think that he's dead, that's what you're saying?' said Mrs Clare.

I nodded and looked into her eyes and tried to make it look as if my opinion might actually count for something.

Her husband was leaning forward, his eyes narrowing as if he had the start of a headache. He looked like a man who had something on his mind.

'Is there something else, Mr Clare? Something worrying you?'

He looked over at his wife and she flashed him a quick, uncomfortable smile. Yes, there was something else, something that was painful that they didn't want to talk about.

'We read something in the paper, about a fire,' said Mr Clare. 'In a nightclub.'

'Jon Junior wouldn't be in a nightclub,' said his wife, quickly.

Too quickly.

The nightclub they were talking about was the Kube. Two hundred and eighteen people had died. A lot had been foreigners. Most of the bodies still hadn't been identified.

I nodded and tried to look reassuring. 'That was last week,' I said.

March the thirteenth, to be exact. A Saturday.

'We wondered...' said Mr Clare. 'We thought...' He shuddered and Mrs Clare reached over to hold his hand.

'Jon Junior doesn't go to nightclubs,' said Mrs Clare. 'He doesn't drink. He doesn't like the music.'

'If...' said Mr Clare, but then he winced as if he didn't want to finish the sentence. I tried an even more reassuring smile to see if that would help. To my surprise, it did. 'If Jon Junior was by any chance involved... in the fire.' He rubbed his face with both hands. 'Would they tell us? Would they even know? They said that the bodies ...' He shuddered.

Burnt beyond recognition. That's what they'd said.

The more salacious Thai newspapers had run pictures of the aftermath of the fire and it wasn't pretty. I could see why the Clares wouldn't want to talk about the possibility of their son being among the dead.

'I really don't think that's likely,' I said, and I meant it.

'But they haven't identified all the bodies,' said Mr Clare, happier to talk about it now that I'd downplayed it as a possibility. 'And there were a lot of foreigners. More than fifty they said in the *Tribune*.'

'That's true. But there are other considerations.'

'Considerations?' echoed Mrs Clare.

'If Jon Junior had been living in Bangkok and had been in the nightclub, his friends would have noticed. Or the people he lived with. Or the people he worked with. Some one would have realised that he wasn't around.'

'That's what I said,' said Mr Clare, nodding. He patted his wife's hand. 'That's exactly what I said.' He flashed a tight smile at me as if to thank me for the reassurance. 'But you will check, right?'

'Of course I will.'

'And how much do you charge?' asked Mr Clare.

'That's difficult to say,' I said. 'I'm not a private detective, I don't charge by the hour.'

'You sell antiques, Mr Richards said,' said Mrs Clare.

'That's my main business, but I've been here for almost fifteen years so I have a fair idea of how the place works. I'll ask around and I can try a few leads that the police wouldn't necessarily think of.'

'He said you used to be a police officer.'

'In another life,' I said.

'In the States?'

I smiled thinly. 'It's not something I talk about, much.'

Hardly at all, in fact. Too many bad memories.

'I understand,' said Mr Clare. 'Mr Richards said you were a good man. And reliable.'

'That was nice of him,' I said, though I figured what Matt Richards was really doing was getting the Clares out of his hair as quickly as possible. 'I'll start by making a few calls, see if I can find out where he was planning to live and work, and take it from there. I'd expect you to cover any expenses, and then when I've finished I'll let you know how much work I've done and you can pay me what you think that's worth.'

'That's a strange way of doing business, Mr Turtledove.'

'It's a strange country, Mr Clare. But things have a way of working out for the best here.'

3

So, ALL I HAD to do was to find one lost American in the Village of Olives. That's how Bangkok translates, I kid you not. Bang means 'village' and kok is an olive-like fruit. Doesn't have much of a ring to it, so the Thais prefer to call their capital Krung Thep, or City of Angels. Actually, the full Thai name gets a place in the Guinness World Records book as the world's longest place name. Krungthep, Maha Nakorn, Amorn Ratanakosindra, Mahindrayudhya, Mahadilokpop Noparatana Rajdhani, Burirom, Udom Rajnivet Mahastan, Amorn Pimarm Avatarn Satit, Sakkatuttiya, Vishnukarm Prasit.

Rolls off the tongue, doesn't it?

It translates as 'The city of angels, the great city, the residence of the Emerald Buddha, the impregnable city of God Indra, the grand capital of the world endowed with the nine precious gems, the happy city, abounding in enormous royal palaces which resemble the heavenly abode where reigns the reincarnated God, a city given by Indra and built by Vishnukarm.'

Bangkok is shorter. But it is still one hell of a big city. Officially it's home to twelve million people but at any one time there could be up to twenty million trying to make a living there. The vast majority are Thais so finding Jon Junior would be difficult, but not impossible.

So, what to do?

First, try the easy options.

I picked up a phone and tapped out the number of Jon Junior's cellphone. It went straight through to a recorded message in Thai that said that the number wasn't available and that I should try later. It didn't give me the option of leaving a message or of using a call-back service which would notify me when the phone was available. I used my cellphone to send a text message in Thai, asking for whoever had the phone to give me a call and I'd make it worth their while.

I reached for my MacBook and switched it on, then sent an email to the address that Mr Clare had given me. While I waited to see if the email bounced back I looked through the letters that Jon Junior had written. There were three letters, mainly just chit-chat about what a great time he was having but that he missed his family and his church.

The first letter contained four postcards – pictures of a floating market, elephants playing in a river, and the Wat Phra Kaew and Wat Arun, the Temple of the Emerald Buddha and the Temple of Dawn. There were scribbled notes on the back – 'been there, done that!'

In the second and third letters were photographs that Jon Junior had taken of more tourist sites, including the Chao Phraya River, the Chatuchak Sunday market, and what looked like shots of the street market in Patpong. Jon Junior was in some of the shots, grinning in knee-length shorts and a baggy t-shirt with the Thai flag on the front. His hair was longer and curlier and his skin was more tanned than it was in the photograph that his parents had given me, and he seemed a lot more relaxed, with a broad grin on his face and a sparkle in his eyes.

I put one of the pictures, in which he was standing in front of a noodle stall, on the scanner and scanned it into my laptop, along with the picture that the Clares had given me.

Jon Junior had obviously been having fun in Thailand.

And he had at least one friend here, because someone must have taken the photographs that he was in. But there was no mention of a travelling companion in the three letters, or any suggestion that he'd met anyone in Thailand.

I sat back in my chair and considered my options.

First, the basics.

Jon Junior had flown into Bangkok at the beginning of January. I needed to know if he was still in Thailand.

I had a good contact who worked for immigration at Suvarnabhumi International Airport. I've not met many Westerners who can come close to pronouncing Suvarnabhumi correctly. There are some in Thailand who think that is exactly why the Thais chose the name, which means Golden Land. Nobody really understood why the airport had been built in the first place because Bangkok had a perfectly serviceable airport at Don Muang. It was fair to say, though, that several wealthy Bangkok families did become noticeably wealthier during the construction of the new $4 billion airport.

I'd met Khun Chauvalit several times through my wife. He's a fan of Chinese art and so is she and we kept bumping into each other at exhibitions and I discovered that he is a big fan of Cajun food and as I'm from New Orleans we had a lot to talk about. During a very long Sunday lunch at the Bourbon Street restaurant he gave me his business card and said that if ever I needed any assistance I shouldn't hesitate to contact him.

I have done just that, several times, and he has always been helpful and never asked anything in return.

I called him on his cellphone and he answered after just two rings.

'Khun Chauvalit, how are you this fine day?' I asked in my very best Thai.

'Working hard for little or no appreciation, as always,' he replied.

He asked me about Noy and I asked him about his wife and five children, and then I got around to the point of the conversation and asked him about Jon Junior.

'He flew in on Delta on January the eighth with a tourist visa. I'd like to know if he's still in Thailand and if so if he'd arranged to have his stay extended.'

'I'm not in my office just now, Khun Bob, so I'll have to call you back.'

I gave him Jon Junior's passport number and date of birth, thanked him and ended the call.

The Clares had been told that the American Embassy had contacted the police and the hospitals, but I've learned from experience that embassies aren't the most efficient of institutions so I didn't think it would hurt to check for myself. I had a list of local hospitals in my desk drawer and I methodically worked my way through them, patiently spelling out Jon Junior's name and his passport number. He hadn't been admitted to any, and there were no unidentified farangs.

Farangs. That's what the Thais call foreigners. It's derived from the word for Frenchman but now it's applied to all white foreigners.

Okay, so Jon Junior wasn't lying in a hospital bed with a broken leg or a ruptured appendix.

So far so good.

I phoned my best police contact, Somsak. Somsak's a police colonel in the Soi Thonglor station, just down the road from my apartment. He's a good guy, his wife's a friend of my wife but our real connection is poker. We play every Friday along with four or five other guys, taking it in turns to host the game. Somsak's a ferocious player with a tendency to blink rapidly whenever he draws anything better than a pair of kings. He never bluffs, either, just plays the percentages. He's a tough player to beat; he either blinks or folds.

Somsak's assistant put me through straight away.

'Khun Bob, how are you this pleasant morning?' said Somsak.

Somsak always called me Khun Bob. I could never work out whether he was being sarcastic or not, but he always said it with a smile. He always spoke in English, too. My Thai was better than his English but he was close to perfect so it was no strain.

'I'm trying to find a missing American,' I said. 'He's a young guy, came here as a tourist but it looks like he's teaching English now. He hasn't been in touch with his parents for a while and they're starting to worry.'

'And you're wondering if he's been caught trying to smuggle a kilo of white powder out of the country?'

'It happens.'

It happens a lot. Despite the penalties – and Thailand still executes drugs smugglers – there are still hundreds, maybe thousands, of backpackers and tourists who try to cover their costs of their trip to the Land of Smiles by taking drugs out of the country.

Heroin is cheap in Thailand.

Really cheap.

A couple of hundred dollars a kilo. For heroin that would sell for a hundred times as much in New York or London.

'I will make some enquiries,' said Somsak. 'You have checked the hospitals?'

'Just before I called you.'

'Why are you contacting the police and not his parents?'

'His parents spoke to the embassy and they said they'd talk to the police. I'm just covering all bases, that's all.'

'He is a good boy, this Jon Junior?'

'He's from a good family. '

'I hope he is okay.'

'Me, too,' I said. 'How are things going with the Kube fire?'

'You think he might have been there?'

'It's not impossible,' I said. 'Unlikely, but not impossible.'

'We still have some unidentified bodies.'

'The identified ones, their relatives have been informed?'

'Mostly,' said Somsak. 'But not all.'

'Two hundred and eighteen dead?'

'Two hundred and twenty-three,' said Somsak. 'Five more died overnight.'

'Terrible business,' I said.

'I'll be there tomorrow with the Public Prosecutor. About nine o'clock. You should come around.'

'I will,' I said. 'Is someone going to be prosecuted?'

'Hopefully,' said Somsak. 'Let's talk tomorrow.'

He ended the call. I didn't hold out much hope that Jon Junior was in police custody. A farang being arrested was always big news. A more likely possibility was that he'd been the victim of a crime but if he'd been badly injured he'd have been in hospital and if he wasn't then why hadn't he contacted his parents?

I had tried to be optimistic while I was talking to the Clares, but I was starting to get a bad feeling about Jon Junior's disappearance.

A very bad feeling.

4

THE HOTEL THAT JON Junior had stayed in was a featureless concrete block in Sukhumvit Soi 9, a short walk from the Nana skytrain station. It was six stories high with air-conditioning units mounted in front of each window. The reception was dark and gloomy; half the fluorescent tubes had been removed from the overhead lighting, presumably to save money.

There was a young woman behind the reception desk, adding up receipts with a calculator when I walked in. There were two wall-mounted fans taking it in turns to play across the desk, and with each pass of air she had to hold the receipts down with the flat of her hand so that they didn't blow away. Behind her was a large wooden unit divided into pigeonholes. A sheet of paper had been taped to the bottom. Child-like capital letters warned that if the room charges were a week late, the electricity supply would be cut off. Two weeks later and the water supply to the room would be turned off.

I smiled when she looked up. 'Sawasdee ka,' she said. She had shoulder-length hair with a Hello Kitty bow behind one ear.

Cute.

I told her that I was looking for Jon Clare Junior and she frowned as if I'd just given her a difficult mathematical equation to solve. 'Where he come from?' she said. 'Have many foreigners here.'

I'd spoken to her in Thai but she had replied in English. That wasn't unusual in Thailand. Many Thais assumed that Westerners couldn't speak their language, and even though they heard the words in Thai they would assume that they had been spoken to in English. Sounds crazy, but it's true.

'America, I think he checked out about three weeks ago,' I said. 'Do you remember him?' I passed over the photograph that his parents had given me.

She looked at it, her frown deepening. Then realisation dawned and she smiled. 'Khun Jon,' she said. 'He check out already.'

She handed me back the photograph and went back to adding up her receipts.

'Did he say where he was going?' I asked, in Thai. 'Did he leave a forwarding address for his mail?'

'I don't think so.' She was still speaking in English and I was persevering with Thai.

'Do you think you could check with the manager?'

'Manager not here today.' She smiled at me and waited for me to go away so that she could get on with her work.

I took out my wallet and gave her a one hundred baht note, which is probably as much as she earned in a day. 'Maybe you could check anyway,' I asked.

She reached under her desk and brought out a heavy ledger, opened it and flicked through the pages. She ran her finger down the hand-written entries, frowning furiously again. One of the fans blew her stack of receipts across the desk and she gasped and tried to gather them up.

I turned the ledger around and looked at it. Most of the guests were foreigners and their names were written in English, as were the dates they checked in and out. All other comments were in Thai.

I found Jon Junior's entry. His name, his address in Utah, his passport details, and the dates he'd checked in and out. There was nothing else.

The girl finished picking up the receipts and weighed them down with the calculator. I turned the ledger around.

'Do you remember Khun Jon?' I asked.

She nodded. 'American boy,' she said. 'Very polite. He say he want to be teacher.'

'Do you know where he wanted to teach?'

She shook her head.

'Did he say if he was going to stay in Bangkok?

'Maybe,' she said.

That could have meant that maybe he said, or maybe he didn't, or that he did and she didn't remember.

'Did any friends visit him?'

She frowned as she thought, then she shook her head slowly. 'No one come to see him.'

'No girlfriends?'

She shook her head a bit more emphatically this time.

'What about when he checked out? He took all his luggage with him?'

'Jing Jing,' she said. Sure. The first Thai she'd used with me. It had finally got through to her that I was speaking to her in her own language.

'Did he have a lot of bags?'

'A rucksack. A black one. And two nylon bags.' She was back to speaking English.

'So did he get a taxi?'

'A tuk-tuk.'

Tuk-tuks were the three-wheeled motorcycle hybrids that buzzed around town. They used to be a quick way of getting around town but the traffic is now so heavy that they weren't any quicker, or cheaper, than taxis. They were usually used by tourists or locals for short journeys down the narrow sois. I asked her if she meant a tuk-tuk or if he'd used one of the small sideless vans that also plied their trade down the smaller roads. She decided that it was a van. A red one. By then I'd pretty much run out of questions so I thanked her in Thai and walked back up the soi to Sukhumvit Road.

I walked down to the traffic lights at Soi 3, and waited for them to change. All the sois to the north of Sukhumvit were odd numbers, those on the south side were even. Fatso's was in Soi 4, also known as Soi Nana and home to Nana Plaza. Nana Plaza is one of the city's red light areas, with forty-odd go-go bars and a couple of thousand bargirls.

The traffic lights were under the control of a middle-aged policeman sitting in a glass cubicle on the Soi 4 side of Sukhumvit. He had a walkie-talkie pressed to his ear. There was no alternative other than to wait patiently.

Jai yen yen.

Relax.

Don't worry.

My cell phone rang. It was Khun Chauvalit, calling me from the airport.

'Your Jon Junior did indeed arrive on a Delta airlines flight from Seattle on January the eighth,' he said. 'He was given sixty days and he left the country by land on March the fifth.'

'By land?'

'To Cambodia. The Ban Laem border crossing. He returned the same day and was given a further sixty days. He had a double entry sixty-day visa granted by the Thai Consulate in Chicago.'

'Did he gave an address?'

'It is listed as simply "Hotel", with no name or address,' said

Khun Chauvalit.

'And so far as we know he is still in Thailand?'

'He has sixty days from March the fifth, though the visa that he has can be extended for a further thirty days if he visits the immigration department.'

I thanked Khun Chauvalit and ended the call.

The good news was that Jon Junior was still in Thailand. The bad news was that he'd arrived back just a week before the fire at the Kube.

The policeman gave the order to change the lights to red and I hurried across the road and down Soi 4.

The early shift go-go girls were starting to arrive at the plaza, more often than not dropped of by their motorcycle-driving boyfriends. Most of the girls wore the standard off-duty bargirl uniform of low-cut black t-shirt, tight blue jeans and impossibly high heels. The ones who were doing well had an ounce or two of gold around their necks and a top-of-the-range cellphone clipped to their belt.

A couple of girls sitting at the beer bar at the entrance of the plaza called over to tell me what a handsome man I was.

Not true, but always nice to hear anyway.

I walked down Soi 4, past the beauty salon, the German restaurant that served a halfway decent wiener schnitzel and the travel agency run by Debby from Rochdale who's been married to a Thai for so long that she speaks English with an accent.

I pushed open the glass door that led into the haven of Britishness that is Fatso's.

Big Ron was sitting in his specially-reinforced chair and smearing butter over two halves of a stick of French bread. His early-evening snack. He didn't really start eating until the sun went down.

The chair was huge, almost three feet across, built from

scaffolding with a massive red cushion. It just about accommodated his huge backside.

'How are they hanging, Bob?' he asked as he began stacking pieces of fried bacon onto one of the slices.

'Straight and level,' I said, sliding onto one of the barstools. 'How's the diet?'

Big Ron chuckled as he piled the bacon higher. He tipped the scales at something like six hundred and fifty pounds, but it had been some years since he'd stepped on a set of scales. Even taxis were reluctant to take him any distance, figuring that the damage to the suspension would be irreversible. He lived in a two-bedroom condo, which was a ten-minute waddle from the bar.

One of the waitresses put an opened bottle of Phuket Beer in front of me and I smiled my thanks. 'How are you, Khun Bob?' she asked. Her name was Bee and she had shoulder-length hair and a cute button nose and a skirt that barely covered her backside when she bent down to pick bottles of cold beer out of the chest fridge behind the bar.

Not that I looked.

Cross my heart.

'I'm fine, Bee, thanks.' She noticed the beads of sweat and my brow and handed me an ice-cold towel in a plastic wrapper.

All the Fatso's waitresses had infallible memories for faces, names and drinks. You could walk into the bar once, order one drink and leave and not go back for a year. But when you did go back, they'd remember your name and what you drank. And whether or not you'd thrown up in the bathroom.

There were only two other customers sitting at the bar. Alan and Bruce, both long-time regulars. Alan was an analyst with a Japanese stockbroking firm; Bruce helped run a furniture factory. I waved at

Bee to buy them both drinks and they raised their glasses in thanks.

Fatso's was a small place with room for about twenty sitting on stools around the horseshoe-shaped bar and another dozen patrons could just about pack into the space by the door. A spiral staircase ran upstairs to a small restaurant area with a dozen tables and the unisex toilets. Big Ron kept a small camera behind the bar so that he could take pictures up the skirts of his waitresses as they went upstairs. The results of his hobby were hanging on the walls of the bar, along with photographs of the Fatso's regulars in various stages of inebriation. There's a couple of me somewhere but I don't go out of my way to seek them out. Part of my past.

I'm not ashamed of my heavy-drinking days. But they're a bit like an old girlfriend that you never really loved and now half-regret sleeping with. I mean it was fun at the time, but looking back I cringe a bit.

Big Ron slapped the top down on his sandwich and began munching on it. Bacon fat and butter dribbled down his chins and he groaned contentedly. The bacon sandwich was just a snack; he'd start eating in earnest at about eight o'clock.

'I'm looking for a Mormon,' I said.

'You've come to the right place, they're all morons in here,' said Big Ron. He grabbed a handful of paper napkins and wiped his chin.

'I resemble that remark,' said Alan prissily.

'Mormon,' I said. 'Salt Lake City and all that.'

'The Osmonds,' said Bruce. 'I'll be your long-haired lover from Liverpool.'

'Not in this lifetime you won't, you bald twat,' said Big Ron. Insulting his customers was as much a part of his charm as his habit of photographing the stocking tops of the waitresses. You either loved Big Ron or you hated him, there was no middle ground.

'He's a young guy, twenty-one. Wouldn't say boo to a Peking Duck. Came to Bangkok to teach English three months ago and he's disappeared.'

'Says who?' asked Alan.

'His mum and dad. They've come here looking for him.'

'What is it with Americans teaching English?' said Alan. 'Shouldn't they be teaching American? I mean, come on.'

Big Ron belched. 'He'll be lying on a beach somewhere with a dark-skinned beauty, smoking dope during the day and screwing like a bunny at night. Trust me.'

'Much as I do trust you, he's not like that,' I said.

Big Ron guffawed again, spitting out bits of bread and bacon in my direction. Bee flashed me an apologetic smile and wiped the bar top with a damp cloth.

'They're all like that,' said Big Ron. 'Americans are the worst. Twenty-four after hitting Bangkok, he'll have been in the sack with a hooker.'

'Twelve,' said Alan.

'Two,' said Bruce, 'including travel time from the airport.'

'He's a virgin,' I said patiently. 'Born again.'

'A born-again virgin?' grinned Bruce. 'Nana Plaza's full of them. Little Puy in Rainbow Two has sold her virginity three times as far as I know.'

'According to his parents, he's saving himself for the right woman.'

'If you save wicked women, save one for me,' said Alan. He reached over and rang a large bronze bell that was hanging just to the right of Big Ron's head. The Fatso's girls started pouring drinks for the guys sitting at the bar. One ring of the bell bought a round of drinks. Two rings bought a round for the customers and a drink each for the staff behind the bar. Three rings and everyone in the bar and in the restaurant upstairs got drinks, along with the kitchen staff.

'I went to his apartment,' I said. 'He'd cleared out.'

'Where was he staying?' asked Bruce.

'Soi 9.'

'He'll have hitched up with a freelancer from the German bar,' said Bruce. 'Soi 7. Or Gullivers in Soi 5.'

'Lying on a beach,' said Big Ron. 'Guaranteed.'

'I don't think so.'

'Do you want to put your money where your mouth is?'

The thing about Big Ron is that more often than not, he's right. 'Maybe,' I said hesitantly.

'If I'm right and he's on a beach with a bird, you ring the bell three times.'

'Okay.'

'On a Saturday night. Between nine and ten.'

That was the busiest time in Fatso's. Maybe two dozen people upstairs eating. Twenty around the bar downstairs. Eight Fatso's girls. Three or four kitchen staff. Not a cheap round.

'And if you're wrong?'

Fingers crossed.

'Free drinks for a week.'

'Deal,' I said. No way was Jon Junior hooked up with a girl. He wasn't the type.

Big Ron grinned, belched, and wiped his chin with the back of his hand.

'Ding, dong,' he said. 'Ding bloody dong.'

THE COCKATOOS THAT LIVE in the garden next to my condominium block woke me up bright and early. The house is owned by a Thai plastic surgeon by the name of Khun Banyat and he lives there with his wife, five children and his collection of exotic birds. I like Khun Banyat and I play tennis with him at the Racquet Club in Soi 49 twice a month but sometimes I would happily strangle his parrots.

I lay looking up at the ceiling wondering what cockatoo would taste like in a hot, spicy soup.

Jai yen.

I rolled over and looked at my wife. Noy.

Noy means small.

She is thirty-two but looks a good ten years younger, with her long black hair spread over the pillow like a raven's wing and long, long eyelashes. She's way out of my league, and not because she's younger and better looking. She's smarter than me, she's a better person than I am and she's kinder to animals. She's fluent in Thai, English, Mandarin and Japanese, she plays the violin and piano like a dream, she has a real estate business that makes twice as much as my antiques shop.

I'm not good enough for my wife. I'm really not. There isn't a day goes by when I don't wonder why she chose me, why she wanted to marry me, and why she stays with me.

She's well connected too, and could have had the pick of any eligible bachelor going. I don't think there's a top Thai politician, Army general or movie star who doesn't know her and usually when we get invited anywhere it's because they want to see her, not me. Her dad is an Air Force General and her mother is on the boards of half a dozen charities and is a regular visitor to the palace. They're lovely people, too, I couldn't ask for better in-laws. To this day I'm still not sure why I've been so lucky.

'I know you're looking at me,' she said quietly.

'How?' I said. 'You've got your back to me.'

'I can feel your eyes,' she said. 'And I can hear you thinking.'

'What am I thinking, then?'

She moved her legs a little. She has great legs. Long, shapely, fit. 'You were wondering if you could get away with killing Khun Banyat's parrots,' she murmured.

'That's impressive,' I said.

'Then you were thinking about pressing yourself against me and kissing the back of my neck and making love to me before I woke up.'

'But you're awake already.'

She sighed dreamily. 'No, I'm still asleep. So was I right?'

'Honey, you're always right,' I said, snuggling up to her and kissing the back of her neck.

Afterwards, she lay in my arms, her hand on my chest. She has perfect hands, the nails beautifully manicured, the fingertips soft, the skin unblemished. 'Do you want to know what I was really thinking?' I asked.

'Oh my Buddha, there's more? Haven't you ravaged me enough?'

I smiled. 'I was wondering why I'm so lucky. Why do you stay with me?'

'Because I'm your wife, Bob. That's what wives do. Through thick and thin.'

'Let me rephrase the question,' I said. 'Why did you marry me?'

'You're asking me that now?'

'It's as good a time as any. The warm afterglow and all.'

She prodded me in the ribs. 'Because I love you.'

'It's as simple as that?'

'And as complicated,' she said.

'Wow,' I said.

'And I love the way you make coffee for me first thing in the morning.'

'You do?'

'And the way you warm the milk first. And serve it with one of those Italian biscuits we got from the Emporium.'

'Really?'

'Yes,' she said. She sighed like a cat making itself comfortable. 'So what are you waiting for?'

I made her coffee, warming the milk and serving it with a biscuit, and then spent another hour in bed with her during which time I forgot all about next door's cockatoos.

After I'd showered and dressed I tried Jon Junior's cellphone again but it was still unavailable. Then I checked my email. There were a dozen or so work-related emails and one from a tourist wanting to know if I could recommend a good hotel near Patpong, but no reply from Jon Junior.

I emailed the two scanned photographs of Jon Junior to half a dozen guys who run Thai-related websites. I asked them to put Jon Junior's pictures and details online and to get back to me if anyone knew where he was. It was a long shot but some of the sites had upwards of twenty thousand visitors a week. I also put the photographs on my site. I sold antiques online at Bangkokbob. biz and had most of my stock on the website. Over the years I'd expanded the website to include advice on living and working in Thailand, and I'd started a question and answer service, more as a hobby than anything else. Now I was getting a couple of hundred hits a day and a reputation as the man who knew all there was to know about the Land of Smiles. I was selling a lot of antiques, too.

It was the website that had got me started as a part-time private eye. A woman in Seattle who'd bought a couple of Khmer statues from me sent me an email asking if I'd go around to her husband's hotel and check that he was okay. He'd gone to Thailand on a golfing holiday with half a dozen of his buddies and she hadn't heard from him for three days.

She'd imagined all sorts of scenarios, most of which involved her husband running off with a sloe-eyed beauty.

There was no great mystery. He'd gone down with food poisoning and was in hospital. His buddies had headed off to Pattaya after the doctors had said that he'd be back on his feet in a day or two. They'd assumed that he'd phone his wife, he'd assumed that they'd done it.

I called her, put her mind at rest, and a week later I received a cheque for five hundred dollars that I hadn't asked for. I hadn't even thought about money. The guy ran a computer business and a few months after he got back to Seattle he called me and me to check out a Thai software firm that he was planning to do business with. I made a few calls and discovered that the two guys running the software company had a history of ripping off Western investors. The Seattle guy was so grateful that he sent me a cheque for five thousand dollars and passed on my name to all his friends.

Now I probably got half a dozen requests for help every week. Most are through the website or word of mouth. A few get pointed in my direction from the Western embassies. I don't take on every case. Just the ones that I find interesting, or where I know that I'll make a difference. I liked Mr and Mrs Clare and I wanted to help.

I wanted to reunite them with their son.

And I wanted to lose the feeling I had that something bad had happened to him.

I looked at my watch. It was time to visit the Kube.

Or at least what was left of it.

6

THE KUBE WAS IN Sukhumvit Soi 71, also known as Pridi Banomyong, named after the seventh prime minister of Thailand who ordered it to be built. He also founded Thammasat University, the country's second oldest. He did a lot of good things for Thailand, and I don't think he would have been impressed with what had happened in the street that bore his name. Two hundred and twenty three young people dead. Many more injured. And all because some Thai wannabe rock star thought it would be a good idea to let off fireworks in the middle of his show.

I paid the taxi driver and waited until a stream of motorcycles had passed by on the inside before opening the door and getting out. The air was stiflingly hot after the blisteringly cold aircon and within seconds my face was bathed in sweat. Panels of corrugated iron had been erected on a scaffold frame to shield the burnt carcass of the building from the road. Two uniformed policemen were standing by their Tiger Boxer motorcycles. One of them was drinking a can of Red Bull.

'I'm here to see Colonel Somsak,' I said in my most polite Thai. 'He's expecting me.'

One of them pointed at a gap in the corrugated iron and I went through. I could smell the ash and seared wood before I saw the building, or what was left of it. It had once been a two-storey building, the lower part built of concrete blocks and clad with wood, and the upper storey made of teak. Only the blocks remained, the grey concrete stained with black soot. The window frames had been reduced to ash and there was broken glass all around.

Somsak was standing in front of a concrete arch on which the name of the club was spelt out in yellow metal letters which had buckled in the heat of the fire. He was wearing his brown uniform that looked as if it had been spray-painted onto his athletic body, a peaked cap with gold insignia and gleaming black boots. His Glock was in its nylon holster on his hip and he was holding a transceiver as he spoke to a pretty woman in a black suit who was carrying a Louis Vuitton briefcase. Standing close by were two more uniformed officers.

Somsak grinned when he saw me and waved his transceiver. 'Khun Bob, come and meet the Public Prosecutor,' he said. 'Khun Jintana, this is the Khun Bob I was telling you about.'

Khun Jintana smiled and managed to wai me which was no mean feat considering she was holding the briefcase. It was a nice wai, too, with eye contact before and after. I figured the wai was more out of respect for my wife than for me but I gave her a wai back anyway.

Somsak grinned again and hugged me and patted me on the back with his transceiver. 'Good to see you, my friend.'

'Terrible business,' I said, nodding at the carnage behind him.

Somsak nodded. 'You should have been here on the night,' he said. 'It was bad.'

Somsak was based at the Thonglor station, not far from my apartment, and the Kube was on his patch.

'Will there be prosecutions, Khun Jintana?' I asked.

She smiled, showing perfect teeth. 'That remains to be seen, Khun Bob,' she said. 'The investigation is on-going.' She smiled again.

I had spoken to her in Thai and she had replied in English. Perfect

English, but then my Thai is perfect, too.

'Two hundred and twenty-three dead,' I said. 'That's terrible.'

'Most of them teenagers,' said Somsak. 'And a lot of them underage. It doesn't look as if they were checking IDs. And it's two hundred and twenty-five. Two more died overnight.'

'And how many have still to be identified?'

Somsak looked pained. 'A lot,' he said.

'Is there are a problem?'

'The bodies are in a mess,' he said. 'The ones with ID are done but if the fire's destroyed ID and clothing then we just have work through missing person lists plus dental records and once we've done that the Central Institute of Forensic Science will start DNA testing.'

'What about the foreigners? How do you about getting dental records for them?'

Somsak looked even more pained. 'It's not my field, Khun Bob. I wish that it was. I've been told that's the way to proceed.'

Hierarchy was everything in Thailand. Bosses were never to be criticised, even when they were wrong.

'I have to be going,' said Jintana. She gave me another wai and walked away, swinging her briefcase.

'Do you know who she is?' asked Somsak.

'The Public Prosecutor, you said.'

'Ah, she's much more than that,' said Somsak. 'She's from a big family. Her father is an MP in Chiang Mai. Went to school with one of the owners of the Kube.'

'That's one hell a coincidence.'

'My father always used to say that there are no coincidences in life, only opportunity,' said Somsak.

'Your father was a wise man,' I said. We both watched her walk through the gap in the corrugated iron and onto the pavement. 'So do you think you'll punish anyone for this? For the deaths?'

'Someone will have to be punished,' said Somsak. 'A lot of kids died here. A lot of hi-so kids. The phones have been ringing off the hook.'

'What about the owners?'

'It's complicated,' said Somsak. He jerked a thumb at the ruined building. 'And after this it's going to get even more complicated, I'm sure. The real owners invested in the place about five years ago, but they did it through an offshore company and used figurehead directors in Thailand.'

'That's interesting.'

'But not unusual,' said Somsak. 'Places like this sometimes get busted for drugs or underage drinking and the great and the good don't like to see their names in *Thai Rath*.'

Thai Rath is one of the bestselling tabloid newspapers and the paper gives a whole new meaning to the word sensationalism.

'And Khun Jintana's father is friends with one of the figureheads or one of the great and good?' I asked.

'The latter,' said Somsak. 'But that's the word on the street, you understand. No one knows for sure who the investors are.'

'So I'm guessing one of the figureheads will be offered up as a sacrificial lamb.'

'That would be a good guess, Khun Bob. Unfortunately two of the figureheads are now in Singapore. The other is somewhere in Isarn.'

Isarn, the north-east of the country, the poorest part of Thailand and the area least amenable to assisting the Bangkok police with their enquiries.

'Do you think the investors can be held accountable?'

'I would think not. They were just money men. But the

figureheads were in the club every night. The club was making money hand over fist.'

'It was an accident, right?'

Somsak grimaced as if he had a bad taste in his mouth. 'It was an accident waiting to happen,' he said. 'There was no insurance, the fire exits were locked, there were more than a thousand people in the building at the time of the fire when it was licensed for seven hundred. There hadn't been a fire inspection for three years and there were twice as many cars in the carpark as there should have been. One reason that so many died is that the fire brigade couldn't get close to the building.'

'Who was in charge, on the night?'

'The sons of one of the owners were there but they were entertaining in the VIP area upstairs,' said Somsak. 'They both died.'

'I'm sorry to hear that.'

'One of the owners was downstairs when the fire broke out. He was one of the first out. Straight into a taxi without looking back. He's the one in Isarn.'

'He didn't try to help?'

'He fled the scene, that's what we were told.'

'What sort of person would do that?'

Somsak shrugged. 'The sort of person who thinks he'll be punished for his actions. His instinct for self-preservation took precedence over helping those who were trapped.'

'And the fire exits were locked, you said?'

Somsak nodded. 'That's why so many died. There was only one way in and out and when the fire broke out there was a stampede and the exit was blocked. Everyone on the upper floor died, except for half a dozen who managed to break a window at the back. They jumped and are all in hospital, smashed up but they will probably live.' He pointed at the left of the shell. 'There was another VIP area in the basement,' he said. 'Everyone died down there. There was only a narrow stairway and when the power went it was pitch dark.'

I shuddered. It wouldn't have been a pleasant way to die. But then again, few deaths are pleasant.

'Why are you interested, Khun Bob?' he asked.

'I'm looking for a missing American boy,' I said. 'His parents are worried that he might have been in the club.'

'I hope that's not the case,' he said.

'You and me both,' I said.

'There were many foreigners in the building,' he said.

'Do we know how many of the dead are farang?'

'The bodies were too badly burned,' he said quietly. 'In the aftermath of an inferno, we all look the same, Thai and farang.'

The two of us stood their nodding in the sunlight, the smell of death all around us. I tried not to imagine what it must have been like in the dark, lungs filling with smoke, everyone screaming and fighting to escape, the strong trampling over the weak, people choking and falling and dying. The lucky ones would have been overcome by the smoke, the unlucky ones would have been conscious as they burned alive.

I wanted to go home and hold my wife and tell her that I loved her and that if she ever went to a nightclub she should never venture far from the emergency exits.

'If the sons were in the VIP area, who was minding the place downstairs?' I asked Somsak.

'The man who fled,' he said, lighting a cigarette. 'And a manager. A farang. From Australia.'

'Where is he?'

Somsak blew smoke up at the sky. 'Bumrungrad Hospital. Soi 3.'

'That's a coincidence.'

'Why's that?'

'I've got an appointment there tomorrow morning.'

Somsak frowned. 'Are you sick?'

'It's my yearly check-up,' I said. 'Nothing to worry about. What about the manager? Is he okay?'

Somsak smiled. 'He's in hospital, Khun Bob. People generally don't go there unless there is a problem.'

It was hard to tell whether he was joking or just taking me literally. Then he grinned.

'Very funny, Somsak,' I said. 'I meant is he seriously hurt?'

'Third degree burns,' said Somsak. 'He will live but he won't be winning any beauty pageants.'

'Do you think he's up to receiving visitors?'

'You want to talk to him?'

'I want to see if he remembers seeing the American boy, that's all.'

Somsak nodded slowly. 'You can try. His name is Ronnie. Ronnie Marsh.'

7

MY APPOINTMENT WITH Doctor Duangtip was at eleven o'clock but I wanted to get there earlier so that I could visit Ronnie Marsh so I caught a taxi in Soi Thonglor at just before nine. It was raining. It was early May and the farmers in the north eastern Isarn provinces had suffered three months of drought that was threatening to destroy the rice crop. The rice paddies were so dry that they weren't able to plant their rice seedlings and many were facing financial ruin. The skies had been cloudy for the best part of a week but the rain had steadfastly refused to come so the Bureau of Royal Rainmaking and Agricultural Aviation had been seeding the clouds with salt and calcium and silver iodide. The clouds had fattened and darkened but then the wind had changed and by the time the rain started to fall they were over Bangkok. The rains had come but it was the citizens of Bangkok who were drenched while the farmers of Isarn were still despairing over their parched farmland and devastated livelihoods. In some of the more remote villages the headmen had given up on the official rainmakers and had organised the hae nang-maew-kaw-fon festival where they dragged a cat around in a wicker basket and drenched it with water. The rains still hadn't reached the north east but the road to Bumrungrad Hospital was under several inches of water.

Bumrungrad Hospital is often touted as the best in Asia. It's in Soi 3, a hop, skip and a jump from Nana Plaza, one of the largest red light areas in the city, and just across the road from Little Arabia, home to most of the Arabs visiting the city. There were more than a dozen Arabs in reception, the men in man dresses and sandals and the women swathed from head to foot in black. I've never understood why the Arabs just didn't build their own hospitals and import the doctor and nurses but whatever the reason it was certainly good for the Thai economy and brought in millions of dollars a year.

I've never liked hospitals but if you've got to go then you might as well go to one that looks like a five-star hotel and is staffed by hundreds of pretty young girls in tight-fitting starched white uniforms. There's a Starbucks on the premises, a McDonald's, a bakery, a top-notch Japanese restaurant, and other restaurants I haven't even seen. When you check into the Bumrungrad for treatment you're asked what sort of room you'd like, up to a two-bedroom suite, and your food is chosen from a room service menu. And you're treated like a valued guest, not a patient.

Eat your heart out, Medicare.

It took me half an hour to get to Soi 3 and then another half an hour to get down the waterlogged street to the hospital but I still had plenty of time to go up to the burns unit before my health check.

The nurse I spoke to in the burns unit didn't ask who I was or why I was there, she just smiled and showed me to the room.

It was a private room and Marsh was the only occupant, lying flat with a rack over his legs to keep the sheet off his legs and chest. There were dressings on his face and neck and what looked like mittens on his hand, but he wasn't connected to any machines making beeping noises which I took as a good sign.

There was a flatscreen television on the wall opposite his bed showing a football match with the sound muted but his eyes were closed and he seemed to be asleep.

'Ronnie?' I said as I closed the door behind me.

His eyes opened. 'Yeah?'

'How are you feeling?'

Not the smartest of questions, I know, but I wanted to get him talking.

'How do you think I'm feeling?'

'It hurts?'

'Not as much as it did when they brought me in.' He looked across at a drip feed that was going into his left arm. 'Whatever it is they're pouring into me, it's doing the trick.'

I nodded at a chair at the side of his bed. 'Mind if I sit down?'

'Who are you?' he asked.

'Bob Turtledove,' I said, which was true.

'From the Embassy,' I added. Which wasn't, strictly speaking.

'You're American,' he said.

'Yes, I am.'

'An American working for the Australian Embassy? That doesn't make sense.'

'I'm with the American Embassy,' I said, which was sort of true in that Matt Richards had sent the Clares to me.

Okay, so it wasn't true.

Sue me.

I took the photograph of Jon Junior from my pocket and held it in front of his face. 'Do you remember seeing this boy, the night of the fire?'

'What?' he said.

'This boy? Was he in the club?'

'I'm lying here in the ICU and you're showing me a bloody photograph?'

'It's important,' I said. 'His parents are looking for him.'

'Yeah, well I've got enough problems of my own, mate.'

I took the photograph away from his face. 'Look, I'm sorry you were hurt,' I said. 'But at least you're alive. This boy might not be so lucky.'

'Lucky? You think I'm lucky? You've no idea what's going on, do you?'

'So tell me,' I said. 'Tell me what's going on.'

He sighed and closed his eyes. 'I'm the fall guy,' he said. 'The farang fall guy.'

'They're going to blame you for the fire?'

He opened his eyes. 'What do you think? I'm the token farang at the club, who else are they going to hang it on?'

'But the papers said that the fire was started by the band.'

Marsh snorted. 'And who hired the band? The farang. And who was responsible for the fire inspections? The farang. And who said that the fire exits should be locked? The farang. And who said it was okay to fill the car park to double its capacity?'

'The farang?'

'Exactly. They're going to hang me out to dry, mate. Life behind bars if they get their way. You know that whatever happens, the farang gets the blame. And I'm the farang.'

'Why do you think you're going to be the fall guy?'

'Because a lawyer came to see me yesterday saying he wanted to discuss my defence. He said that the police were preparing to press charges and he wanted to make sure that I was ready.'

'He wasn't your lawyer?'

'He works for a firm that one of the partners uses,' said Marsh. 'I told him to go screw himself.'

I nodded. Telling Thais to go screw themselves wasn't the smartest course of action.

Especially Thai lawyers.

'I wouldn't think that the police would be looking to charge you, unless you'd done something wrong.'

Marsh tried to sneer at me but he grunted with pain instead. 'How long have you been in Thailand, Turtledove?'

'A few years.'

'Yeah, well you should have learned by now that people who do things wrong often end up getting away with it, and people who've done nothing often end up in prison. Getting punished here has more to do with who you are and how much you have rather than what you did.'

Marsh was a cynic.

But he was probably right.

'The fire exits. Was it your idea to lock them?'

'Of course not,' he said. 'What do you think I am?

'Whose then?'

'Thongchai. He's one of the owners.'

'From Isarn?'

'Udon Thani,' said Marsh. 'He ran away as soon as the fire started. Saw the flames and just turned and ran.'

'And he wanted the fire exits locked?'

Marsh sighed. 'We'd been having problems with people sneaking in through the back. One guy would pay to get in and he'd kick open a fire door and a dozen of his mates would pile in. I said we should just station security guards at the exits but he said we didn't have a budget for that.' Marsh shook his head. 'Two hundred baht would get you a guard for the whole night. The price of one beer in the club. Cheap bastard.'

'So he had the exits locked?'

'Chains and padlocked. Did it himself and carried the keys. I screamed for him to come back and open the doors but he didn't stop.'

'They're saying that it was fireworks that started the fire.'

'Yeah. The idiot lead singer set them off halfway through his set.'

'Didn't anyone know what he was going to do?'

'It was their first time in the club. I was there at the sound check during the day and there was no mention of fireworks then. I was near the entrance keeping an eye on things because we had a hundred or so kids trying to get in even though we were full. First I knew of it was when he takes a lighter out of his pocket and he lights these black things. Next thing I know there are white sparks everywhere and the crowd is cheering. Then the showers of sparks get bigger and then the ceiling catches fire and everyone starts screaming. That's when Thongchai ran for it.'

'How did you get burned? You said you were by the entrance.'

'I was trying to get people out. The power went so all the lights went out. There was a surge to get out and people fell. I stayed as long as I could but...'

He closed his eyes.

'You know what I don't understand?' he said.

'What's that?'

He opened his eyes. 'When I did get out there were hundreds of people watching and most of them were holding up their cellphones, taking pictures and videoing. Why didn't they help?'

'I don't know.'

'Why were they standing there taking pictures of people dying? They could have helped but they didn't.'

It wasn't a question that I could answer.

I don't thing anyone could.

It was the way of the world in the twenty-first century. People preferred to be observers rather than participants, and nothing was real unless it had appeared on YouTube.

'They could have helped, but they didn't. I helped and I got third degree burns and now they want to hang me out to dry. It's not fair.'

He was right, of course. It wasn't fair.

I held out the photograph again. 'Ronnie, did you see this boy in the club that night?'

He squinted at the picture. 'I don't think so.'

'You were at the door all night?'

'That's the thing, I wasn't. I was moving around.'

'So he could have gone in when you weren't on the door?'

'It's possible.'

I sighed. 'Well, it was worth a try.'

'Who is he?' asked Marsh.

'Young American kid on his gap year. His parents are worried sick. They haven't heard from him in a while and then they read about the fire.'

'Close family?'

'Mormons,' I said.

'I left home when I was sixteen and I don't think my parents even noticed.' He sighed. 'I am in so much shit, Bob.'

'It might not be as bad as you think.'

'The lawyer said the prosecution were looking to put me away for life.'

'I spoke to a Public Prosecutor yesterday and she said the investigation was ongoing.'

'Maybe she doesn't know what's going on behind the scenes. The lawyer said that I was going to get the blame for the fire certificate not being up to date, for the locked exits and for the underage kids there. He said the best thing to do was to just admit everything and throw myself at the mercy of the court and that I'd probably only get ten years and that would get cut in half at some point.'

I nodded.

The bit about the sentence being cut was right. That's how it worked in Thailand. On major holidays like the King's birthday thousands of prisoners had their sentences reduced. It happened so often that a guy sentenced to thirty years for murder could easily be back home in five years. The only sentences that weren't reduced were those of drug dealers.

'Sounds to me like you need a lawyer, Ronnie. Someone with your best interests at heart.'

'Do you think?' he said, his voice loaded with sarcasm.

'Do you know anyone?'

'Never needed one before,' he said.

'I've got a friend who knows what he's doing,' I said. 'I'll get him to drop by.'

'Thai?'

'For this sort of thing, you need a Thai lawyer,' I said. 'And you need a good one.'

I stood up and both knees cracked. Marsh grinned. 'You're getting old, Bob.'

'We all are,' I said.

'Can you see the remote?'

It was on a shelf next to his drip. I picked it up.

'Put the sound up so I can hear it, will you?' I boosted the volume and he thanked me. 'You could try talking to Lek and Tam. They might have seen your boy.'

'They were on the door?'

'Yeah. They're kickboxers, they train at the gym in Washington Square most days. You'd better say you're a friend of mine or they'll not talk to you.'

'Thanks, Ronnie.'

'No sweat. Just don't forget that lawyer.'

8

THERE WERE HALF A dozen girls giggling at the reception desk when I got out of the elevator on the second floor. I was there for a battery of tests as part of a yearly health check. The sort of annual service that would cost you several grand back in the States and costs a couple of hundred at the Bumrungrad, and you're waited on hand and foot every step of the way. A nurse who looked sixteen smile coyly and took me to a seat where a girl who could have been her twin took a blood sample that I swear to God caused me not one iota of discomfort. I don't know if they used extra sharp needles or if the sight of two beautiful creatures in nurse's uniforms dulled the pain, but I felt nothing.

I was taken to a waiting area where after five minutes another nurse apologised for the delay and gave me a coupon for a free cup of coffee or a portion of French fries. Two minutes later I was in to see the doctor who would be overseeing the tests.

Doctor Duangtip.

There was a battery of framed certificates on the wall behind him. Bangkok. London. San Francisco. You could buy similar certificates in any print shop in the Khao San Road, but his were the real thing. I'd been coming to see Doctor Duangtip every year for the past four years, so I knew the drill. A physical, blood tests, a cardiac test that had me running on a treadmill with electrodes strapped to my upper body, a chest X-ray and a lower abdomen ultrasound. Two days later a brief chat about the results and a suggestion that I should try cutting down on fatty foods and alcohol to lower my cholesterol. My cholesterol levels, good and bad, had remained a few per cent higher than average since I'd been having the yearly check-ups, and cutting back on fatty food and going to the gym three times a week hadn't made any difference either way so I'd cancelled my gym membership and eaten what the hell I wanted.

Doctor Duangtip ran through my medical history and then sent me of for the first of the tests. I was totally relaxed.

I was fine.

I was fit.

I was healthy.

I was going to live forever.

Little did I know.

9

WASHINGTON SQUARE IS A hangover from the days when Thailand was an R&R destination for American troops fighting in Vietnam. The main venue slap in the middle was the Washington Theatre, a huge cinema with more than a thousand seats. Around the theatre were dozens of bars, clubs and massage parlours, all just a few hundred yards from the intersection of Asoke and Sukhumvit roads. After the war ended the troops went home but the Square stayed much as it was, frequented by vets who preferred to stay in Asia rather than return to the real world. Time took its toll, on the vets and on the area, and these days Washington Square is a pale shadow of what it once was. Some of the bars are still there, and you can still get a soapy massage, but the cinema became a transvestite cabaret show and then a sports bar, and every year there's talk of the area being demolished to make way for a shopping mall or condominiums.

I've always had a soft spot for Washington Square. The Bourbon Street restaurant, tucked away behind the cinema building, serves great Cajun food, and the bars are quiet havens where you can have a drink and watch American sport and listen to American voices mumbling around you. And I'm a big fan of the Dubliner, an Irish pub at the entrance to the square which serves breakfast all day and a decent cup of coffee most days. The Muay Thai gym wasn't a place I'd ever visited, mainly because they didn't serve breakfast or coffee and because these days my preferred exercise is a game of tennis with my next door neighbour.

It was a hot day, probably in the low forties, but there was no air-conditioning in the gym. Instead they had opened all the windows and had half a dozen floor fans on full power, and the contrast with the blisteringly-cold air-con of the taxi that dropped me outside had beads of sweat forming on my forehead within seconds.

I took off my jacket and wiped my forehead with a handkerchief. 'I'm looking for Lek, or Tam' I said to a stocky man sitting behind a metal table reading a Muay Thai magazine and chewing on a toothpick.

The man looked up and frowned, confused because I'd spoken to him in Thai. 'You speak Thai?' he said.

'This is Thailand, right?' I said, and he laughed.

'Why is your Thai so good?' he asked, switching to Khmer. He had nut-brown skin and a snub nose and I figured he was probably from Surin or Sisaket, close to the Cambodian border. He was wearing a t-shirt with a picture of two kickboxers slamming into each other and baggy tracksuit bottoms.

'I watch too much television,' I answered, speaking in Khmer and throwing in a few curse words for emphasis.

He nodded, impressed. 'Thai girlfriend?'

'Thai wife,' I said.

'From where?'

'Chiang Rai.'

'Children?'

'Not yet,' I said. Thais had no reservations about asking the most personal questions of people they had only just met.

'Is Lek here? Or Tam?' I asked.

He took the toothpick out of his mouth and jabbed it towards the far end of the gymnasium where a lanky trainer in a baggy tracksuit was holding a punchbag for a bald-headed Westerner who was grunting every time he launched a kick which thudded against the canvas with the sound of a seal being clubbed to death. 'That's Lek.'

I sat down on a wicker chair and waited for the session to finish. The bald guy wasn't a fighter, and he certainly wasn't fit. After a minute or two he was bathed in sweat and he was barely getting his kicks above knee height. Eventually he waved Lek away and bent double, gasping for breath. Lek patted him on the back and draped a towel around his shoulders before helping him over to the changing rooms. Lek reappeared a couple of minutes later holding a bottle of water.

'Farang here wants a word!' shouted the guy with the newspaper.

Lek looked over at me and jutted out his chin. 'You here to train?' he asked in accented English.

'Me?' I patted my stomach. 'My fighting days are over.' I spoke in Thai, and gestured at the changing rooms. 'What about him, when will we be seeing him in Lumpini?' I asked, referring to the city's main Muay Thai stadium.

'He thinks he's Rambo,' said Lek. 'Wants to get fit so that he can be a mercenary in Iraq.'

'Sounds like a plan,' I said.

Two more Westerners appeared at the entrance. They were in the twenties with the sort of muscles that only came from steroids. They both had their names tattooed in Thai across their left forearms. Michael and Martin. They waied Lek but spoiled the effect by grunting at the same time. They looked at me with hard faces as they walked to the changing rooms as if daring me to pick a fight with them.

I smiled.

Smiling is the best way of dealing with aggression, I've always found.

Unless you've got a gun strapped to your waist, of course.

I didn't have a gun, so I smiled.

'Ronnie Marsh sent me,' I said. 'I took the photograph of Jon Junior from my pocket and showed it to him. 'The night of the fire, was this boy there? In the club.'

Lek wrinkled his nose. It was a nose that had been hit so many times that it was almost flush against his face giving him the look of a confused monkey. 'Maybe,' he said.

'Maybe?'

'Farangs all look the same to me,' he said. He shrugged. 'Was he with anyone?'

'I'm not sure.'

'Because if he was with a girl I'd probably remember the girl. Girls are more memorable. Especially pretty girls.'

'Yeah, I get it. Is Tam around?'

Lek pointed upstairs. 'He's sleeping.'

'Okay if I go and ask him?'

'He doesn't like to be disturbed when he's sleeping.'

'I'll be gentle.'

I went up the stairs. They opened into a landing where there were three chipboard doors. There was a buzz-saw snoring coming from one of the rooms and I pushed open the door to find a stocky Thai man wearing nothing but red and gold Muay Thai shorts lying face down on a stained mattress.

'Khun Tam?' I said.

The snoring continued so I bent down and shook him by the arm.

Big mistake.

He let out a shriek, jumped up into a fighting crouch and threw a punch that I only just managed to avoid by falling backwards and staggering against the wall.

'Whoa!' I shouted. 'I come in peace.'

Tam drew back his right fist but then he checked himself. 'Did you touch me?'

'Not in a bad way,' I said. 'You were snoring.'

'Who are you? He put his hands on his hips. He was dark-skinned and his chest and abdomen were the texture of seasoned mahogany.

'My name's Bob,' I said. 'Ronnie Marsh sent me.' I took out the photograph of Jon Junior. 'He wanted me to ask you if you remember this boy from the night of the fire.'

Tam looked at the picture and rubbed his nose with the back of his hand. 'No,' he said.

'You're sure?'

'I was on the door all night and I didn't see him.'

I put the picture away and thanked him.

'How is Khun Ronnie?' he asked.

'Not good,' I said. 'He's in the Bumrungrad.'

'He saved a lot of people. Stayed inside to help them get out.'

'What about you?'

'I went outside, phoned the fire brigade.'

'What about Khun Thongchai? What did he do?'

His eyes narrowed as he looked at me suspiciously. 'Why do you care about him?'

I shrugged. 'Khun Ronnie said he ran away.'

Tam avoided my gaze and didn't reply, letting me know that whether Thongchai had stayed or run away was none of my business, or his.

I thanked him and went downstairs. Lek had gone and the guy

with the newspaper smiled as I left.

I had a definite 'no' and I had a 'maybe' from a bouncer who only remembered girls so I was fairly confident that Jon Junior hadn't been in the Kube on the night that it had gone up in flames.

It would just be nice to be sure.

10

THE KEY TO FINDING an English teacher to Bangkok is remember that the job pays really badly. An expatriate teacher is doing well if he earns thirty thousand baht a month. That's twice what a Thai would get, but it's still only about a thousand dollars which doesn't go far, even in Thailand, which means that they spend a lot of time hunting down cheap places to eat and drink. The Londoner Pub on Sukhumvit Road is one of many drinking holes that's realised how hard-up teachers are and offers them a two drinks for one deal every Thursday. I left it until just before nine o'clock before heading there, figuring that the more they'd had to drink, the chattier they'd be. It had started raining again. I don't know if it was the real thing or the result of more misplaced cloud seeding.

The pub's down a basement under an office building, right next door to a bowling alley. The décor is standard dark wood and brass fittings and the only nod to the London theme were the Beefeater dresses that a couple of the staff were wearing. Two televisions were showing a British football match but nobody was paying them any attention. The clientele were almost without exception young men in knock-offs of designer shirts and shabby chinos.

A girl in a regular waitress uniform of white shirt and black trousers waved at an empty table but I shook my head and told her that I was there to see a friend.

I wandered among the tables letting the conversations wash

over me.

Moans about working conditions. Long hours, low pay.

Places that sold cheap beer.

Why Singha beer always gave you a headache.

Go-go dancers who offered free sex in exchange for English lessons.

Not much talk about the education system or lesson-planning. That's the way it is in the Land of Smiles – the vast majority of English teachers aren't here on a mission to educate. They're here to drink cheap beer. And hang out in go-go bars. Teaching is just a means to an end.

I took out Jon Junior's photograph and went over to a table where half a dozen guys in their twenties were standing guard over bottles of Singha and Carlsberg. 'Sorry to interrupt, but have any of you lads seen him?' I said, handing the picture over to the teacher nearest to me. He shook his head and handed it around the table. 'He's an American,' I said. 'Salt Lake City.'

'A Septic?' said one of the guys. 'Just what Bangkok needs, another Septic teacher.'

Septic Tank. Yank.

British humour.

'He arrived a few months ago,' I said. 'Now his parents are worried. Jon Clare's his name. Jon Clare Junior.'

The picture went around the group and back to me. They all shook their heads.

'You a detective?' asked one of the teachers. He was the smallest of the group with shoulder-length blonde hair tied back in a ponytail.

'Just a friend of the family,' I said.

'No reward or anything, then?'

I shook my head and slid the photograph back into my jacket.

A waitress hovered at my shoulder and I ordered a Phuket Beer. She smiled apologetically and said they didn't stock it so I ordered a Heineken.

'He came over as a tourist a couple of months ago, then decided to stay on as an English teacher,' I said.

The guy with the ponytail sniggered. 'Story of my life,' he said.

'How easy would that be?' I asked.

'To teach English?' said the guy on my right. He was in his early twenties, overweight with slicked back hair and a gold earring in his left ear. He had a computer case slung over his shoulder and three cheap ballpoint pens in the breast pocket of his shirt. 'Depends where he wanted to teach. There are some schools who'll take anybody. Was he qualified?'

'Not really.'

'He had a degree, though?'

'Sure.'

'Then he'd get a job no problem. The Thai universities would insist on a teaching qualification like an RSA. The good ones, like Thammasat and Chula would want a Master's degree. But most of the language schools will take on any farang provided they've got a degree.'

'What's an RSA?' I asked.

'Four-week course that supposedly prepares you for teaching,' said the overweight guy. 'That and a degree would get you into most schools. You can go on a course at the EEC in Siam Square. Set you back about sixty thousand baht.'

'Or you can buy a fake one for a fraction of that,' said Ponytail. 'I got mine for two thousand baht on the Khao San Road.'

Khao San Road.

Uncooked Rice Road.

The jumping-off point for most backpackers embarking on a South East Asian experience. Cheap food, cheap lodging, cheap transport to anywhere in the country and beyond. You can buy pretty much anything on the Khao San Road. Fake certificates, fake passports, fake driving licences. Drugs. Weapons.

'Don't they check?'

'Depends where you go,' said Ponytail. 'Some places are desperate they'll take anyone. There's an Indian at my school who can barely speak English. He just gets the students to read the text books. But he's got a degree certificate from the UK. I don't think the ink's dry yet, but the school doesn't care.'

'What about the students? They must realise that they've been fobbed off with an incompetent teacher?'

Ponytail grinned. 'They wouldn't say boo to a goose. It's not the Thai way. They'd probably just stop going after a few lessons. But there's always more students joining. Most pay in advance so the schools don't care about drop-outs.'

I made a mental note to ask Mr and Mrs Clare if Jon Junior had taken his educational qualifications with him.

'So you're saying that anyone can get off a plane and start teaching English in Thailand?'

The teachers nodded in unison.

My two bottles of Heineken arrived. I asked the waitress to bring a round of drinks for the guys and they all beamed at me like I was Father Christmas.

'So where's the best place for me to go looking for Jon Junior?'

'If he's legit and an American, you could try the AUA,' said the guy with earring. 'The American University Alumni. They're one of the biggest schools in Thailand. But he'd need real qualifications and references. You could try the Thai universities and high schools.

And the International schools. They're the best payers and the most selective. If he's using dodgy documents, then you'd drop down to the second division English schools.'

'How many of those are there?'

'Dozens,' said the guy with the earring.

'Hundreds,' added Ponytail.

'Needle in a haystack,' added one of the teachers.

It wasn't too daunting. There'd be a list of language schools somewhere. All I had to do was to telephone them all and ask if there was a Jon Clare on their staff.

The drinks arrived, two for each of the teachers. I paid the bill and then went around the bar, showing Jon Junior's picture to anyone who looked like a teacher.

An hour later and all I'd seen were shaking heads and blank faces.

I went home. At least it had stopped raining.

Maybe my luck was starting to change.

11

I COULD NEVER GET the hang of changing time zones. I know that if I fly to Hong Kong I lose an hour and that if I fly back to Bangkok I gain an hour. And I know that the clocks in the UK are moved an hour during the winter months so that farmers don't have to get up in the dark, and that the Americans change their clocks a week after the Brits. But other than that it's a mystery to me. I couldn't work out if Salt Lake City was ahead or behind Bangkok time, but I figured that as it was pretty much on the opposite side of the world, the difference would be about twelve hours either way. I left it until nine o'clock in the evening before calling the Clares. Mrs Clare answered and she sounded wide awake so I guess I hadn't woken her up.

'Is he okay, Mr Turtledove?' she asked as soon as she realised it was me.

'I haven't found him yet, Mrs Clare,' I said. 'But I've checked with the police and the hospitals and he's not been in any trouble. And I'm fairly sure that he wasn't in the nightclub. I've spoken to some of the people who worked there and no one remembers seeing him that night. So that at least is good news.'

I was trying to sound as optimistic as possible but she was obviously close to tears. I asked her about Jon Junior's degree. Had he taken it with him or asked her to send it to him in Bangkok? She said that he hadn't mentioned it to her and that so far as she knew his degree was framed and hanging on his bedroom wall.

I asked her to go and check. I waited for almost four minutes. The Clares must have lived in one hell of a big house.

While I waited I booted my laptop and went to the Google Mail page. I tapped in Jon Junior's user name and clicked the button that said I'd forgotten my password. It asked me for Jon Junior's date of birth so I waited until Mrs Clare came back on the line.

'It's still on the wall,' she said.

'Is it possible he took a copy before he left?' I asked.

'I don't think so,' she said. 'It's in a frame.'

'And did he take some sort of teaching class before he came to Bangkok?'

'No,' she said. 'We had no idea that he was considering teaching as a career until we got his phone call.'

'He wouldn't have done it in secret?'

'Why would he have done anything in secret, Mr Turtledove?' she said archly.

'Perhaps if he knew that you wouldn't approve.'

'I thought I made it clear in your office. We support our son fully in whatever he decides to do. Our philosophy in raising our children has always been to offer guidance and support, not to lay down the law.'

That's not quite what the Clares had said in my office and I didn't have to look at the notes I'd made. They'd wanted Jon Junior to join the family business. And if he was set on becoming a teacher, they wanted him to teach in Utah, not Thailand.

'Did he mention taking a teaching course in Thailand?' I asked.

'No, he didn't.'

'I'm told it would cost about sixty thousand baht for a four-week course. About one thousand five hundred dollars. Nothing like that showed up on his credit card statements did it?'

'Definitely not.'

'Did he have that sort of money on him?'

'He was on a tight budget, Mr Turtledove. I don't think he would throw away fifteen hundred dollars on a teaching course. Would you mind telling me why you have this sudden interest in my son's educational qualifications?'

'I'm trying to find out which school he was teaching at. It would make it easier if I knew what qualifications he had.'

I didn't want to tell her that if Jon Junior's degree was hanging on the wall in a frame then he'd probably had a counterfeit copy made in the Khao San Road. I figured that a devout Christian would probably regard that as a sin.

'Is there anything else I can help you with?' she asked.

'Actually there is,' I said. 'Can you give me his date of birth?'

She did and I entered the details and hit 'enter'.

The next stage was to answer Jon Junior's security question. 'What was the name of your first pet?'

'And can you tell me the name of Jon Junior's first pet?' I asked.

There was a long pause during which time she was no doubt wondering whether I'd gone insane.

'I'm trying to access his email account,' I explained.

'Isn't that illegal?' she said.

That was a good question, and the answer was probably yes.

'It'll be a big help to see if he's still sending emails,' I said. 'And with any luck there might be clue to his whereabouts in his inbox.'

'Jeeves,' she said. 'He had a cat called Jeeves. He was a big fan of P.G. Wodehouse at school.'

I tapped in 'JEEVES' and the server allowed me to reset the password on the account.

'All right, Mrs Clare, I'm in,' I said. 'Please stay on the line and

I'll see if there's anything useful here.'

I opened Jon Junior's inbox. Nothing had been opened for two weeks. There were more than fifty unopened emails, about half of which were spam offering cheap Viagra, millions of dollars from Nigerian bank accounts and cheap flights. I clicked on a personal message, from a friend back in Utah asking him why he hadn't been in touch.

'I don't see anything recent, Mrs Clare,' I said.

'That's not good, is it?' she asked.

'It might not mean anything,' I said. 'He might just be away from a computer. Did he have a laptop with him?'

'It's here, at home,' she said. 'He wanted to travel light. This isn't good, is it, Mr Turtledove?'

'He could be travelling,' I said, trying to put her at ease, even though I was beginning to share her concern. 'A lot of backpackers go up north to visit the hilltribes or over the border into Laos or Burma. Not everywhere has internet coverage.'

'Tell me one thing, Mr Turtledove. If Jon Junior has started working as a teacher in Bangkok, why hasn't he called us?'

It was a good question. One that I couldn't answer.

'We're not bad parents,' she said.

'I'm sure you're not.'

'We love our son.'

'I'm sure you do.'

She was upset.

I'd upset her.

I thanked her, promised to call her when I had any news, and cut the connection.

12

THAILAND'S IMMIGRATION policy is different to most developed countries – they just put out a welcome mat and pretty much allow everybody in. There are a few countries where Thailand insists on visas and generally anyone who arrives is given permission to stay for thirty days. Anyone who wants to stay longer can apply for a tourist visa at a Thai consulate or embassy in their own country and they'll be given a sixty-day visa, good for either one or two stays. The Thais are happy to let visitors in because all employment of foreigners is strictly regulated through a work permit system – a system that leads straight to jail if it's abused.

I guess the way the Thais think is that providing visitors aren't working, they're bringing money into the country which can only be a good thing. But what they didn't bank on was the visa run, where foreigners working illegally in Thailand simply leave and return once a month. Coaches packed with illegally-employed Westerners now shuttle back and forth between Cambodia and Laos so that they can be legally in the country, albeit working without a work permit. Once the authorities realised the extent that the system was being exploited, they slashed the number of days that would be granted to a visitor arriving by land from thirty to fifteen. But that didn't stop the illegal workers, it just doubled the number of visa runs and increased the profits of the companies, mostly Western-owned, that ran the coaches.

I googled 'Thailand visa run' and got almost a quarter of a million hits. I went through the first few pages, looking for companies based in Bangkok that did same-day visa runs to the Ban Laem border crossing that Jon Junior had used. Most of the companies only offered overnight trips for people who needed to get a new visa from the Thai Embassy in Phnom Penh. They spent the night in a cheap hotel and then picked up the visa the next day.

Jon Junior didn't need a new visa, all he had to do was to leave the country and return to activate the second half of his double re-entry visa. After half an hour of scrolling through the Google search results I had about twenty possibles, and I started calling them. I got lucky with the seventh company. The phone was answered by a Thai girl who spoke English with an American drawl that she had probably picked up at an international school in Bangkok. I spoke to her in Thai and asked if Jonathon Clare had been on her company's run to Cambodia on March the fifth. She put me on hold for a couple of minutes and then came back on the line and said yes, he been on the bus.

I punched the air in triumph.

'Is there a problem?' she asked, and I reassured her that there wasn't. I explained that his parents were looking for him and asked if she had an address or phone number for him. She only had a number and it was for a cellphone, the one that the Clares had given me.

'I don't suppose you know if he was sitting next to on the coach, do you?'

'I know the bus was almost full,' she said. 'My boss was on it, he might remember, but he isn't in at the moment. I'll ask him and give you a call.'

I gave her my number and ended the call.

I figured the next line of attack should be to track down the school where Jon Junior was teaching. For that I needed a list of English language schools and I figured my old friend Stickman would be able to help. Stickman runs a website about Thailand and in a former life he was an English teacher until he started to earn more from the internet than he was paid to stand in front of a group of unruly teenagers. Before I went to bed I emailed him to see if he had a list of English language schools. When I switched on the computer again at eight o'clock in the morning he'd replied with a list of thirty but warned me that it wasn't an inclusive list. 'The fly-by-nights open up for a few months, shut down and then open up under another name,' he said in his email.

Top of his list was the AUA school. I called and an efficient secretary confirmed within minutes that there was no Jonathon Clare on staff.

Sometimes it was important to be specific when talking with Thais so I got her to check Jon Clare and J Clare, and also to check using Junior as the family name.

It took me the best part of two hours to work my way down the list. None of the schools had heard of Jon Junior. He was either working for a school that wasn't on the list, or he was using another name.

That worried me.

If Jon Junior wasn't using his own name, then he was hiding. But from whom? And why?

I went through to the kitchen where Noy had made breakfast for me. A cheese omelette with a slice of wholewheat toast and a cup of tea. She sat and watched me as I ate.

'What are you doing today, light of my life?' I asked.

'I'm showing an American around three apartments. He's got sixty million baht to spend.'

'What does he do?' I asked, my fork poised over the omelette.

'He's a banker,' she said. 'Works in Hong Kong but wants a place here.'

'Where did I go wrong?' I asked.

'Are you unhappy with your lot?' Her eyes sparkled with amusement.

I grinned back. 'No honey, I'm the luckiest man alive.'

'Because you've got me?'

'Exactly,' I said.

And I meant it.

13

I was in the shop helping Ying wrap a bronze statue of a Khmer dancer that we'd sold over the internet to a collector in Texas when my cellphone rang. I didn't recognise the number or the voice, but it was a Frenchman speaking accented English and he said that his name was Philippe and that he was the owner of the company that had taken Jon Junior to Cambodia. I asked him if he remembered Jonathon Clare but he ignored the question.

'Who exactly are you?' he asked.

'My name's Bob Turtledove, I sell antiques. I'm trying to help Mr and Mrs Clare find their son.'

'And where are you now?'

'My shop. Soi Thonglor.'

'Can you come and see me?'

'You can't tell me on the phone?'

'I'd be happier talking to you face to face,' he said. 'I'm in On Nut. Not far from the Skytrain station. There's a coffee shop under the station. I'll be there in an hour.'

I looked at my watch. It was ten o'clock in the morning and On Nut was only half an hour away by taxi. 'Okay, I'll come,' I said.

'And bring your passport or photo ID with you,' he said. He ended the call before I could say anything.

I finished helping Ying wrap and box the statue, then called Federal Express to come and collect it. I left Ying filling in the paperwork while I went outside and flagged down a taxi.

When I got to the coffee shop, the Frenchman was sitting at a table by the window. He was in his sixties, balding with a greasy comb-over and wearing a rumpled linen suit. He stood up and shook my hand and immediately asked to see my passport. I gave it to him and he put on a pair of reading glasses and he looked at my photograph, then checked my name before giving it back to me.

'I'm sorry if I seem over-cautious,' he said as he sat down. 'But my assistant said that you spoke perfect Thai and the Government isn't very keen on the service that we offer.'

'But visa runs aren't illegal,' I said, sitting down opposite him. A waitress came over and I ordered an Americano. The Frenchman already had a frothy cappuccino in front of him.

'Not illegal, but the authorities would rather they didn't happen. They think that too many people are using the visa runs as a way of staying in the country indefinitely.'

'And you thought, what? That I was a Government spy?'

The Frenchman chuckled. 'I didn't know what to think,' he said. 'But I thought better safe than sorry.' He sipped his coffee. 'The thing is, the majority of people using our service are using visa runs to stay in the country. And a lot of them are regular customers working in Thailand without work permits. They obviously want to keep a low profile.'

'Obviously,' I repeated. I took out the photograph of Jon Junior and gave it to him. 'He was on the bus on March fifth, right?'

The Frenchman nodded. 'First time he'd used us.' He handed the picture back to me. 'Hadn't been in Thailand long. You could tell, most of the regulars watch the movie or sleep, he was looking out of the window the whole way there and back.'

'Did you talk to him?' My coffee arrived and I stirred in a

spoonful of sugar.

'Just to say hello and take his money. It was a straight through and through run and we were late setting off so we didn't even stay for lunch in Cambodia.'

'Did you take any details from him? Address, place of work, anything like that?'

'All we ask for is a name and to be honest we don't even check that. We take bookings but anyone can turn up on the day and if there's a seat they're on the coach.' He gestured around the coffee shop. 'This is where we meet. Seven in the morning and we head off at seven-thirty.'

'Was he travelling alone?'

The Frenchman nodded. 'Sat near the back next to the window.'

'Anyone sit next to him?'

'One of our regulars, he got here just before we left. Almost missed us.'

'Can I talk to him?'

The Frenchman looked as if I'd asked him to give me a couple of pints of his blood. 'He's not the sort to talk to people he doesn't know,' he said. 'I'm not sure that he'd want me to give you his name.'

'I really don't care who he is or what he's done, I just want to know if Jon Junior said anything that might help me locate him.'

The Frenchman dipped a biscuit in his coffee and then bit into it. A large chunk fell into his cup but he pretended not to notice. 'He's working illegally, that's the problem. He runs a go-go bar in Soi Cowboy. His boss won't apply for a working visa so he's here on tourist visas and that means at the moment he's doing a run every two weeks.'

'Like I said, what his visa status is no concern of mine.'

'He won't want to talk to strangers, that's the problem.' He took an iPhone out of his jacket pocket. 'I'll give him a call.' He stood up and went outside. I watched him through the window as he paced up and down, talking animatedly into the phone. After a couple of minutes he came back and gave the phone to me. 'He'll talk to you now.'

I took the phone from him and he sat down. 'This is Bob Turtledove,' I said. 'Thanks for agreeing to talk to me.'

'Philippe says you're cool,' he said. He had a British accent, Liverpool maybe, as if he was talking through his nose and not his mouth.

'That was nice of him,' I said.

'You are cool right?'

'As a cucumber.'

'Because I don't like busybodies sticking their nose in my business.'

'I understand,' I said. 'I just want to know about Jon Clare. The American boy you were sitting next to on the way back from Cambodia.'

'The Yank, yeah. Total newbie. Didn't know his arse from his elbow.'

'What did you talk about?'

'Not much, I was asleep most of the way. He asked me about what I did for a living and I told him about Soi Cowboy. He'd never been inside a go-go bar, can you believe that?'

'He's a Mormon,' I said. 'His family's religious.'

'Yeah? He seemed like a mummy's boy.'

'Did he say where he was working?'

'Some English school. I don't think he said where. He was complaining about it, said it was run by some dodgy Russians. He thought they were up to something.'

'Did he say what?'

'I don't think he knew. But he wanted out.'

'Was he in trouble?'

'I'm not sure. He wasn't exactly opening his heart to me, it was just chit-chat.'

'Did he say where he was living, where he hung out? Any clue as to where I might find him.'

'He said he had a girlfriend. We were talking about the bars and he said he'd never been inside a go-go bar and he didn't think that his girlfriend would like it if he did.'

'So she's Thai?'

'I assumed so,' he said.

'Didn't he say?'

There was a pause of several seconds. 'Hand on heart, I can't remember. But a single guy in Thailand, why would he be hanging out with a farang girl?'

'And when you got back to Bangkok, did he say where he was going?'

'He didn't say anything. Just goodbye and then he took his bag and went.'

'Taxi?'

'Motorcycle taxi,' he said. 'Just down from On Nut Skytrain station. I saw him go by.'

'Heading which way?'

'Back to lower Sukhumvit,' he said. 'And he was talking on his cellphone.'

I thanked him for his help, ended the call and gave the phone back to the Frenchman.

'Any help?' he asked.

'Maybe,' I said. 'We'll see.'

14

THERE WERE SEVERAL VANS lined up in the road outside Jon Junior's former hotel. Two were red, one was yellow and one was a green so dark that it was almost black. The drivers were huddled in a tight group at the front of the queue, smoking cigarettes and laughing. One of the saw me walking across the road and waved. 'Tuk-tuk?' he asked.

I shook my head and showed him the photograph of Jon Junior. 'Did you ever pick this boy up at the hotel and take him somewhere? He had two bags with him.'

The driver looked at the photograph and shook his head. I showed the photograph to the rest of the drivers. They blew tight plumes of smoke as they studied Jon Junior's picture.

'He went in a red tuk-tuk,' I said. 'He probably went to another hotel. Or an apartment block.'

The first driver took back the photograph and looked at it again. 'Maybe,' he said. 'Maybe I took him.'

'Where?' I asked.

The driver pointed down the soi. 'That way.'

Right. Fine.

'What was the name of the building you went to?'

The driver shrugged.

'Are you sure it was him?'

The driver scratched his neck with the nail of his little finger that seemed to have been grown extra long specifically for the purpose of scratching.

'I think so.'

'Your tuk-tuk is red?'

The driver nodded.

'Which one is yours?' I asked, in case he was just telling me what I wanted to hear.

He pointed at one of the two red tuk-tuks. That was a good sign.

'Was he with anyone?'

'No, he was alone.'

'And he went to another hotel?'

'Condominium,' he said.

'Condominium?' I repeated. 'Are you sure?'

The driver shrugged and scratched his neck as he frowned at the photograph. 'Old building,' he said. 'Sukhumvit Soi 22.'

'Can you take me?' I asked.

'A hundred baht,' he said quickly.

'Let's go.'

There are two sorts of tuk-tuks. There's the three-wheeled type that is powered by a two-stroke scooter engine, covered with a canopy and with a seat just large for three people at the back. They're noisy, smelly and uncomfortable and part of the Thai tourist experience, usually for a vastly-inflated fee. There are also four-wheeled versions with larger engines and with two facing seats at the back. They're more for locals with too much baggage or shopping to get onto the bus. I'm not a fan of either but sitting in the back with my head jammed against the roof was the only way that I was going to get Jon Junior's forwarding address.

Getting to Soi 22 from Soi 9 meant braving the traffic on the main Sukhumvit Road, a white-knuckle ride in any vehicle but a near-death experience in the back of a tuk-tuk, no matter how many wheels it has. The air was stifling hot, and every time we stopped it seemed that there was a bus next to us, belching out black smoke.

We shot down Soi 22 past a row of massage parlours and drove by the Imperial Queen's Park Hotel and then made a quick left turn into one of the side sois. We slowed to a crawl past a woman who cooking at a roadside stall and I got a blast of burning chilli in my eyes. By time the tuk-tuk had stopped there were tears streaming down my face.

I used a handkerchief to wipe my eyes as I looked up at the building. It was hard to tell whether Jon Junior's new address was a step up or a step down from the cheap hotel in Soi 9. From the look of the outside I'd probably say that he was paying a bit less but getting a bit more for his money. He was a good fifteen minute walk from the nearest Skytrain station, Phrom Pong, but there was a motorcycle taxi rank across from the building so transport wouldn't be a problem. The building was a soot-stained, grey oblong, eight floors high, with windows that didn't appear to have been cleaned in decades. There was no sign that I could see, no way of telling if the building was a hotel or an apartment block or an abattoir. Or a combination of all three.

'You're sure this is it?' I asked the tuk-tuk driver as I climbed out of the back of the van. I had to bend my head low, the tiny vans were designed to ferry around slightly-built Thais, not six-foot-tall farangs.

The driver was smoking a roll-up and he took the remnants from between his lips, coughed and spat into the street. 'I didn't see him go in, but this is where I dropped him.'

'With his bags?'

'Yes.'

'Just him?'

'Like I said, him and his bags.'

'But no one brought him here?'

He frowned, not understanding. 'I did.'

Jai yen yen. It was my own fault for not phrasing the question properly.

'You brought him and his bags, but did you bring anyone else?'

The driver took a last drag on his roll-up and flicked it into the gutter. 'He came alone.'

I gave him a hundred baht note and he sped off in a cloud of black smoke.

There were two double doors at the entrance and I pushed through them into a small reception area. There were two rattan sofas and a glass-topped coffee table at one end of the room and a small booth at the other. There was a woman sitting in the booth watching a Thai soap area on a tiny television.

On the wall behind her were rows of keys on hooks and pigeon holes for mail. 'Excuse me, is this a hotel or serviced apartments?' I asked.

'You want a room?' she said, not taking her eyes off the TV. A middle-aged woman with hair piled high on her head was bemoaning the fact that her husband had taken a mia noi, a minor wife. The friend she was confiding in was nodding sympathetically and produced a box of tissues as the betrayed wife burst into tears. Heart-rending stuff.

I told the receptionist that I was looking for a friend and showed her Jon Junior's picture. She glanced at it and handed it back to me.

'He check out already.'

'Jonathon Clare,' I said. 'From America.'

'I know,' she said. 'He check out.'

'When?'

'Last week.'

'Where did he go?'

She sighed but kept looking at the television. I couldn't tell if she was sighing because she was bored with my questions or if she was moved by what she was seeing on the television.

'He didn't say.'

'But he paid his bill and left?'

She nodded.

'He was a teacher,' I said.

'I know.'

'Do you know where he was teaching?'

On the television the middle-aged betrayed wife collapsed onto a sofa and dabbed at her cheeks with a handful of tissues. The receptionist put her hands together and clasped them to her chest. She was close to tears. 'No,' she said.

'Did he have any friends?' I asked. 'Anyone who came to see him?'

The soap opera hit a commercial break. The receptionist gasped.

I repeated my question.

'There was a girl,' she said, looking me in the eye for the first time since I'd walked into the building.

'A Thai girl?'

The woman nodded. 'Young.'

'How young?'

'A teenager.'

'What did she look like?'

'Short hair, hi-so maybe.'

'She went to his room?'

The woman nodded. 'Once. Mostly she waited for him here.'

'She came often?'

'Three or four times.'

'Do you think she was a girlfriend? Or a student?'

She shrugged. 'I don't know. She was dressed like a student.'

'Do you know which school she went to?'

She shook her head.

'And this is a hotel, right? Not a condominium block.'

'Both,' she said. 'You can rent rooms by the day or week, or you can stay for a year. Some people buy the rooms.'

'What about Jonathan Clare? Was he renting by the day or the week?'

She picked up a ledger and flicked through it. 'By the month,' she said.

'So he paid a deposit?'

The woman nodded.

'And he got that back when he checked out?'

'Usually we give people their deposits the day after they check out.'

'That doesn't make any sense.'

'It's our policy. We have to check for damage and that phone calls and electricity and water bills have been paid.'

'And he came back for his deposit?'

She looked at the ledger and nodded.

If Jon Junior waited around for his deposit then he probably wasn't running away from anyone. He'd just moved on. But why? And where?

I asked her if anyone had moved into Jon Junior's room. She flicked through the ledger and shook her head. 'It's still empty,' she said.

'Can I look around?' I asked.

I could see the look of concern flash across her face so before she could say anything I slipped her a five hundred baht note. Probably more than two days wages. She stared at the note, then the adverts ended and the soap opera restarted. She gave me the key to room 31. 'Second floor,' she said, her eyes back on the TV set.

There was an elevator but I took the stairs, figuring that I could do with the exercise.

The room was large with a queen size bed, a cheap black plastic sofa and a glass-topped coffee table that was a twin of the one in reception. There was a wardrobe and a dressing table and a door that led to a small bathroom. Western-style toilet, washbasin and a shower stall.

The wardrobe was bare except for a line of pink plastic coathangers.

There as nothing in the dressing table drawers.

I looked under the bed. There was a roach trap and a lot of dust, but nothing else.

I lifted the pillows. Nothing. Lifted the mattress. Nothing.

I went over to the plastic sofa and lifted the cushions. Nothing.

I wasn't sure what I expected to find. A map showing where he'd gone? A letter? But whatever I was hoping to find, I was disappointed.

I went back to reception. The woman there was wiping her eyes as the end credits of the soap opera rolled across the television screen.

I gave her back the key.

'And he definitely didn't leave a forwarding address?' I asked.

She shook her head.

'Did he take a taxi or a tuk-tuk when he left?'

'I didn't see him leave,' she said.

'Why not?'

'He must have checked out at night,' she said.

'Who was here then?'

'The night man,' she said. 'Gung.'

Gung. It means prawn.

'Does he work every night?'

'He's the night man,' she said patiently.

Stupid question.

Jai yen.

'How did he pay his bills?' I asked.

'Cash.'

'No credit card?'

'Just cash.'

'And the only visitor he had was this girl?'

'She was the only one I saw.'

I'd have to talk to Gung to find out if Jon Junior had had any nocturnal visitors. I was running out of questions for the receptionist. It looked like a dead end. Jon Junior had been here. Now he wasn't. End of story.

The receptionist looked at me blankly. I felt that I was missing something. That if I asked her the right question then the puzzle would be solved. I looked at the mailboxes.

'Did he get any mail while he was here?'

'No.'

Okay, so that wasn't the magic question.

'Any phone calls? Did anyone call here asking for him?'

'I don't think so.'

'But any calls would come through reception, right?'

There was a small switchboard on the desk. The receptionist nodded.

'So, did anyone call for him?'

'Maybe. I don't remember.'

I figured that it was unfair of me to expect her to remember every call she answered.

'He did make some calls, though.'

I stared at her in surprise. 'Really?'

She twisted around and opened the bottom drawer of a filing cabinet and pulled out a sheaf of papers. She licked her index finer and flicked through them. They were receipts. She smiled triumphantly and pulled out a sheet and handed it to me.

It was dated three weeks earlier and was a computer print-out of half a dozen phone calls, the time and date of each call and how long the call lasted. I wanted to reach over and plant a kiss on her cheek but I slipped her another five hundred baht note.

'Can I keep this?' I asked.

She shook her head. 'It's for our records,' she said.

I quickly copied down the numbers, dates and times and gave the receipt back to her. Another soap opera was starting and she hurried to put the receipt back into the filing cabinet drawer as I left.

I found a Starbucks, ordered a low-fat latte and sat down at a corner table. There were two numbers on the receipt. One was a cellphone. Jon Junior had called it five times on three different days. Two of the calls had been short, just a few seconds so I figured he'd left a message, and the three others had all been over half an hour.

Interesting. Half an hour was a long time to be talking on the phone.

I took out my cellphone and tapped out the number. I went straight through to the answering service which suggested that the phone was switched off. It was the standard recorded message and it gave no clue as to who owned the phone. I thought about leaving a message but then decided against it.

The other number had the prefix 02 which meant that it was a

Bangkok landline. Jon Junior had made a two-minute call. I tapped out the number.

A Thai woman answered, speaking English. 'Betta English Language School,' she said briskly.

Interesting.

I asked her for the address of the school and scribbled it down in my notebook. It was a short walk away from Jon Junior's apartment. I cut the connection.

Very interesting.

The fact that Jon Junior had switched rooms suggested that he'd wanted to move closer to the Betta English Language School. But the Betta English Language School had been on the list that Stickman had given me. And they'd denied all knowledge of Jon Clare Junior.

15

Petrov Shevtsova was a big man who looked as if he worked out a lot. He was wearing a too-tight black t-shirt and khaki chinos and brown suede loafers with tassels on them. He had a couple of days of stubble on his chin, or maybe his hair just grew faster than mine. He wore a thick gold chain on his right wrist, a gold Rolex on his left, and he had a gold chain with three Buddhas on it around his neck. I knew his name was Petrov Shevtsova because that was the name on his office door. He hadn't introduced himself when I'd walked into his office. 'So where did you teach before?' he asked.

'New Orleans,' I said. 'Night school.'

'You're qualified?' There were three cellphones on the desk close to his right hand. All brand new Nokias, the sort that let you surf the internet, take a five megapixel photograph, pinpoint your position to within a few feet and, on a good day, allow you to make a phone call.

'Sure.' I handed over a degree certificate showing that I'd got a degree in English from New Orleans University, and a TEFL certificate from a college in New Orleans. A print shop in the Khao San Road had made them up for me for five hundred baht. The owner of the shop had asked for two thousand but I'd bargained him down. It took him five minutes on a computer and I had perfect fake qualifications.

I'd faked the qualifications but I'd used my own name just in case I was asked to show my passport or driving licence.

'References?'

'I'm having some sent over.'

'We pay four hundred baht an hour,' said Petrov, tossing the certificates back to me. 'You'll get a minimum of six hours a day. Most of our classes are early mornings or evenings and weekends. Weekends are our busiest time.'

'So that's two thousand four hundred a day, right?'

Petrov squinted at me as if he had the start of a headache. 'I just said, four hundred an hour. If there's no class, you don't get paid. If there's a class, you get paid. Most of our students attend regular schools and use our school to get extra English lessons so most of the classes are early morning, in the evening and at weekends.'

'How many pupils in each class?' I asked. I was asking the questions I figured a job applicant would ask, but all I seemed to be doing was annoying the Russian. His frown deepened.

'A class is a class,' he said. 'One, ten, a hundred. You teach, they learn. Do you want the job or not?'

So that was it. Interview over. 'Sure,' I said.

Petrov waved at the door. 'Start tomorrow. Talk to the secretary, she'll give you a schedule.'

'What about a work permit?'

'Teachers fix up their own permits.' One of his cellphones started to ring.

'But I'm okay to teach without one?'

'Immigration don't bother us,' said Petrov. 'If it worries you, wait until you've got your permit.'

He answered his phone and spoke a few sentences of rapid Russian. When he cut the connection he glared at me as if he was annoyed that I was still in his office. He waved at the door again and looked at his Rolex.

'A friend of mine used to work here,' I said. 'Jon Clare.'

'So?'

'I just wondered if he was still here.'

'If he is, you'll see him. If he isn't, you won't.'

'Do you have a number for him?'

'A number?'

'A phone number. So I can call him.'

Petrov sighed. 'I can't be expected to remember all the teachers who work here,' he said. 'Talk to the secretary.' He picked up one of his cellphones and tapped out a number, then swung his feet up onto his desk. He was barking in Russian as I left his office.

Petrov's secretary was a Thai woman in her fifties with permed hair and Chanel glasses with pink frames. She was wearing a pink shirt with a fern pattern on it and peach slacks. I told her who I was and she gave me a photocopied sheet of times and classroom numbers and a dog-eared textbook. 'The book is four hundred baht,' she said.

'I have to buy my own book?'

'All teachers buy their own books,' she said. 'It is the company policy.'

I gave her four one hundred baht notes. 'Does my friend Jon Clare still work here?' I asked.

'Is he a teacher?'

'Sure. He started about three months ago.'

She went over to a filing cabinet by the door and asked me to spell out his name. She pulled out a drawer, ran her fingers over the files, then pushed the drawer closed. 'No one called Clare,' she said.

'I'm sure he worked here,' I said.

She sat down at her desk again. 'No file.'

'He's an American. Twenty-one, good-looking.' I took the photograph from my jacket pocket and showed it to her.

She shook her head before she'd even looked at the picture. 'No file,' she said.

'But do you recognise him?'

She shook her head again.

So that was it. The school where Jon Junior had worked for three months didn't have a file on him.

Interesting.

'Would you show me around?' I asked.

She nodded and I followed her out of the office. There wasn't much to see. Six classrooms, three on each side of a corridor. There were glass panels in the doors so that anyone walking down the corridor could see inside. I pictured Petrov striding up and down, cracking a whip and urging his underpaid teachers on. There were classes in four of the rooms and two were empty. Each room had a dozen wooden chairs with panels screwed to the side so that the students could take notes. On the wall, a large whiteboard. Two windows with the blinds drawn and fluorescent lights overhead. At the end of the corridor was a staffroom. Two teachers were sitting on a wooden bench, blowing cigarette smoke through an open window. They looked up guiltily as the secretary opened the door and showed me in. There was a no-smoking sign by the window. Along one wall was a line of metal lockers. Half were padlocked. There was a coffee percolator and a microwave and a stack of stained cups in a grubby sink.

Salubrious.

Not.

The teachers nodded at me but said nothing as they made a half-hearted attempt to hide their cigarettes. The secretary blinked amiably at me. The unspoken question hung in the air like the stale smoke: had I seen enough? I nodded. More than enough.

Opposite the school was a shophouse with a few tables on the ground floor and a glass-fronted fridge containing beer and soft drinks. I sat down at one of the tables and ordered a Phuket Beer but they didn't have any so I said I'd have a Heineken, one from the back of the fridge, and no ice because it didn't look like the sort of place that bought in ice. There was probably an old man in the back with a sweat-stained t-shirt and a rusty knife hacking away at a big block of the stuff, and while my immune system was well up to speed when it came to dealing with Thai microbes and viruses, there was no point in tempting fate.

At four o'clock a bell sounded from somewhere up on the second floor and a couple of minutes later a stream of boys and girls flowed out of the main entrance. The girls wore the standard Thai uniform of white shirt and black skirt and I was too far away to see the small badges that identified the individual schools. A few had regulation haircuts, no longer than shoulder length, a sign that they were from the city's public schools. The majority of the girls with longer hair, shorter skirts and Gucci high-heeled shoes were from the international schools, where fees were higher and the pupils were given more leeway dress-wise and were allowed to grow their hair longer. There didn't seem to be any mixing between the two groups. The public schoolgirls headed for the bus stop, the up-market pupils walked together in small groups, presumably to wherever they'd parked the cars that their doting parents had given them.

It was just as easy to spot the social status of the boys. The few who were in the public school system had crew cuts, with well-worn white shirts tucked into black shorts. The private school kids had their shirt tails out, their ties at half mast, wore their hair fashionably long and had cellphones pressed to their ears.

As one lot of pupils flowed out, a new lot flowed in. More upper-class pupils arrived by the luxury car-load while the poorer kids walked from the bus stop.

My bottle of Heineken arrived with a handful of shaved ice in a glass so I drank it from the bottle. There was a stack of Thai newspapers on one of the tables so I leaned over and picked up a copy of *Thai Rath*, the local scandal sheet. They specialised in close up photographs of road accident victims or Burmese girls hiding their faces but not their breasts after being busted in a local massage parlour. The old woman who'd bought me my beer nudged her husband in the ribs and nodded at the farang reading a Thai newspaper. He snorted and closed his eyes again.

Five minutes after the bell the pavements were empty again. I read the paper from cover to cover and ordered another Heineken, without ice. The old woman put a fresh bottle on the table, with a fresh glass of shaved ice. I smiled. Sometimes it didn't matter how fluent you were in the language, whatever you said went in one ear and out of the other. The trick was not to let it annoy you.

Jai yen.

Cool heart.

Forget about it.

The next time the bell rang three farangs were among the throng of eager-to-leave pupils. All men in their twenties wearing polo shirts, jeans and cheap shoes and carrying plastic briefcases.

Teachers.

They headed over to the shophouse, flopped down at the table next to mine and ordered three Singha beers. I've never been fond of Singha. It's too sweet and on the few occasions I've had more than a couple of bottles I've always ended up with a fierce hangover.

I sipped from my bottle of Heineken and listened as they swapped gossip, war stories of a day at the chalkface. The one in the pale blue shirt was British with a girlish giggle and a rash of acne across his cheeks and neck. The one in the red polo shirt was Canadian with receding hair and nicotine-stained fingers, and the one in the green shirt was from New Zealand or Australia, I can never tell the difference between the accents, a good-looking guy with piercing blue eyes and a dimpled chin. The Brit was describing a girl in one of his classes in a way that would annoy the hell out of me if she'd been in any way related to me. The other two nodded enthusiastically as if it was the most normal thing in the world for teachers to be discussing the breasts and thighs of a fifteen-year-old girl who'd been entrusted to their care.

I leaned over. 'Are you guys teachers?' I asked.

The Brit stopped his girlish giggling and his cheeks flushed. Maybe he thought I was the father of one of the girls at the school, or maybe it was just the Singha beer kicking in. 'Why?' he asked defensively.

I smiled amiably. 'I've just been offered a job over there,' I said, nodding in the direction of the school. 'Supposed to start tomorrow.'

'You talked to Petrov, yeah?' said the Canadian.

'Yeah, what's his story? Bit strange to find a Russian running an English language school, isn't it?'

The Canadian shrugged. 'There's all sorts running schools out here,' he said. 'Any man and his dog can set up a school. Where did you teach before?'

'Back in New Orleans,' I said. 'Came out here on spec.'

The Kiwi grinned. 'Well you sure didn't come out here for the money,' he said.

'The son of a friend of mine told me it was a good place to work,' he said. 'American guy, Jon Clare. Do you know him?'

'Jon Boy? Haven't seen him around for a couple of weeks.'

'He quit, didn't he?' said the Brit.

'I didn't know that,' said the Kiwi.

'From Salt Lake City,' I said.

'Yeah, a Mormon,' said the Canadian. 'Could never get him inside a go-go bar.'

'I thought he was gay,' said the Brit.

'Just because he didn't want to watch naked girls swing around silver poles doesn't mean he's gay,' said the Kiwi.

'Yeah, but it's a good indication,' said the Brit, and giggled. It was the sort of giggle that made me want to lean across and slap his acne-scarred face.

Jai yen.

'Jon Junior wasn't gay,' I said. 'Just a well-brought up kid. Any idea where he went? It's been a couple of months since I spoke to him.'

All three men shook their heads.

'Petrov could have sacked him,' said the Brit. 'Jon Boy was forever in his office complaining about one thing or another.'

'Complaining about what?' I asked, and took another sip of my Heineken.

'He needed to kick back and relax,' said the Kiwi. 'He took it all too seriously.'

'Took what all?'

The Kiwi shrugged again. 'We're not teaching brain surgery, right? Mainly we're teaching rich kids to speak English. Most of them don't want to be there, it's their parents who want them to learn. So they resent it. They resent us and they resent their parents. Our job is to stand in front of them for an hour and talk to them in something approaching a Western accent. If Petrov could get away with it he'd staff the school with Indians and Malaysians but the parents want to know that they're getting genuine native speakers so he has to hire us.'

The Brit giggled girlishly. 'Yeah, but sheep-shaggers don't really qualify as native speakers, do they?'

'It's your language in name only,' said the Kiwi.

'What's this crap about lingua franca, anyway?' said the Brit. 'Why use a French phrase to say that English is the common language. I've never understood that.'

'It's Italian,' I said.

'What's Italian?' said the Brit, frowning.

'Lingua franca. It's Italian.'

His frown deepened. 'Are you sure?'

'Yeah, I'm sure.' I waved for a round of beers. 'On me,' I said. 'Tradition back at my old school was that the new guy buys the beers.'

'I'll drink to that,' giggled the Brit. I was giving serious consideration to hitting him over the head with my bottle of Heineken.

Jai yen.

'So you're telling me that job satisfaction isn't high on your list of priorities?' I said.

'You get bitter and twisted,' said the Canadian. 'Some of the kids do want to learn. Some of them work during the day and spend their own money on the courses. But in the main, yeah, it's rich kids doing what their parents want. If you want job satisfaction, join one of the international schools or the Thai universities.'

The fresh beers arrived and the teachers toasted me. 'So what's your reason for coming to Thailand, Bob?' asked the Kiwi.

'To teach.'

The Brit sniggered but didn't say anything.

The Kiwi shook his head. 'You're not being interviewed now,' he said. 'No one comes to Thailand to teach. There's no money in it. You must have talked money with Petrov, right? You'll be getting a quarter of what you'd be getting in the States.'

'It's not about money though, is it?'

All three of them laughed. 'No, it's not,' said the Kiwi.

The Canadian took a long pull on his beer and wiped the back of his mouth with his hand. 'There are three reasons for coming here,' he said. 'Sex, sex, and sex.'

'You forgot sex,' said the Brit.

'You put up with the low wages, the students who don't give a shit, the cockroach-infested classrooms, because a couple of times a week you can go out and get laid by some of the best looking women in the world,' said the Canadian, warming to his theme.

'Or men,' said the Brit. He waggled his eyebrows suggestively.

'That's just the way it is,' said the Canadian. 'The only ones not here for the sex are the ones running away from something.'

'So which are you, Bob?' asked the Kiwi.

I shrugged. 'I'm sorry to disappoint you guys, but I enjoy teaching. I've been doing it almost fifteen years and I wanted to see a bit of the world. And I don't think Jon came here for sex, either.'

'Born again virgin,' sneered the Brit.

'Yeah, you could never get Jon Boy into a go-go bar,' agreed the Kiwi.

'Any sort of bar,' agreed the Canadian.

'There you go,' I said. 'Not everyone's here for sex. And I don't see Jon sticking at a job he didn't like. Do you think that he just found a better job?'

The Kiwi shrugged. 'It's possible. More likely that Petrov sacked him, I'd have thought.'

'Why do you say that?'

The Kiwi took a sip from his bottle of Singha. 'Nothing was good enough for Jon. He argued about the classrooms, the state of the textbooks, the fact that classes were merged if we were a teacher short, the rattle and hum from the air-con. He was never out of Petrov's office, always in there with one complaint or another.'

'And Petrov didn't give a damn, right?'

'The school's a business, that's all. He doesn't care if the students come out speaking the Queen's English or not, so long as the fees are paid. The kids don't care one way or another. So why should we? I put in the hours, I get paid, end of story.'

I took a sip of my beer. 'So do you think Jon quit? Or Petrov sacked him?'

'Either's a possibility.'

'You've all got lockers at the school, right?'

The Kiwi frowned at the change of subject. 'So?'

'I'm just wondering if Jon cleaned his out.'

The frown deepened. 'Do you think something's happened to him?'

'I'd feel a lot easier knowing that he'd cleared out his locker, that's all.'

The Kiwi put down his beer. 'You think Petrov did something to him?'

I put my hands up. 'I'm just considering all angles, that's all.'

'You don't shoot a guy just because he objects to teaching from photocopied text books,' said the Kiwi.

'Who said anything about shooting?' I said.

'That's what you were suggesting.'

'You're the one who mentioned shooting,' I said. 'Is Petrov like that?'

The Brit screwed up his face as if he'd just swallowed a wasp. 'We did see him with a gun once. In his office.'

'Once,' said the Kiwi.

'He was playing with it,' said the Brit. 'Looked like he was practising a quick draw.'

Guns aren't difficult to get in Thailand, and just because a man has one doesn't mean he's going to use it.

But it wasn't a good sign.

'Look, we make jokes about it being a school run by the Russian mafia, but the school is a business,' said the Kiwi. 'And Petrov is a businessman.'

'A businessman with a gun,' I said.

'He does hang out with some pretty heavy characters,' said the Brit.

'So now we're condemning a man for the friends he's got,' said the Kiwi. 'Look, he pays my wages and leaves me alone. What more can you ask for from a boss? Jon Junior was a pain in the arse and I wouldn't be surprised if Petrov had sacked him.'

'Fine. So if Jon Junior was sacked, where is he?'

The three teachers shrugged.

'Who knows?' said the Kiwi. 'People come, people go. Bangkok's a city of transients.'

'Who cares?' said the Brit. 'He was a stuck-up prick. So where are we going tonight? I fancy Nana Plaza.'

Jai yen.

I caught a taxi back to the shop and as I sat in the back I dialled the cellphone number that Jon Junior had called. The answering service kicked in again. This time I left a message.

16

'YOU'RE GOING TO WHAT?' Noy asked me over breakfast. This time I'd cooked for her. A Thai omelette stuffed with pork, boiled rice, and a glass of freshly squeezed orange juice with added salt, just the way she likes it. It's one the strange things about Thais – they put salt in their orange juice and sugar in their soups. Go figure.

'Just for a day or two,' I said. I sipped my coffee and tried to look as if teaching English was the most natural thing in the world for me to suggest.

'Would you like to tell me why at this stage in your life you've suddenly decided to teach English?'

'It's a case.'

'Honey, you're an antiques dealer. You don't have cases.'

'I'm looking for a boy.'

Her fork froze in the air on the way to her lips. 'Oh my Buddha,' she said.

'That came out wrong,' I admitted.

'I hope so.'

'There's an American boy gone missing, his parents have asked me to find him. He taught at an English school and I want to see if his students know where he went.'

She put down her fork. 'And you're going to do this by pretending to be an English teacher?'

'A teacher of English, yes,' I said. 'How hard can that be?'

'You were a policeman,' she said. 'And now you sell antiques.'

'It's English, honey. It's not rocket science.'

'And when are you going to start this new career?'

'In a couple of days. And it's not a career, honey.' I sipped my coffee.

'And what about the medical? How did that go?'

'I get the results this afternoon.' I patted my stomach. 'But I feel good. I weigh about five pounds less than the last time I had a medical and I'm playing more tennis.'

'I'll keep my fingers crossed,' she said. 'Just in case.'

'It'll be fine,' I said. 'The nurse who took my blood pressure said I had the heart of a twenty-five year old.'

'Well I just hope he doesn't ask for it back,' she said, and giggled at her own joke.

She has a lovely giggle, my wife.

We finished breakfast and then I spent the morning in the shop, pricing a consignment of opium pipes that I'd had shipped over from Vietnam. They were copies of Chinese antiques and looked just like the real thing but at a fraction of the price. I didn't sell them as genuine antiques, of course, but I have competitors who do. I put them on the website with a clear warning that they were decorative and not antiques.

I had lunch at Fatso's. Big Ron wasn't there and a tourist in a Singha beer sweatshirt and union jack shorts was sitting in the big chair while his wife took a photograph with her cellphone.

I sat at a stool at the other end of the bar and drank a Phuket Beer and had one of Big Ron's famous steak and kidney pies with French fries and peas before walking along Soi 3 to the Bumrungrad.

I was due to see Doctor Duangtip at two o'clock but I got there at one and went up to see Ronnie Marsh in the burns unit. I'd spoken to a Thai lawyer who I sometimes played tennis with and he wanted Marsh to call him but I wasn't sure if he had access to a phone. I knocked on the door to his room and pushed open the door and then stopped as I saw a teenage girl lying on the bed, an oxygen mask over her face. 'Sorry,' I said, and closed the door. I frowned as a looked at the room number. It was definitely the right one.

A nurse was talking down the corridor pushing a trolley and I asked her what had happened to Khun Ronnie. The look on her face gave it away before she even opened her mouth to speak.

'I'm sorry,' she said. 'Khun Ronnie passed away.'

'What happened? He was okay when I spoke to him,' I said.

'He passed away last night.'

'Passed away?'

'He had heart failure.'

'Heart failure?'

The nurse nodded. 'Are you a relative?' she asked.

'Just a friend. Is there somebody who can tell me what happened to him?'

The nurse took me along to an office and introduced me to a doctor who looked as if he was in his twenties. He shook my hand solemnly and asked me to sit down, then explained that Ronnie had suffered a massive heart attack in the middle of the night.

'Is that usual with burns victims?' I asked.

He pushed his spectacles higher up his nose and shifted in his seat. 'It can happen,' he said. 'But Mr Marsh did seem to be recovering. We had a resuscitation team in his room within seconds of the alarm sounding but they were too late.' He tapped away at his computer terminal and squinted at the screen. 'We don't have a next of kin for Mr Marsh,' he said. 'Do you know where his family is?'

'I don't,' I said.

The doctor frowned. 'That's a pity,' he said.

'I'll ask around,' I said. "Look, I know this might sound a little strange, but it isn't possible that something caused his heart attack?'

'Such as?'

I shrugged. Like somebody injecting him with potassium chloride, sodium gluconate, or even a straightforward air bubble, is what I wanted to say.

But I didn't.

'I don't know,' I said. There was no point because if someone had killed Ronnie then there'd be no way of proving it. Potassium chloride and sodium gluconate disappeared from the system within hours and an air bubble was almost impossible to spot. 'It's just that he seemed fine when I spoke to him last.'

'These things do happen,' said the doctor. 'Burns of the sort that Mr Marsh suffered cause a massive shock to the system.' He leant back in his chair. 'There will be a post mortem of course. I am sure we will know more then.'

On the way out I dropped by the nurse's station. There were three young nurses sharing a box of cookies and I asked them if Khun Ronnie had received any visitors before he died.

One of the nurses had been working the night shift and she said that yes, two men had come to see Khun Ronnie and brought him some oranges.

I asked her to describe them and I was pretty sure it was Lek and Tam, the kickboxers.

Funny that.

I wouldn't have pegged either of them as fruit fans.

17

'WELL, IT'S GOOD NEWS, bad news, Khun Bob,' said Doctor Duangtip, flicking the corner of my file with his thumbnail.

That wasn't exactly what I'd been hoping to hear. The last three times I'd been in for the chat about the yearly check-up it had been a beaming smile and a pat on the back and see you next year.

And this time I was five pounds lighter.

And I'd been playing a lot of tennis.

And I'd cut down on my drinking.

Good news, bad news didn't sound reassuring.

The last time I'd had to break good news, bad news to anyone it had been a data processor from Manchester who'd asked me to run a check on his Thai fiancée. I don't normally get involved with relationship cases because when you tell people something they don't want to hear about their loved one, they tend to lash out at the messenger. Besides, I also figure that what people do in the privacy of their bedrooms or a short-time hotel is up to them and their consciences. I'd taken Jason's case, though, mainly because he wasn't the normal case of a tourist falling head over heels for a bargirl. Jason worked for a website design company in Hua Hin and he'd met the girl of his dreams. Her name was Fun. It means rain. Jason was planning to marry her and then take her to Manchester to meet his parents and introduce them to his new bride. While he was in the UK he planned to sell a flat he had there. With the money he was planning to buy a piece of land near the beach in Hua Hin and build a house where he and Fun could live happily ever after. Under Thai law, foreigners can't own land, so Jason wanted to be one hundred per cent sure that he was doing the right thing. He'd heard horror stories of expats who'd lost everything after marrying local girls and so he wanted me to check that there wasn't a Thai husband waiting to come out of the shadows once all Jason's assets were in Fun's name. He was a friend of a friend so I agreed to help.

It was an easy job. Fun was from Udon Thani, in the North East. Jason gave me her full Thai name, her date of birth and her parents address. I drove up to Udon Thani and spent an hour drinking tea with two middle-aged ladies in the local amphur – the district office.

Good news, bad news.

The good news was that Fun was totally loyal, totally faithful, loved Jason to bits and would probably make him a great wife.

The bad news was that Fun was a man.

Oh yes, it happens. It happens a lot in Thailand. A snip and a tuck and a six-month course of hormones and Mr Fun was Miss Fun.

Good news, bad news.

Jason took it quite well, I thought. So far as I know, they're still together. He's given up any thoughts about taking her back to Manchester. Tells everyone that she'd hate the rain and the cold but the real reason is that all her legal documents, including Fun's ID card and passport, show that she's male. The British Embassy would laugh in his face if he applied for a visa for her. So they live happily ever after, sort of, in Hua Hin. He processes data for a couple of Bangkok companies, and Fun does whatever men who have had their penises surgically removed do. They're thinking about adopting a baby, apparently.

'The good news,' said Doctor Duangtip, 'is that your cholesterol level is on the way down at last. You must be exercising.'

I shrugged.

'Your heart is strong, your chest x-ray is clear and your vision and hearing are exceptional.'

Good news.

Great.

Fantastic.

So what's the bad news?

'No diabetes, blood pressure normal, your prostate is fine.'

More good news.

'Your lower abdomen ultrasound shows no problems, your liver is functioning exactly as it should.'

She loves you, Jason. Loves you to bits. There's just one thing you should know ...

Doctor Duangtip took a deep breath. 'There is however a slightly raised level of CEA.'

That's the bad news. It didn't sound so bad. But then, I hadn't a clue what a raised CEA level was.

Doctor Duangtip looked pained. 'It's not hugely high, but it is abnormal and is generally regarded as a red flag.'

A red flag.

Now that sounded like bad news.

It sounded like train crashes and road accidents and bodies lying bleeding in the road.

'It's what we call a marker,' said the doctor, looking over my shoulder at a spot somewhere on the wall.

I nodded. A marker didn't sound quite as bad as a red flag.

'It can, in certain cases, be an indication of an intestinal tumour,' he said.

'A tumour? Cancer, you mean?'

'Yes. Cancer of the colon.'

Right then. There it was, finally out in the open. Definitely bad news.

Cancer.

Worse than a red flag.

A lot worse.

'Wouldn't that have shown up on the ultrasound?' I asked. Throw me a lifebelt. Something.

He looked even more pained and flicked the file again. 'The ultrasound gives us a view of the outside of the various organs in the abdominal cavity, but we can't see inside them.' He leaned forward and clasped his hands together as if about to say a prayer. 'Khun Bob, it is a marker, that is all. The fact that you have a raised level of CEA is an indication that something might be wrong. That is all. It just means that we have to carry out a few more tests. And you should see a specialist.'

Something might be wrong.

That sounds better than a red flag.

Better than cancer.

Cancer.

Shit.

What the hell am I going to tell my wife?

18

NOY WAS SITTING on the terrace playing something by Bach. I stood in the shadows watching her for the best part of ten minutes. She's always beautiful, but there was something incredibly sexy about her when she concentrated on her violin. Her eyes half open, a look of rapture on her face as her lithe body swayed in time to the music. I wanted to rip the violin from her, to take her in my arms, to force my lips on her hers and to take her there and then on the terrace. She'd have killed me on the spot, of course. For a start the violin is a Stradivarius and worth almost as much as our apartment. And her playing is as close to perfection as you can get. Interrupting her for something as basic as sex would have been a mortal sin. So I stood and listened and worshipped.

Thailand is famous for its beautiful women, and there are head-turners in every department store and on every street corner, but my stomach still turns over whenever I see Noy. When I first met her hair was almost down to her waist, jet black and glossy, but she's had it cut since so that it's just down to her shoulders. She's got high cheekbones and a cute nose and skin the colour of milk chocolate and a body with curves in all the right places. She was wearing a red dress that ended above the knee showing off one of the best pairs of legs I've ever seen. There isn't a day that goes by that I don't thank the Lord that I found her and married her.

Actually, she found me.

I first met Noy when she came into my shop and bought a small nineteenth-century Burmese Buddha. She asked me lots of questions about its authenticity and how it had come into the country, and then she asked a few similar questions about my own authenticity. I figured she just liked to talk and I was happy to stand and listen and gaze at her.

She came back a week later and bought a Khmer wall hanging that I'd had in the shop for almost three years. She barely looked at it and spent most of the time asking me about where I lived, which restaurants I liked, where I went for holidays. I thought she just liked to talk. On the way out she gave me her card. Back then she was working for one of the glossy magazines that were full of advertisements for dresses that cost twice the national average wage. She was a stylist, whatever that meant.

I had two assistants back then, middle-aged sisters called Start and Stop. They were born two years apart and yes, the first one born was optimistically called Start but the second was delivered by Caesarean and the mother had decided that enough was enough. I'd only been in Thailand a couple of years and my Thai wasn't up to much so when the two sisters put their heads together and started laughing I didn't know what had amused them but figured that it almost certainly involved me.

The next week Noy was back. I was dealing with a German who wanted to take two eighteenth-century Buddhist statues back to his loft in Paris and my French was even worse than my Thai so it was taking forever to explain the regulations about taking religious figures out of the country. Noy wandered around the shop apparently aimlessly but she always seemed to be in my field of vision, smiling, brushing her hair behind her ear, cocking her head coquettishly. Start went over to see if she could help but Noy said that she was just browsing. She browsed for a full fifteen minutes until I'd finished with the German, then started talking to me about an antique Khmer dancing figure that I had in the window. It was bronze and I was pretty sure that it was more than two hundred years old but there were some very clever forgers working out of Vietnam so I had to admit that I wasn't absolutely sure of its provenance I'd found it in an old house in a small village about thirty miles outside Udon Thani, and persuaded the old lady who lived there to sell it to me, along with half a dozen wooden carvings that were easier to date.

We chatted for a while and she was asking me about restaurants in the area. She told me that she was thinking about changing jobs and becoming an estate agent and she asked me where I lived. Back then I lived in the small apartment above the shop but I told her that I was looking for somewhere bigger. She bought the statue and she paid me in cash. I boxed it for her and took it out to her car, a new model Porsche SUV. It was one hell of a car and I figured it must have belonged to her husband, which shows you what a chauvinist I was back then.

After she'd gone, Start and Stop came over, grinning like they knew something I didn't. Which as it turned out, was absolutely the case.

'She isn't interested in the statue,' said Start.

'She's only interested in one thing in the shop,' said her sister.

The giggled like naughty schoolgirls.

'What?' I asked, totally confused.

They giggled even more and finally I realised why they were laughing.

'Oh come on, why would she be interested in me?' I asked.

It was a fair point, all things considered. I was probably ten years older than her and while I'd managed to hang on to my own hair and teeth I'd also managed to pile on a few extra pounds.

'She was looking at you all the time, Khun Bob,' said Start.

'All the time,' said Stop, for emphasis.

'She's beautiful,' I said.

'Very,' said Start. 'You should ask her out next time she comes in.'

'Why do you think she'll come back?' I asked and they both giggled.

'She'll come back,' said Stop.

'For sure,' said Start.

They were right.

Three days later she was back in the shop, this time to look at a Japanese stair tansu, a chest in the shape of stairs. It was a good piece, the wood polished to perfection and the fittings made of aged bronze.

Start wasn't in the shop when she came in but Stop was and she wagged her finger at me to let me know that I shouldn't waste any more time.

I felt like a gawky teenager even thought it had been more than twenty years since anyone had described me as either gawky or a teenager. I stumbled over the words because I was sure she was going to turn me down but I asked her if she'd go for dinner with me one evening and she said she'd love to and she sounded as if she meant it.

We had dinner in a terrific Italian restaurant down the road from the shop and a few days later we had dinner again and then we went to see a Martin Scorsese movie but for the life of me I can't remember which one because all I could think about was Noy and the fact that she was on a date with me.

Two months after we first met she introduced me to her parents. We flew up to Chiang Rai and I slept in a hotel while she stayed in their house because her parents were very traditional and, frankly, so was she. Three months after that, we were married.

Anyway, that was then and this is now. If anything I think Noy is even more beautiful now then when I met her. She's confident, smart, and can make me smile without even trying. I can't imagine living without her.

She finished playing and stood looking out across the Bangkok skyline, the violin at her side.

'Beautiful,' I said quietly.

'Bach is always beautiful,' she said, turning around.

'I meant you,' I said. I stepped forward and kissed her on the lips. She pressed herself against me, holding the violin to the side.

'I missed you today,' she said.

'I missed you, too.'

'No, I really missed you,' she said, pressing herself harder against me.

'Oh,' I said. 'That's nice.'

'Nice?' she said, caressing the back of my neck. 'I'll give you nice.'

So what did I tell Noy? About the hospital?

Nothing.

Not a damned thing.

I carried on kissing her.

We went to bed.

We had great sex.

Then we went to sleep.

I didn't think about cancer the whole night. Until I woke up.

19

I GOT TO THE Betta English Language School at just after six o'clock. The list that Petrov's secretary had given me showed the first classes starting at six-thirty and I figured that the teachers wouldn't be turning up much before then. I was wearing my English teacher's outfit. Cheap khaki chinos with imitation leather belt, fake Lacoste polo shirt, scuffed shoes and carrying a canvas briefcase. I nodded at the security guard at the main entrance and headed up the stairs. The door to the school was locked but I only had to wait fifteen minutes before Petrov's secretary arrived. She was wearing a pale blue skirt suit with a white bow holding her hair back in a ponytail.

'You are early,' she said.

'The early bird catches the worm,' I said.

She frowned and I explained the proverb as she unlocked the door.

Once inside she unlocked the door to the staff room for me before walking along the corridor and opening the classrooms.

I closed the door and went over to the metal lockers. Most had name tags glued to them, other had names scratched into the metal. Jon Junior's name was on a locker on the bottom row. Padlocked. I'd seen the padlock last time Petrov's secretary had shown me the room so I had come prepared.

I figured the padlock was significant.

If Jon Junior had quit or been sacked, why would he have left his locker padlocked?

It was a combination lock with three dials. Nine hundred and ninety nine combinations. A thousand if you included treble zero. You wouldn't have to be a safecracker to open it, just patient. But I didn't have time to go through all the combinations so I took the boltcutters out of my briefcase and snipped the cheap steel hasp.

There was a photograph taped to the inside of the locker. Jon Junior in his graduation get-up, father to his left with his hand on his shoulder, mother beaming proudly at the camera from underneath a wide-brimmed hat. There was a blue laundered shirt on a metal shelf next to a plastic bottle of ozone-treated drinking water and a dog-eared copy of a John Grisham novel. At the bottom of the locker was a squash racquet and a pair of old tennis shoes.

Nothing that you'd particularly want to take with you if you did a moonlight flit. I picked up the book. There was a Foodland receipt among the pages. A bookmark, halfway through the novel. Not many people gave up halfway through *The Firm*.

So maybe Jon Junior hadn't had time to clear out his locker.

Or maybe somebody had prevented him.

The door handle started to turn and I quickly shut the locker.

It was Petrov's secretary.

'I can use any of these, can I?' I asked, pocketing the padlock.

'Any that aren't already being used,' she said. She was holding a computer print-out. 'Your first class isn't until eight.'

I feigned surprise. Opened my mouth. Raised my eyebrows. Hardly Oscar-winning material but she got the message. 'You thought you had an early class?' she asked.

'I thought seven,' I said. 'Oh well, I might as well go home and come back later.'

She smiled brightly. 'We have a class at seven and the teacher has just called to say that he's sick today.'

'Right ...' I said hesitantly.

'So you could teach the class.'

I smiled. I shrugged. I frantically tried to think of a reason to turn down her offer but nothing sprang to mind.

'I thought classes start at half past the hour,' I said. 'Seven-thirty?'

'Not always,' she said. 'It's in room four.' Her smile widened. 'The early bird really does catch the worm, doesn't it?'

Indeed it does.

By the short and curlies.

I looked at my watch. Three minutes to seven.

She held the door open for me. 'Most of the students are already here.'

Terrific.

I followed her down the corridor and she showed me into one of the classrooms. 'This is Khun Bob,' she said, by way of introduction. 'He will be taking your class today.'

The door closed behind me with a dull thud. I smiled. Twelve faces smiled back. Three teenage boys. Nine girls. I looked at my watch. One minute gone. Fifty-nine to go.

So far, so good.

'So what did you do in your last lesson?' I asked.

No one spoke. A boy with shoulder-length hair and a diamond earring in his left ear opened his book at Chapter Five and pointed at it.

'Right then, let's open our books at Chapter Five,' I said.

I walked over to the girl nearest me and looked down at her book. The chapter was headed 'At The Post Office'.

Half of the pupils had photocopies of the text book, the pages stapled together. Twelve faces looked at me expectantly.

Right then.

How hard can it be, teaching?

'So, who's been to a post office then?' I asked.

No reaction.

'Some of you must have been to a post office. To buy a stamp. Post a letter.'

Twelve smiles.

'Hands up who's posted a letter?'

Nothing. Just smiles.

I was obviously going about this the wrong way.

'Why don't we read the first paragraph out loud?'

Blank looks.

I pointed at the books. 'Read,' I said slowly.

The students haltingly read through the first paragraph then looked at me.

I looked at my watch again. Fifty eight minutes to go.

'So, are there any words there that anyone doesn't understand?'

Twelve smiling faces.

'Anything at all?'

I sat down on the table and smiled amiably. 'How long have you been studying here?' I asked. This time I spoke in rapid Thai. A few of the girls exchanged looks of surprise. I presumed that they hadn't come across many English teachers who spoke their language fluently.

'Three months,' said a girl with shoulder-length hair and a Gucci bag.

'How many hours a week?'

'Five.'

'What do your teachers do in class?'

'We just read from the book,' said one of the boys.

'Which other teachers have you had?'

'Khun Bill,' said the boy with the earring.

'Khun Peter,' said one of the girls.

'Khun David, from New York.'

Several of the girls nodded excitedly. Khun David of New York had obviously left an impression.

'And they all just get you to read the book?'

Twelve nods.

Right then.

'Anybody remember a Khun Jon? From America? Jon Clare'

Twelve frowns.

I took the photograph from my jacket pocket and handed it to the girl on my left. She looked at it and handed it to the girl next to her. The fourth girl to look at the picture smiled and nodded. 'Khun Jon,' she said. 'From Salt Lake City.'

'He taught you?'

The girl nodded.

Three of the girls in the class and one of the boys said that they remembered Jon Junior. None of them had seen him in the last two weeks.

'Does anyone know where he went?' I asked.

'I thought he went back to the States,' said one of the girls.

'Did he say that?'

She shook her head. 'I just assumed ...'

'Did he have any friends at the school? Anyone he was close to?'

The girl with the Gucci bag giggled and whispered something to the girl next to her. It sounded like 'Tukkata'.

Doll. That's what Tukkata means.

The theme from James Bond started playing and one of the boys pulled a cellphone from his pocket. He started talking into it in Thai, his hand cupped over the phone. He was obviously talking to his girlfriend. I wagged my finger at him and he flashed me a dirty look and turned away.

'Can you take that outside?' I said.

He ignored me and carried on whispering into his phone.

I walked over to his seat and tapped him on the shoulder. 'Outside,' I said in Thai.

'I'm on the phone,' he snapped sullenly.

'I can see that,' I said. 'Take it into the corridor.'

He glared at me and left the room, still whispering into his phone.

'Do your other teachers let you use your cellphones in class?' I asked the rest of the students. I'd given up speaking to them in English.

'They don't care,' said one of the girls. The one who'd said Tukkata. 'They don't care about much.' She looked me in the eye without a trace of shyness. A teenager going on thirty-five. The others looked away. It's not in the Thai psyche to be critical. Especially of one's teachers.

I stood up again. 'Okay, let's forget the textbooks. Close them. Close your books.'

They did as they were told.

'Let's not talk about the Post Office. Let's talk about people.' I held up the photograph. 'Let's talk about Khun Jon,' I said in English. 'I want you to describe him in as many different ways as you can.' I was faced with confused looks so I repeated what I'd said in Thai.

'American,' said one of the girls.

'Good,' I said.

'Handsome,' said one of the girls, who blushed and hid her mouth with her hand.

'Tall,' said another of the girls.

'Good,' I said. There was a black marker pen on a shelf below the whiteboard. I wrote on the board. 'American'. 'Handsome'. 'Tall'.

'Teacher,' said a boy with gelled hair and a silver chain around his neck.

I wrote 'Teacher' on the board.

'Yellow hair,' said one on the girls.

'Blond,' I said. 'We say blond.'

More words were thrown out. 'Serious.' 'Kind.' 'Lonely.'

Interesting.

The girl who'd said lonely was in her late teens with short hair and a gold Rolex watch. Like the rest of the girls she was wearing a white shirt and short black skirt with a leather belt. There was a small gold pin on her shirt pocket that showed she went to one of Bangkok's most prestigious schools. It wasn't the most expensive but it was one of the hardest to get into. You needed connections to get your children accepted. The sons and daughters of Thailand's top politicians and generals were on the school role and the school's alumni ran many of the country's top companies and financial institutions. I asked the girl her name. 'Kai,' she said.

Kai. It means chicken.

'What makes you think he's lonely, Kai?' I asked. She was one of the girls who'd nodded when she'd seen Jon Junior's photograph.

'He used to sit on his own sometimes, reading.'

The girl who'd said 'Tukkata' nodded. 'He was always reading.'

'Just because you read doesn't mean you're lonely,' I said.

'He didn't talk to the other teachers,' said the boy with gelled hair.

'So he didn't have many friends?' I asked, looking at the girl who'd said Tukkata.

She shrugged but didn't say anything.

'He didn't talk to the teachers, but was he friendly with the students?' I asked.

The girl smiled but didn't say anything. The boy who'd been using his cellphone came back into the room, scowled at me and flopped down onto his chair.

'Enthusiastic,' said Kai.

I wrote 'enthusiastic' on the board.

'Was he a good teacher?' I asked.

Several of the girls nodded. I wrote 'good teacher' on the board.

'Okay,' I said. 'Let's play a guessing game. Let's see if we can guess where Khun Jon has gone.'

I stood there with the marker pen in my hand, smiling encouragingly.

Twelve faces looked back at me, blankly.

Just when things were going so well.

20

As soon as my hour was up I went into see Petrov's secretary and asked her if there was a student at the school with the nickname Tukkata.

'That would be Somchit Santhanavit,' she said.

'Is she in school today?'

The secretary tapped on her computer keyboard, then shook her head. 'She should be.' She frowned. 'She should have been in your class today.'

'She wasn't. Do you have a list of pupils?'

'It's not your regular class,' she said. 'You probably won't be teaching them again.'

'I know, but if there's a problem we should know about it.'

'What sort of problem?'

'I don't know. Maybe there isn't a problem. But shouldn't we know whether or not the pupils are in class?'

'Not really.'

'Don't you have a roll call each morning?'

'We're not a government school, our pupils don't have to attend.'

'But you must know who's in each class to check that they've paid.'

'The pupils pay each term in advance. If they don't choose to attend after they've paid, that's up to them.'

'Which regular school does she attend?'

The secretary told me. It was the same as Kai's. Tukkata must have been from a good family.

'Maybe I should phone, check that everything's okay.'

'There's no need,' she said. She looked at the clock on the wall. 'Don't forget that you have an eight o'clock class,' she said.

'I'd feel happier, knowing that she wasn't ill.'

'She isn't one of your pupils,' she said.

It was clear from her tone that she wasn't going to budge. I wanted to know why she'd lied about Jon Junior working in the school despite the fact that he still had a locker in the staff room but I knew I'd be wasting my time. So I smiled. And I left.

The end of my teaching career.

I don't think I was a great loss to the profession.

Or vice versa.

21

KHUN WICHIT WAS a portly man in his early fifties wearing a neatly pressed white shirt with oval gold cufflinks and a blue silk tie. His hair was thinning and flecked with dandruff and he had a large mole under his left nostril. I introduced myself and handed him a business card. I had spoken to two female secretaries and a male assistant and waited in a corridor for the best part of an hour before getting into Khun Wichit's office.

'I'm not sure what it is you want from me, Khun Bob,' he said.

That was understandable. I'd spoken to all his subordinates in rapid English and pretended to misunderstand virtually anything they'd said to me. If I'd used Thai they'd have come up with a million and one reasons why I couldn't talk to their boss. But rather than admit their inadequacies with English, they'd passed me up the food chain. Sometimes it paid to be the idiot farang. But there was no point in playing that game with Khun Wichit. His framed university diploma was on the wall behind him and it was from Bangkok's Assumption University where courses were taught in English.

'I need some tax advice.'

Khun Wichit took out a pair of gold-framed reading glasses, perched them on his stub of a nose, and frowned as he studied the business card.

'You are an antiques dealer?' he said eventually.

'That's right.'

He placed the business card on his desk like a poker player revealing a winning ace. 'We are tax collectors, Khun Bob,' he said softly. 'For advice you require the services of an accountant.'

I nodded. I knew that.

And I knew that information held by the Tax Office was confidential.

So I lied.

I told Khun Wichit, graduate of Assumption University with a second class degree in Information Technology, that I was looking for an English school for a friend's teenage daughter and that I wanted to make sure that the school I recommended was a reputable one.

Khun Wichit's frown deepened.

'I thought that one way of checking that a school is reputable would be to see that if it was paying its taxes,' I said. 'One hears so many stories these days of schools interested only in making a quick profit,' I said. 'I want to ensure that the school that my friend's daughter attends is a responsible one.'

Khun Wichit nodded slowly. 'That is admirable,' he said. 'It may be that I can offer you some assistance in that regard. What is the name of the company?'

'The Betta English Language School in Sukhumvit Soi 22.'

'Betta?'

I spelt it for him. He frowned. 'What does it mean, Betta?'

I shrugged. 'It might be a way of spelling better,' I said. 'Or they might have mis-spelled Beta.'

'Beta?'

'Alpha, Beta, Gamma.'

'Why would they spell it incorrectly?'

'By accident, maybe.'

'It is confusing.'

'It is,' I agreed.

There was a computer on a side table next to his desk and Khun Wichit carefully adjusted his cuffs before pecking at the keyboard with the index finger of his right hand. He peered at the screen, tutted, and then pecked at the keyboard again. He smiled in triumph as a spreadsheet appeared on screen and he studied it for almost a full minute before nodding to himself.

'Everything is in order, Khun Bob,' he said. 'The Betta English Language School has been registered with us for the past three years and they have been most prompt in paying their taxes.'

I smiled easily. 'That is good to hear,' I said. 'So there is nothing untoward, nothing that my friend should be concerned about?'

'I wish that all companies were as diligent as this one in filing their tax returns,' said Khun Wichit.

'I wonder if it would be possible to have a copy of that file,' I said. 'So that I could give it to my friend. Just to show him how reputable a school his daughter would be attending.'

'Quite impossible, I'm afraid,' said Khun Wichit. 'The Data Protection Act prohibits the sharing of our database with members of the public. The information we collate has to remain confidential.'

'Absolutely,' I said. 'But I wonder if perhaps the payment of a fee might facilitate the process. The information would remain confidential, of course. It would only serve to reassure my friend that his daughter's education is in the hands of reputable people.

'How much of a fee were you thinking about?' he asked.

I smiled amiably as I looked him over. Assumption was a private university and while it wasn't the best in Bangkok it wasn't the cheapest which meant he came from a reasonably well-off family. His shirt had a Ralph Lauren logo on it and it looked like the genuine article. His watch was gold but not a make that I recognised and was probably plated. He wore a simple gold wedding ring but there was nothing simple about a Thai wife. On the desk was a framed photograph of two small boys in dark blazers. Private education wasn't cheap in Bangkok. No photograph of the wife but he didn't look as if he was taking care of himself so maybe there was a minor wife somewhere in the building. Minor wives weren't cheap.

The trick was not to offer too little so that he wouldn't be offended. But there was no point in overpaying. There could be a negotiation, but only if my first offer was somewhere in his ballpark.

His smile was as amiable as mine as he looked me over. What did he see? A Rolex Submariner that was scarred and chipped from twenty years of diving. A cheap suit that I'd had knocked up by an Indian tailor in a Sukhumvit backstreet for a couple of thousand baht. The material, a wheat-coloured linen, was fine but the stitching was suspect and I'd had to ask the tailor to redo some of the stitching around one of the buttonholes. Expensive shoes because I never scrimp on footwear but they were under the desk so he couldn't see them. A hundred baht haircut, a hundred and twenty if you count the tip.

'I thought perhaps a thousand baht,' I said, as if I was thinking out loud. Probably equivalent to a day's salary.

His smile tightened a little.

'Two thousand?' I added quickly.

He looked at his wristwatch.

Message received.

'Three thousand?'

A pained smile. Close, but no cigar.

'Five thousand?'

'That sounds satisfactory,' he said. He opened the top drawer of his desk and passed a pale green file over to me. He looked at me expectantly. I took five one-thousand baht notes from my wallet, slid them inside the file and gave it back to him. The file disappeared back into the drawer. He hit a few keys on the keyboard, then gave me a curt nod. 'Please, I shall only be a few minutes.'

He left me alone in the office. I looked at the clock on the wall as it ticked off the seconds, wondering if he was going to return with the police and I was going to end up sleeping on the floor of a Thai prison for the next five and a half years. When Khun Wichit returned he didn't have Bangkok's finest with him but he did have a computer print-out which he gave me with a knowing smile. 'If there is anything else I can do for you, don't hesitate to call, Khun Bob,' he said. 'I am at your service.'

I'd overpaid.

You live and learn.

22

THE SPECIALIST THAT Doctor Duangtip sent me to see was a kindly looking man in his late fifties with greying hair and metal-framed spectacles with round lenses. I waied him as I walked into his office. He seemed momentarily confused at being waied by a farang but he waied me back half-heartedly, then stood up and shook hands. His hand was as dry and cool as a lizard. Mine was bathed in sweat and I wiped it on my trouser leg as I sat down. His name was Doctor Wanlop and he was, according to Doctor Duangtip, one of the most experienced intestinal cancer specialists in Asia.

There was that word again.

Cancer.

Doctor Wanlop had more certificates than Doctor Duangtip, but his were all from Thai institutions. Like Doctor Duangtip he had a computer on his desk and he tapped on the keyboard and studied the screen for several minutes before turning to smile at me.

'My colleague explained about CEA?' he said, peering over the top of his spectacles. He spoke in English, which was fine with me.

'He said it was a marker for ...' I hesitated. I didn't want to say the word. I wanted to use something less final. Something I could tell my wife.

'For colorectal carcinoma,' he said.

Whoa there, hoss. That sounded a hell of a lot worse than cancer. Colorectal carcinoma? Where had that come from?

I took a deep breath. I didn't want my voice to tremble when I spoke. 'For cancer, he said.'

There. I'd said that. The world didn't end. The sky didn't fall in. But I didn't feel any better.

Dr Wanlop smiled. It was a reassuring smile, a smile that told me not to worry, that he knew what he was doing, that he would cure me of whatever ailed me. My heart was pounding like a jackhammer. The heart of a twenty-five year old.

'Carcinoembryonic antigen, to give it its full name, was used as a test for cancer of the colon for a few years, but I'm not convinced that CEA levels are a valid marker for tumours,' he said.

That sounded hopeful. It sounded a hell of a lot more hopeful than colorectal carcinoma. And he was smiling reassuringly. That had to be a good sign.

Right?

'In fact, I can say with confidence that of the last twenty people who passed through that door with elevated CEA levels, not one had a tumour.'

I frowned. 'But Doctor Duangtip said that CEA was an indication that there was a problem.'

'It can be. And it's only right and proper that he had you come and see me. But I don't think you should worry too much. These days we tend to use CEA more as a treatment marker. If after we've carried out a procedure we get a sudden elevation in CEA, then we know that our procedure has not been effective.'

Thais aren't great at breaking bad news. In the old days, when they're going to execute a criminal, they hid the machine gun behind a sheet. The condemned man didn't even know that he was going to be shot until the bullets ripped through him.

Doctor Wanlop was certainly making me feel a lot better, but

I wasn't a hundred per cent sure that he was just sugar coating his diagnosis to stop me worrying. Maybe he just wanted me to feel better, right up until the moment that the cancer ripped through my guts.

'So what happens next?' I asked.

'We should have a look inside,' he said. 'Reassure ourselves that there isn't a problem. Assuming that we don't find anything, we will know that you have a naturally high level of CEA.'

'An operation, you mean?'

'Not exactly. We can put a very small camera inside your intestines. We give you a small injection, just to relax you.'

Right.

Fine.

That doesn't sound so bad.

Not really.

'And you'll do that for me?' I asked.

Doctor Wanlop smiled and shook his head. 'I used to, but I'm too old these days,' he said apologetically. 'You need nimble fingers, and a lot of practice. I do so few these days that it takes me forever. But I can recommend a colleague who is an expert in the technique. She can do the entire procedure in less than thirty minutes.'

She?

A woman was going to run a camera through my intestines?

Interesting.

23

THERE ARE ALL SORTS of rumours about Big Ron. One is that he once lost more than two hundred pounds on a crash diet. Grapefruit and tomato, or something like that. He lost weight so quickly that his skin hung around his waist and down to his knees like a deflated Zeppelin. A local surgeon cut out three square feet of skin that Big Ron had made into lampshades that now stood either side of his specially reinforced bed. Then he started eating again and the weight was back on within a year. I don't know if that's true or not but sometimes when he's drunk and the Fatso's Fools are in full mad mode, he'll lift up his enormous t-shirt and show off the scars across his stomach and hips. They look as if a great white shark had bitten out huge chunks of his skin. That's what he says happened, scuba diving near the Great Barrier Reef. I'm not sure I believe that any more than I believe about the lampshades. Big Ron's more of a floater than a swimmer.

The other big rumour about Big Ron was that he was almost taken hostage by Saddam Hussein during the Gulf War. The first one, with George Bush Senior running the show. The one that didn't end in an absolute disaster. Big Ron, so the story goes, hid out in a disused water tank on the top of his apartment building in Kuwait City, only leaving at night to go downstairs for food. Three months he was there, and he only left when the Americans moved in. Big Ron was chief accountant with one of the big Arab banks. The Iraqis had looted the main branch before running home, but when Big Ron gets there he finds that the Iraqis hadn't been able to open one of the vaults. Big Ron still had the key on his key chain and he opens the vault to find ten million dollars. The story is that Big Ron filled two suitcases, drove to the airport and flew straight to Bangkok. True or not? Only the Shadow knows. But Big Ron bought Fatso's from a former British publican who wanted to swap the bright lights of Bangkok for the seedy underbelly of Pattaya and he did it with cash, by all accounts. And he bought himself a nice two-bedroom condo, again with cash. True story or not, Big Ron has never been short of money and he has one of the best financial brains I've ever come across.

There were only a handful of tourists sitting around the bar when I pushed open the glass door. Young guys with shaved heads and tattoos and t-shirts with wittily amusing slogans like 'I FCUK FOR ENGLAND' and 'SOD OFF, I DON'T NEED ANYMORE FRIENDS' and 'MY MOTHER LOVES ME, LET'S HOPE MY DAD DOESN'T FIND OUT' and half-drunk pints of lager in front of them.

I smiled at Bee and she pointed upstairs as if she'd read my mind. She hadn't, of course, she was just being typically Thai, anticipating my needs and meeting them without having to be asked. She knew I wasn't a daytime drinker and it wasn't lunchtime so the fact I was there meant I wanted to see Big Ron, and Big Ron was where he usually was on a Thursday afternoon, in the upstairs restaurant sitting at a back table, going through the Fatso accounts.

I went up the spiral staircase. I heard the tap, tap, tap of ebony balls before I reached the upper landing. Big Ron doesn't use a computer. Won't even touch a calculator. Doesn't believe in them. He does all his calculations on a hundred-year-old abacus that he claims he won in a Mah Jong game in a Kowloon brothel. I'm not sure I believe that. Sure, I can picture Big Ron in a Kowloon brothel, but his hands are way too big to hold the tiny Mah Jong tiles. But the abacus is the real thing, polished rosewood frame with gleaming brass dragons at either end and black ebony balls on thin brass rods and Big Ron uses it effortlessly. And he's fast. Fast and accurate.

Big Ron's argument goes like this. Computers make mistakes. Not the people who use them. They make mistakes, of course. Everyone knows that. Human error. But computers make mistakes all on their lonesome. Not very often. Maybe once in a trillion trillion calculations. An electron doesn't do exactly what it should. There's a slight fluctuation, a flicker in the atomic structure, and a decimal point is misplaced or a three becomes an eight. Ninety nine point nine nine nine nine per cent of the time the mistake doesn't matter. It's a computer in a coffee maker or a washing machine or a cash register in a short-time hotel, and the error goes unnoticed. But sometimes the mistake does matter and when it does an aeroplane crashes into a hillside or New York loses all its electricity or a pacemaker goes into overdrive and a middle-aged man with three kids and a mistress keels over and dies. Computers make mistakes so Big Ron won't use them.

I think he's making it up. I think the real reason he hates computers and calculators is because his massive fingers keep on hitting the wrong keys. But whatever the reason, he's fast on the abacus. Seriously fast. And accurate.

I was in Fatso's once when Relentless challenged him to a duel. Relentless is a real estate broker for one of the big Thai-Chinese property developers. He had his BlackBerry with him and bet Big Ron a month's bar bill that he could add up a list of figures faster using new technology than Big Ron could do with the abacus. Big Ron had been drinking for most of the day and the Fatso's girls tried to talk him out of it, but the bet was on. Relentless had brought two sheets of numbers with him, but Big Ron wasn't having any of that. He got the business section of the Bangkok Post and turned to the stock market listings. The challenge, he told Relentless, was to add up all the individual prices of the shares that were listed on the Bangkok exchange. There were hundreds. Thousands, maybe. Relentless looked a lot less confident then, but a bet was a bet and the Fatso's Fools were baying for blood. They sat at the bar with the stock market page in between them.

Bruce had one of those fancy digital watches with a stopwatch so he was appointed timekeeper. He gave them a quick ready, steady, go, and then Big Ron and Relentless were off. Relentless bashed away on his BlackBerry, his head down close to the paper, eyes flicking from the prices to the keypad. Click, click, click. Then stabbing at the '+' key.

Big Ron sat back in his specially reinforced chair, totally relaxed, his eyes scanning down the columns of figures, barely looking at the abacus as his fingers played across the balls. Tap, tap, tap, tap. The sound of a pool game played at breakneck speed.

Half an hour into it and Relentless was soaked in sweat and he had a manic look in his eyes. He was having trouble focussing and his index finger was hurting so he tried using his middle finger. Every now and again he'd hit the wrong key and curse vehemently. Big Ron just smiled contentedly and carrying on manipulating the ebony balls. Tap tap tap. Tap. Tap tap tap.

Sweat poured off Relentless. It dripped around his chair. It splattered onto the newspaper. It ran into his eyes and Bee passed him a cold towel with a sympathetic smile. She'd bet fifty baht with one of the new waitresses that Big Ron would win. He did, too. By a full five minutes. He sat back with a smile of contentment and waited for Relentless to finish. Eventually Relentless sagged on his stool and ordered a Singha beer.

Big Ron had written a number on a Fatso's chit. He compared it to the number on the BlackBerry. It was the same. Big Ron held up the chit and the BlackBerry for all to see. 'Who's the daddy?' he shouted.

'You are, Big Ron!' we chorused.

He leaned over and rang the bell, twice. It was the last time that anyone challenged Big Ron over the use of the abacus.

He looked up as I got to the top of the stairs.

'How's it going, Bob?' he said.

'I'll know better tomorrow,' I said. 'They're shoving a camera up my bum.'

'Hope it's not one of those digital video jobbies with the big screens,' he said. Then he looked suddenly serious. 'Hey, everything okay?'

I shrugged as if the possibility of a slow and painful death by colon cancer was nothing to write home about. 'Had a medical at the Bumrungrad. One of the cancer markers was a bit high so they want to go in for a look-see.'

'You can live without ninety per cent of your colon,' said Big Ron.

'That's reassuring.'

'You can lose a kidney, two-thirds of your liver, half your brain and most of your stomach, and still live.'

'Yeah, but would you want to?' I said, sitting down at his table.

'Anything I can do?' he asked.

I shook my head. 'It'll be fine.'

'Make sure you get a copy of the video.'

'What?'

'They'll video it for you. We'll have a movie night at Fatso's. Popcorn, hot dogs. Journey to the Centre of Bob's Arse. The Voyage of No Return. I mean, how many times do you get to look up a friend's back passage?'

'I'll pass.'

'You're no fun.'

I handed him the print-outs from the tax office. 'Can you cast your expert eyes over these?'

Big Ron flicked through the sheets of paper.

'It's an English school over in Soi 22. Russian guy runs it. There's something not right about his set-up but I can't work out what it is.'

'Mafia?'

'Ethnic cliché,' I said. 'Not all Russians are Mafia, not all Italians are the Mob, not all public schoolboys are gay.'

'It wasn't a public school,' said Big Ron. 'It was a grammar school. And just because we had to swim naked in the pool once a week doesn't mean we were gay. It was a bonding thing.' He waved the print-out at me. 'What's your interest?'

'That missing Mormon. He used to work there but Petrov, the Russian, comes over all forgetful when I mention his name.'

Big Ron went back to the first sheet and read it carefully. He frowned and scratched his chins. Then he raised his eyebrows. 'I'm in the wrong bloody business,' he said.

'How come?'

'He turned over two hundred and fifty six million baht two years ago. That's what these figures are for, the year before last. That's close to five million quid. Staff costs of twelve million, three hundred and sixty thousand, most of that the teachers. Rent and utilities amount to a shade over fifteen million. Total profits of two hundred and forty million, six hundred and forty thousand baht profit. That's one hell of a return.'

'And he pays his taxes?'

Big Ron's sausage-like fingers played across the abacus. Tap, tap, tap. Tap tap tap tap. He studied the ebony balls. 'To the baht,' he said. He frowned. 'There's something not right about this,' he said.

'What's wrong?'

'No one pays this much tax unless they have to,' he said. 'Every businessman in Thailand has two sets of books, one for the taxman and one showing how much money he's really making. This guy's taking the piss. If he paid ten per cent of what he's paying the taxman would still be grateful.' He scratched his chins and studied the print-out. 'Okay, let's look at this another way,' he said. His fingers rattled the shiny black balls. 'Total income two hundred and fifty six million baht.'

Tap, tap, tap.

'How much do the students pay? Per hour?'

'A hundred baht.'

Tap, tap, tap. Tap tap.

'Three hundred and sixty five days a year,' he said. 'Forget all the public holidays, royal birthdays and the like.'

Tap, tap, tap. Tap.

How many hours a day is he open for business?'

'From seven in the morning until nine at night.'

'Fourteen hours a day.'

I nodded but he wasn't looking at me.

Tap, tap, tap, tap. His forehead creased into a deep frown. 'How many classrooms?'

'Eight,' I said.

Tap, tap, tap. Tap tap.

Big Ron sat back and grinned. 'Sixty-two,' he said.

'What's that, the answer to life, the universe and everything?'

'It's the number of people in each classroom. Sixty-two. Sixty-two pupils, every hour for fourteen hours a day, for three hundred and sixty five days a year. That's the only way you get a turnover of two hundred and fifty six million baht.'

'But there's only a dozen chairs in each room.'

'Five to a chair, then? Be like the black hole of Calcutta. Standing room only.'

I shook my head. 'None of the rooms I saw were close to capacity. I saw fifty pupils at most when I was there.'

'There you go then.' Big Ron's grin widened.

'What?' I didn't get it.

'It's not about teaching English. It's about laundry.'

I still didn't get it.

24

THE SCHOOL THAT Kai attended was in Soi 15, not far from one of the city's busiest red light areas, Soi Cowboy. Over the years the city's hookers and transsexuals had spread out from Nana Plaza in Soi 4 and Soi Cowboy in Soi 23 and now most of the lower reaches of Sukhumvit Road were fair game for the city's purveyors of vice. Every now and again the police would go on the offensive and for a few weeks the streets would be clear but like cockroaches the hookers always returned.

The school was far enough from the main road to be untouched by the drug-dealing and hooking fraternity but even so I didn't think it would be a good idea to loiter outside a school where more than half the pupils were girls. There were a couple of noodle stalls on the pavement about a hundred feet from the main entrance so I took a seat with a good view of the gate and ordered a bowl of red pork and noodle soup, which as it turned out wasn't half bad. I was half way through it when I saw Kai. She was wearing a short black skirt, a white shirt that was so tight the buttons were straining at the material, and black Gucci heels. To go with the Gucci bag on her shoulder.

How did I know the shoes were Gucci?

Because my wife has a pair of the very same shoes. And they were very expensive. I know because I bought them.

Kai was nodding her head strangely but as she got closer I saw that she was listening to an iPod. I stood up and smiled but she didn't see me until she was almost in front of me, then her mouth opened in surprise showing perfect white teeth with pink braces. I saw the panic in her eyes so I smiled again and held up my hand in greeting.

'Miss Kai,' I said, 'how are you today?'

She didn't hear me and she frowned as she took out her earphones. I repeated what I'd said, and smiled again.

She frowned, not recognising me at first, then realisation dawned. 'Khun Bob,' she said. 'You're not a teacher here as well are you?'

'No, I'm happy enough where I am,' I said, which wasn't exactly a lie but it was close. 'Would you like a Coke?'

She looked at her watch. It was slim, gold and obviously expensive. 'I have an appointment,' she said. She looked up and down the road, and then back to me. She smiled again, showing me a flash of her braces.

'I wanted to ask you about Tukkata,' I said. 'She goes to your school, doesn't she?'

Kai nodded.

'Was she at school today?' I asked.

'I didn't see her,' she said. 'But we're not in the same class.' She giggled. 'We're not in the same year.'

'Do you know when she was last at school?'

Kai ran a hand through her shampoo-commercial hair. 'Is she in trouble?'

'No, I wanted to talk to her about Khun Jon. I thought she might know where he is.'

'Why?' she asked, which was a good question.

I didn't like lying to a kid who thought I was a teacher, but telling her why I was trying to find Jon Junior would be way too complicated. And would involve me explaining why an antiques dealer had been trying to teach English.

'I found some personal stuff in his locker,' I said. 'I wanted to send it to him.'

She pouted and looked at her watch again.

'When was she last at school?' I asked.

Kai shrugged. 'A week ago, maybe. Like I said, we're not in the same class so I don't always see her. I'm year nine, she's year twelve.'

'You're only fifteen?' In her designer shoes and carrying her Gucci bag she looked older, but now I was looking carefully at her unblemished skin and slim figure I realised that she was just a kid. And that Tukkata wasn't much older.

'Do you think Tukkata might know where Jon is?' I asked.

'Perhaps,' she said. She frowned and ran a hand through her hair. Her nails were a deep red, the colour of blood. 'I think he might be a janitor now.'

'A janitor? Why would you think that?'

'The last time I saw him, he was talking on the phone. He said something about working in a boiler room.'

A top-of-the-range black BMW came down the road towards the school. Kai stiffened when she saw it and clutched her bag to her chest. 'I have to go,' she said.

I figured it was probably her father, come to collect his darling daughter. I wanted to ask her more about the boiler room but she was already walking towards the car. 'Hey, Kai, wait,' I said. I took a pen from my pocket and scribbled down my cellphone number on an old Emporium receipt. I gave her the piece of paper. 'If you see Tukkata, get her to give me a call.'

She took the number and as she drew level with the car, the back door opened. I caught a glimpse of a large Thai man in a suit and then she got in and the door closed.

As the car drove by all I could see was my own reflection in the tinted windows. Then it was gone.

A janitor?

That didn't make any sense.

But a boiler room. That definitely did.

25

PEOPLE COME TO LIVE in Thailand for a host of reasons. Retired people come for the climate and the relatively low cost of living, men come because it's easier for them to get a girlfriend even if more often than not have to pay by the hour, others come because they're fed up with what has happened to their own countries and hope that they'll have better lives in the Land of Smiles. There are Vietnam vets living around Washington Square who never wanted to go back to the States after their tours were over, and criminals in Pattaya who would be arrested if they ever set foot in their own countries. But almost everyone is in Thailand by choice. They want to be there.

Not Brent Whittington.

He was practically forced onto the plane at gunpoint, kicking and screaming all the way to Bangkok.

Well, maybe that's an exaggeration. But Brent never wanted to come to Thailand, and neither did his wife and two sons. They were perfectly happy in London, where Brent headed up a hugely profitable stockbroking operation for one of the big banks, one of the ones that didn't nearly go belly-up in the financial crisis that hit Europe and the States. There are those who say that Brent had a lot to do with the fact that his bank did well while so many others almost went to the wall. Brent is far too modest to ever say as much, but he is pretty contemptuous of most of the UK's banks and says that they deserved what happened to them.

Back in 2005, Brent's bank went into partnership with a stockbroking firm in Thailand, owned by a wealthy family with Royal connections. Try as they might the joint venture just couldn't make money, and Brent's bosses decided that the only way to salvage the situation was if he went out to run it.

At first Brent point-blank refused, but eventually his bosses made him an offer he couldn't refuse, which is why he now has a seven-figure salary, a luxury villa in a gated community, a Bentley and driver on call twenty-four hours a day, unlimited first class travel between London and Bangkok, and places in one of Thailand's top schools for his boys. It was one hell of a good deal and one that made him the envy of the rest of the stockbroking community. Brent still wasn't happy to be in Thailand, though, and had a cast-iron guarantee that after five years he and his family would be back in England.

I met Brent through his wife, Samantha, who wandered into my shop one day and walked out with a nineteenth-century fifty-thousand baht reclining Buddha. She came back with Brent a couple of weeks later and we hit it off and he's been a friend ever since. He's still counting the days before he gets back to London but he seems happier than when he first arrived. Brent and I don't agree about much, as it happens. He thinks cricket is the best game in the world and I know for a fact that it's baseball. He thinks Thailand is a Third World hellhole and I can't think of anywhere that I'd rather live. And he's sure that the best steaks in Bangkok are served in the Rib Room on the thirty-first floor of the Landmark Hotel while I'm sure they're only available in the New York Steakhouse of the JW Marriott Hotel on Sukhumvit Soi 2. I was the one who wanted something so I arranged to meet him at the Rib Room and told him that the evening was on me.

'Are you playing poker on Friday?' he asked as he sat down and took the menu from one of the Rib Room's many pretty waitresses.

'Sure,' I said. 'You?'

'Probably not,' he said. 'I've got to go to Singapore and probably won't get back until late. At least I'll save money, I've lost pretty badly the last few weeks.'

'Yeah, Somsak's been on a bit of a winning streak. And Tim.'

'You don't think they're cheating, do you?'

I laughed. 'A Thai policeman less than honest? Perish the thought.' I shook my head. 'Somsak plays for fun, he doesn't care if he wins or loses. And Tim's just a good player. '

'And we're on losing streaks.'

I waved over a waitress and ordered a bottle of red wine that I know he likes, and we spent the next hour eating perfect steaks and chatting. I waited until we'd finished our meal before getting around to the reason that I'd invited him. It seemed only fair.

'I could do with some advice,' I said as he stirred brown sugar into his coffee.

'Buy cheap, sell high,' he said.

I grinned. 'I knew I was doing something wrong.' I put a spoonful of sugar into my coffee, even though Noy is always nagging me to give up on the sweet stuff. 'I want to pick your brains about the boiler room situation.'

'Are you looking for another job? Because I have to warn you it's a young man's game.'

'It's a young man that I'm looking for,' I said. 'And before you say what I know you're going to say, it's a missing person case. A young American, a Mormon. His parents are frantic and I'm trying to help.'

'A young American in Bangkok?' He raised his glass of red wine. 'Try Soi Cowboy, then Nana Plaza, then Patpong. If that fails then try the Khao San Road.'

'He's a Mormon, Brent. Doesn't drink, doesn't go out with girls, wouldn't say boo to a goose.'

'And you think he's working in a boiler room? I don't think so, my friend.'

'Someone heard him on his phone, talking about working for one.'

'It's a high-pressure job, Bob. Not for the faint hearted.'

'Do you know anyone who's hiring?'

Brent chuckled. 'I hope you're not implying that I hang out with those guys.'

'You know every trader in the city,' I said.

'That's true.' He swirled his wine around the glass. 'Did he have any experience?'

'None,' I said. 'He was doing some English teaching.'

'But he had a good head on his shoulders, did he?'

'I think he's a normal American kid. Why?'

'It's a tough job, boiler room guys have to be pushy yet personable, and while they work from a script they have to be able to think on their feet. You know how it works, right?'

'Selling worthless shares to people who should know better,' I said.

'You old cynic, you,' he said. 'But basically that's it. The boiler room boys have been chased out of the States and Europe so a lot of them have set up in Asia. International phone calls are so cheap these days that it doesn't matter where they are. Hong Kong and Singapore have been clamping down so more have been moving here in recent years.'

'So what are you saying, he could have gone anywhere?'

Brent shook his head. 'Nah, a lot of them are quite small

operations, half a dozen or so traders who all know each other. They rarely bring in outsiders. But there are a couple of larger set-ups where they do recruit. Most of them are run by Aussies selling into Australia or New Zealand.'

'Offices?'

Brent shook his head. 'Low, low profile,' he said. 'They don't want to be found.'

'So how would my guy have found them?'

'Word of mouth,' said Brent. 'Followed by a chat in a pub, then they'd make a few checks and if he panned out then he'd be shown the office.'

'Dead end, then?'

'Not necessarily,' he said. 'There's one group I know off who drink at the Dubliner most evenings. They've got a place in Soi 33 somewhere and then walk to the Dubliner to wind down. The boss is an Aussie called Bear. Huge bloke, bushy beard. Used to be a legit broker years ago in Hong Kong but got done for insider trading. If you can find Bear he might have come across your lad. They take backpackers on and train them. His name's Alistair Wainer but everyone calls him Bear.'

'Bear it is, then.'

'Just be careful, Bob. They're a suspicious bunch at the best of times.' He finished his wine and held up the empty glass. 'Another?'

'It's the least I can do,' I said.

26

I LEFT BRENT IN the hotel's reception area. He was waiting for his chauffer to arrive. He lived about thirty minutes drive north of Bangkok in a gated community on the campus of the International School of Bangkok. The school was mainly for Americans and the Nichada Thani expat community was one of the most secure areas in the country, with its own supermarket, medical facility and shopping plaza. Brent liked the fact that his kids could cycle safely to school and that his wife had plenty of friends and had insisted that his company set him up in one of the biggest villas on the site. Getting to my humble abode in Sukhumvit 55 meant crossing over Sukhumvit Road and catching a taxi. I'd decided against driving because I knew that Brent and I would get through at least two bottles of wine at dinner. I wasn't worried about losing my licence because like most traffic violations in Thailand, a few hundred baht would make the problem go away. But I was worried about driving while under the influence because even when stone cold sober Bangkok was one of the most dangerous places in the world to be behind the wheel of a car.

Even at ten-thirty the road was busy so I headed for a concrete overbridge. It stank of urine but it was safer than trying to dodge the traffic. As I came down the stairs I saw the red light of a taxi for hire in the distance and I held out my hand.

The taxi slowed but before it reached me a large black SUV with darkened windows pulled up next to me. I figured the driver was dropping someone off so I walked to the rear, still waving at the taxi.

The front passenger door opened and a man got out. The door slammed shut and then someone grabbed my arm and swung me around.

I put my hands up to defend myself but my wrist was grabbed and my arm twisted up behind my back and before I could react I was thrown against the side of the car. The rear door on the far side of the car opened and slammed shut and a second man came around the back of the car. He was wearing a denim jacket, camouflage cargo pants and impenetrable wraparound sunglasses. It was Lek, from the kickboxing gym in Washington Square.

'Someone wants to see you,' said Lek.

'Yeah, well someone can come around to my shop, any time he wants,' I said.

The man who was holding me dragged me back so that Lek could open the door, then they both bundled me inside. As I fell onto the seat I felt something hard press against my side and I looked down to see a large shiny automatic. 'Be quiet,' he said.

'I'll be quiet, you be careful,' I said. It was a .45 and would blow a hole as big as baseball in my gut if he pulled the trigger.

The man on the pavement slammed the door and jogged around to get in the other side, boxing me in. It was Tam. Like his colleague, he was wearing dark glasses, even though it was late at night.

Gangster chic.

The driver stamped on the accelerator and the SUV sped off.

'What's this about, Lek?' I asked.

'Just keep quiet and you'll know soon enough,' he said.

We turned left on Asoke, the wide road that runs north-south across the city. Lek jabbed the gun in my ribs.

'Get down on the floor,' he said.

'Why?'

He jabbed the gun, harder this time. 'Just do it.'

'If you don't want me to see where I'm going, I'll close my eyes,' I said. 'It's no big deal.'

Tam grabbed me by the back of the neck and forced my head down behind the front seats. I could hardly breathe but he was strong so I went with the pressure and slid down onto my knees.

We drove for about twenty minutes with several turns and once I was pretty sure we doubled back. Whoever they were taking me to see didn't want me to know where I was. That was a good sign, because if something bad was going to happen to me they wouldn't care one way or the other.

We stopped twice which I figured was because we'd come to a red light, but the third time we stopped I heard a gate rattle back and then we drove slowly and made a left turn and the driver switched off the engine.

'We're here,' said Tam, patting me on the shoulder. 'You can sit up now.'

I did as I was told. We were parked next to a traditional Thai house made from old teak that gleamed in the moonlight. Tam opened the door and got out and Lek prodded me with the gun to let me know that I was to follow suit.

They took me up a flight of wooden stairs and Tam, knocked on a large door and pushed it open. Lek prodded me with the gun again, this time in the small of the back. It wouldn't have been too difficult to have swung around and knocked the gun to the side and pushed him down the stairs but there were two of them and they were both trained kickboxers and besides I really wanted to know who was on the other side of the door.

'Shoes,' hissed Lek.

'What?' I said.

'Take off your shoes.'

I sighed and did as I was told. Lek and Tam took theirs off, too, and we lined them up by the door.

The room was in near darkness, the only light coming from a small bulb mounted in what looked as if it had once been the axle of a buffalo cart. There was a man sitting in a teak planter's chair. He was wearing dark clothing and had set the light up so that he was sitting in shadow.

Tam pointed at a wicker sofa and motioned for me to sit down. I did as I was told and looked around the room. There were two doors leading off to the left, both closed, and one to the right that was open and through which I could see a kitchen. An open stairway of thick teak planks led to the upper floor.

'You are Bob Turtledove,' said the man, in accented English. It was a statement rather than a question.

'If I'm not, you've all been wasting your time,' I answered. I was pretty sure that if they were going to do anything nasty to me they'd already have done it. The man wanted to talk, which was fine by me.

Lek tapped the gun against my leg as if he wanted to remind me that he was still holding it.

'Please don't try my patience,' said the man, again in English.

'Yes, I'm Bob Turtledove,' I said in Thai. 'Who are you?'

I wanted him to speak in Thai because then I'd have a pretty good idea of where he came from.

'You're not here to ask questions,' he said. I couldn't make out his face but he was tall for a Thai and had stretched out his long legs. 'You went to see Marsh in hospital. Why?'

'What business is that of yours?' I asked, again in Thai.

Lek put the barrel of the gun against my forehead. I could feel sweat trickling down my back. I've never been happy at people pointing guns at me, especially loaded ones with the hammer cocked. I didn't think that Lek intended to shoot me but his finger was on the trigger and guns sometimes went off unintentionally.

I knew that from experience.

'No one will hear the gunshot, except for us,' said the man, still in English. 'And anyone who does hear will not care. Why did you go to see Marsh in the Bumrungrad?'

'I'm looking for an American boy who has gone missing,' I said. 'His parents are worried. They thought that he might have been in the nightclub when it burned down.' I switched to the Isarn dialect, which is close to Thai but has a lot in common with the language of neighbouring Laos.

The man settled back in his chair and I could feel him staring at me, trying to work out if I was telling the truth or not.

'What is his name?' asked the man, this time speaking in Isarn. 'This missing boy?'

'Jon Clare,' I said.

'And that is all you wanted from Marsh?'

I nodded. His accent sounded as if he was from the north of Isarn. Udon Thani, maybe. Which meant that it was probably Thongchai, Lek and Tam's boss who had disappeared after the fire.

'And why did you go to the kickboxing gym?'

'Same reason.'

The man crossed his legs slowly. 'You were at the Kube with the police.'

'I was there when the police were there, yes.'

'And you spoke to the Public Prosecutor.'

'Khun Jintana. Yes.'

'Did you think that Public Prosecutor might know where the

boy is?'

'No,' I said.

'So what did you talk about?'

'I was just there to see the club,' I said.

'And it was a coincidence that one of the investigating officers and the Public Prosecutor were there?'

'I went there to see a friend of mine who's in the police,' I said. 'But I don't see that that's any business of yours.' I leaned forward. 'What are you so scared of, Khun Thongchai?'

He stiffened. 'How do you know me?' he asked.

'You owned the Kube and these two work for you,' I said. 'What I don't understand is why you're here and not in Udon Thani.'

'Because the police are looking for me and Udon Thani is the first place they'll look,' he said.

'So you're hiding?' I said.

'I'm not scared of the police,' he said. He reached over and flicked a switch on the wall and the room was flooded with light. The walls, floor and vaulted ceiling were all made of polished teak and two wooden-bladed fans slowly stirred the air above our heads.

Thongchai was tall and thin, wearing a dark blue Mao jacket, baggy pants and rope sandals. There was a gold watch on one wrist and a thick gold chain on the other, and five Buddha amulets were hanging from a heavy chain around his neck. Thais wear amulets for a whole host of reasons. Some are passed down from father to son, others are gifts from nearest and dearest, some are worn as good-luck symbols, some for protection.

Protection?

That's right. There are amulets that are supposed to protect against bullets, others that are proof against poison, or car crashes. I couldn't get a good look at the ones hanging around Thongchai's neck but I would have bet my last dollar they were amulets that offered protection of one form or another.

He took off his dark glasses and stared at me with cold eyes. 'Who told you about me?' he asked.

'You're not an official secret,' I said. 'The police know that you are one of the owners.'

'And you talked to Marsh about me?'

'Your name come up.'

'And you went to see Lek and Tam to find out where I was?'

I shook my head. 'I already told you, I was looking for Jon Clare.'

'You have a picture?'

I nodded and reached into my jacket. Lek pushed the gun against my neck and I slowly took out the photograph and gave it to him. Lek passed it to Thongchai.

'You think he was in the club the night of the fire?' said Thongchai as he studied the photograph.

'It's possible, but your men don't remember him.'

'Neither do I,' said Thongchai, passing the picture back to Lek. 'I think you can assume that he wasn't there. One of us would have seen him.'

Lek gave me the picture and I put it back in my pocket.

'You know that Marsh is dead?' I said.

'You think I killed him?'

'The thought had entered my head, yes,' I said.

'And why would you think that?' asked Thongchai.

'Marsh thought that he was going to be blamed for the fire.'

'It was the band that set off the fireworks,' said Thongchai. 'That was what started the blaze.'

'Marsh said that the club was overcrowded and the fire exits were blocked. He seemed to think that he'd get the blame.'

'He's a farang,' said Thongchai. 'They will want the head of a Thai for this.'

'You ordered the exits to be locked?'

Thongchai shook his head. 'No. I said it was a bad idea, I said it was illegal and dangerous, but I was overruled.'

'But you're the owner.'

'I own ten per cent and I have to work like a dog,' said Thongchai. 'The other investors put in most of the money but they don't lift a finger.'

'But you run the place, right?'

'Marsh was the manager but I was there every night. The exits kept being opened from the inside. One guy would pay to go in, then he'd open the door and let in his friends. It happened a lot.'

'So you had the doors locked?'

'No, I told the other owners that we needed more security, a static guard stationed at each fire exit. I'd already brought the men in but I was told to let them go and to lock the doors instead.'

'Told by who?'

His eyes narrowed. 'Why do you care?'

I shrugged. He was right. It was none of my business. But a lot of people had died so yes, I cared. 'Marsh said it was the owners. I assumed that he meant you.'

'I wanted the doors guarded. But I was overruled.'

'By who?'

'The sons of one of the big investors. They used the VIP rooms three or four times a week. They'd bring in their girlfriends and order the best champagne and not pay for a thing. They liked to throw their weight around.'

'Marsh said it was your idea to lock the doors.' Thongchai's face tightened and I put up my hands. 'I'm just telling you what he said.'

'I told him to lock the doors, yes. But I was only telling him what they had told me.'

'And he said you left the building as soon as the fire started.'

Thongchai pursed his lips. 'He said a lot, didn't he?'

'He was scared. And now he's dead.'

'That was nothing to do with me.'

'He said a lawyer had been around to see him. Was that your idea?'

Thongchai shook his head.

'Marsh reckoned that the lawyer wanted him to take the blame for the fire. Or for the locked door and the overcrowding, at least.'

'It wasn't his fault,' said Thongchai. 'It wasn't mine either. It was the boys. But they're dead now so there's no one to back me up.' He sneered. 'Not that they would, even if they were alive.'

'They died in the fire?'

'Everyone in the VIP room died. There was just one narrow stairway up to it.'

'Why did you run, Thongchai? And why are you hiding now?'

Thongchai sat back in his chair and steepled his fingers under his chin. 'How long have you been in Thailand, Khun Bob?'

'A long time.'

'So you understand Thai people.'

I smiled. 'The longer I am here, the less I understand,' I said.

'But you know about Thais and revenge?'

I nodded. I knew what he meant. The boys had died and the parents would want retribution. It wasn't just the police who were looking for him.

'So someone will have to pay the price for what happened, and it won't be a farang.'

'Do you think they killed Marsh?'

Thongchai shrugged. 'I don't know. But I am sure they'll kill me if they find me.'

'So go to the police. The guy I went to see at the Kube, he's a police colonel investigating the case and he's as straight as they come. He'll give you a fair hearing.'

'It doesn't matter whether he's corrupt or not,' said Thongchai. 'Do you think he can protect me?'

It was a good question.

And the answer was probably no. Somsak might want to help but I doubt that he would be any more effective than the amulets hanging around Thongchai's neck.

'My men will take you wherever you need to go, Khun Bob,' said Thongchai. 'Good luck with your hunt for the missing boy.'

'Good luck yourself, Khun Thongchai,' I said.

Of the two of us, I suspected that he would need it more than me.

27

Dr Ma-lee was in her mid-thirties and seemed happy in her work. She was slightly plump and wore round spectacles and there were framed photographs of her husband and three equally plump daughters either side of her computer. She was wearing a white coat and had a stethoscope hanging around her neck and she inhaled the steam from the cup of Chinese tea that she was holding as I sat down in her office. She'd called me in for a chat about what she would be doing to me in a few days. There were framed certificates on the wall behind her showing that she'd studied in Chicago and Seattle, which was reassuring.

'Dr Wanlop explained what it is we'll be doing?' she asked, putting her cup down on its saucer.

'A colonoscopy, just to check that my colon is okay,' I said, trying to be as optimistic as possible.

'Exactly,' she said. 'Basically there are two systems we can use. The latest device is in the form of a capsule containing a camera which the patient simply swallows. It works its way through the system and we then plug it into our computer and obtain a view of the entire alimentary canal.'

'Sounds great,' I said.

Well, maybe not great, but it sure sounded better than pushing a camera up the other way.

'So, is that what you want to use?'

Her smile widened. Her teeth were slightly grey but perfectly even. 'Actually, Khun Bob, I am more old school,' she said. 'I prefer the old-fashioned method.'

That didn't sound so great, because old-fashioned basically involved shoving a camera up where the sun doesn't shine.

I smiled. 'Why's that, Dr Ma-lee?' I asked.

'Two reasons, really,' she said. 'First, the capsule method really only allows us one pass. We see what we see and that's the end of it. But with the camera I can spend as long as I need in there. I can view any problem from different angles which helps better to assess what needs to be done.'

'Right,' I said. 'I see.'

I didn't like the way she was talking about problems before she'd even started. I wanted her tell me that everything was going to be just fine, that there was nothing to worry about.

I didn't want to hear about problems.

Or red flags.

Or cancer.

'But the big advantage is that the equipment I use allows me to deal with any polyps that we find there and then. All the capsule does is tell us where there is a problem, we would then have to go back in and deal with it. So on balance, we're better off doing it the old-fashioned away.'

I smiled but really I didn't feel like smiling.

Before the colonoscopy had been an abstract procedure, but now it was a looming reality, and it wasn't something that I was looking forward to. Not one bit.

'And you understand there are preparations before we can do anything?' she said, smiling and nodding.

Preparations?

That didn't sound good.

28

IT WASN'T HARD finding out where Somchit Santhanavit – alias Tukkata – lived. Thai surnames are usually very distinctive. In fact, a hundred years or so ago there weren't any surnames. The entire population had just first names. It was King Vajiravudh who realised that knowing his subjects on a first name basis wasn't conducive to good governorship. If nothing else it made taxation difficult. He issued an edict that henceforth every family should have a family name and even came up with several hundred surnames himself.

Vajiravudh was one of the great kings of Thailand. He was educated at Sandhurst, studied law and history at Oxford, and was a real Anglophile. He replaced the traditional flag of Siam – a white elephant on a red background – with its present version of red, white and blue stripes and introduced the Boy Scouts to Thailand.

The fact that there were no surnames until the twentieth century meant that there were no common family names, no equivalent of Smith or Jones or Williams. There were also hundreds of thousands of them. Surnames were distinctive and often ran to more than five syllables. There were also so hard to remember that outside of official business Thais generally didn't use them. They would introduce themselves by their first names, or their nickname, and often close friends of many years might not know each other's family names.

The fact that Thai surnames were so distinctive also meant that once you did know the full name of the person you were looking for it was often reasonably easy to track them down. The phone book was often all that you needed, provided that you could read Thai.

I could.

The Santhanavit residence was on Sukhumvit Soi 39, not far from the Emporium Department Store. I like the Emporium. It's one of the most up-market department store in Bangkok, jam-packed with designer label clothing, state-of-the-art electronics and the prettiest girls you've ever seen selling perfume on the ground floor. It's also got a great food court, one of the best-kept secrets of culinary Bangkok. You buy coupons which you can exchange for Thai dishes that you'd normally find on the street: stewed pork knuckle; wanton noodle soup; chicken and rice. You get the street hawker culinary experience but with an unbeatable view over the city.

I could just about see the top of the Emporium tower while I was parked outside the big house midway down Soi 39 where the Santhanavits lived. I couldn't say exactly how big because it was surrounded by a wall twice my height and the gate was solid metal. All I could see from the street was the roof. It was a big roof. Maybe eighty yards from end to end. Attached to the all at the side of the gate were metal tubes for newspapers, two for leading Thai papers and one for the *Bangkok Post*. The newspaper delivery boys didn't throw the papers onto the garden American-style or push them through the letterbox, British-style. They went into the tubes and the maid or security guard came out and collected then.

Under the newspaper tubes was an oblong red box with Thai writing on it.

Interesting.

It was a police box.

The Thai police aren't the hardest working law enforcement officials in the world, and their bosses are always looking for ways of making them more efficient. One scheme was to attach the red boxes at points around the various beats in the city. Inside the red boxes were cards which had to be signed every hour by patrolling police officers. At first the red boxes were placed at random, but before long the city's wealthier citizens realised that having a police officer turning up at your gate every hour was a pretty good way of deterring criminals. They started offering hard cash for the privilege of having one of the red boxes.

That meant that my idea of sitting outside the house and waiting for Tukkata to leave was a non-starter as cops would be turning up every hour or so and they'd be sure to spot my car. A black Hummer is pretty hard to miss.

Time for Plan B.

I drove home.

29

THE DUBLINER IS an Irish pub at the entrance to Washington Square, all green paintwork and shamrocks with Guinness signs and dark wooden tables, some of them made from barrels. I sat down at a corner table and ordered a coffee and waited for the boiler room boys to put in an appearance. The pub was just around the corner from the kickboxing gym where Lek and Tam trained so I kept my face turned away from the window just in case either of them walked by.

Sitting at the table next to mine was a couple in their sixties from England with a man who was obviously their son and a girl who was obviously a bargirl, or a former bargirl. The parents were stick-thin and grey-haired with worn, tired faces, but they were clearly proud of the fact that their son had acquired a beautiful Thai bride-to-be. Their son was slack-jawed and shaven headed and had his name tattooed in Thai across his forearm. Derek. He was wearing a Chang beer vest and baggy shorts and plastic flip-flops and a fake Rolex watch and he spent a lot of time scratching himself.

He was educating his parents on the best way to treat Thais which seemed to involve speaking slowly and loudly and offering them bribes, and telling mum and dad that it was the best country in the world unless you were into drugs because they shot drug-dealers. He didn't seem the sharpest knife in the drawer, but his proud parents were nodding and grunting at his pearls of wisdom as they ate their way through the Dubliner's massive all-day breakfasts.

The girl sitting with them was in her very early twenties, dark-skinned with the high cheekbones you usually find on girls from Surin, close to the border with Cambodia.

Why did I think she was a bargirl?

The tattoo of a scorpion on her left shoulder was a clue.

As was the ornate tattoo across the small of her back, revealed every time she leaned forward to pick up one of the French fries off Derek's plate.

The way she was dressed screamed bargirl – tight blue jeans and even tighter low-cut black t-shirt, with a heavy gold necklace that Derek had no doubt bought for.

But the clincher was the fact that she was on the phone to her Thai boyfriend while Derek and his parents chatted obliviously.

I couldn't believe it, and neither could the two waitresses within earshot who kept giggling at the outrageous things the girl was saying.

Derek was from Wolverhampton, in the middle of England pretty much, and he had only known her for a month. He had already proposed and his parents had flown over to attend the wedding in Surin. It would be a proper ceremony but the girl, Apple, swore to her boyfriend that she would never sign the paperwork to make the marriage official. She told her boyfriend that it would be the third time that she had done the marriage ceremony with a customer and that it didn't mean anything.

Derek had promised to build her a house in Surin, and had already paid the deposit for a Toyota pick-up truck, which the boyfriend was driving around in. And Derek, bless him, had agreed to pay a sinsot of three hundred thousand baht.

Sinsot? It's a dowry, paid by the groom to the parents of the bride. I paid a sinsot of half a million baht when I married Noy. Plus another half a million in gold jewellery. A total of a million baht, about thirty-five thousand dollars back then.

Was she worth it?

Every cent.

Noy's parents gave it all back after the wedding, of course. Noy kept the jewellery but used the cash towards the deposit on our flat. That's part of the tradition – the parents return most if not all the sinsot to the newlyweds to give them a good start in life.

I doubted that Derek would be getting any of his sinsot back.

The fact that he'd agreed to pay a sinsot at all showed that Derek really didn't understand Thailand. His bride-to-be clearly wasn't a virgin, wasn't from a good family, and the scorpion tattoo suggested that she either been in prison or been dancing around a chrome pole in one the city's red light areas. Any one of those three would have meant a much-reduced sinsot, and the fact that he'd pulled a hat trick meant that really the parents should have been paying Derek to take her off their hands.

As she carried on her conversation with her boyfriend, half in Thai and half in Khmer, Apple kept winking at Derek and blowing him the occasional kiss.

'She loves me,' he told his parents. 'Not like the girls back in Wolverhampton, hey, dad? These Thai birds really know how to treat a man.'

Apple was telling her boyfriend that she was on the pill so there was no way that she could get pregnant, and that once the house was finished she would send him packing. 'Or you could kill him,' she laughed, and I couldn't tell if she was joking or not.

I sipped my coffee as I watched the drama unfold.

Another lamb to the slaughter.

Derek was saying that he wanted children and that his mum would soon be a grandmother. His mum beamed and nodded.

'We're going to have kids soon, aren't we Apple?' he asked, jabbing at her with his knife.

Apple took the phone away from her mouth and nodded. 'Soon, darling,' she said. 'I want your baby too much. I want handsome son, like you.'

So why didn't I warn Derek that his bride-to-be didn't really love him and was only after his money?

Because it was none of my business.

Most countries in Asia have a saying along the lines of you don't mess with another man's rice bowl, and I've been in Asia long enough to respect that philosophy.

Apple was doing what she had to do to survive.

If Derek was too dumb to see that, then really he deserved what was coming to him. I reckoned he was in his late thirties, a good fifteen years older than her. He was overweight and clearly hadn't bothered to learn any of the language, so why would he think that a pretty girl would see him as anything other than a cash cow?

I finished my coffee. I knew that the Dubliner didn't sell Phuket Beer so ordered a half pint of Guinness instead. I was half way through it when Bear came in, followed by three young men in sharp suits. Bear was as big as his name suggested, a little over six feet six inches tall, broad shouldered and pot-bellied with a bushy beard and a pair of black horn-rimmed spectacles.

He sat down on a stool at one of the circular tables fashioned from a barrel and ordered three beers as his colleagues joined him.

I picked up my beer and went over. 'Alistair?' I asked. 'Alistair Wainer?'

Bear screwed up his eyes as he looked at me. 'You look like a cop,' he said suspiciously.

'I used to be one,' I said. 'In another country and in another life.

But I sell antiques now.' I took out one of my business cards and gave it to him.

He frowned as he read the card. 'If it's about shares, I work in administration, you need to talk to your broker.'

'Relax, Bear, I'm more of a cash-under-the-mattress sort of guy.' I took out the photograph of Jon Junior and gave it to him.

'He owe you money?' asked Bear.

I shook my head. 'He's missing. His parents have asked me to look for him.'

Bear nodded. 'Jon, right? Jon Clare. That's his name, yeah? A Yank?'

'He came to see you?'

Bear gave me back the photograph. 'A week or so ago.'

'Can you remember when exactly?'

Bear frowned. 'Why does that matter?'

I put the picture back into my jacket. The waitress brought over three pints of beer and put them down on the table. 'Remember the nightclub that burned down? The Kube?'

Bear nodded. 'That was some serious shit,' he said.

'Yeah, well his parents are worried that he might have been caught up in it.'

Bear picked up his pint and took a long drink. 'Yeah, he came to see me a few days before the fire, looking for a job. I asked him back for a trial and he came to the office last Monday, which was what, two days after the fire?'

'Yeah, the fire was on Saturday.' I couldn't stop myself from grinning. At least I had definite proof that Jon Junior was alive and well after the Kube had burned down. 'Did you offer him a job?'

Bear took a drink, then wiped his mouth with the back of his hand. 'He didn't have the balls,' he said. 'Absolutely zero killer instinct.' He nodded at one of his companions. 'Jimmy took him under his wing, gave him a script and watched as he made a few calls.'

'Bloody disaster,' said Jimmy in an upper-class English accent. 'Couldn't sell smack to a heroin addict.'

Nice analogy. But I got the drift.

'Did he say where he was going? What he was doing?'

'He was teaching English at some school,' said Bear. He clicked his fingers at a waitress and asked for a menu. 'I figure he'd make a better teacher than broker.'

'He's left the school,' I said. 'That's the problem. Did he say why he wanted the job?'

'The money, probably. But he wasn't happy at the school. He thought there was something not right about it.'

'In what way?'

'It's run by some Russian guy and he thought he was Mafia. Kept seeing shady characters hanging around the office.'

'The thing is, he was only supposed to be in Thailand for a year, he was going back to work for the family firm. And he already had a job, teaching English.'

Bear and his two companions laughed. 'Teaching English isn't really a job, Bob,' said Bear. 'I spend in one night what a teacher earns in a month.'

'He's a Mormon,' I said. 'They're not driven by money.'

'The Osmonds performed for free, did they?' laughed Bear. 'Everyone's driven by money, trust me. If they weren't, we wouldn't make the living we do.'

'Greed is good?' I said.

Bear laughed. 'It might not be good, but it keeps me in booze and hookers and puts gas in the Ferrari.' He took a long pull on his pint.

'You ever thought about sales, Bob?'

'I told you, I sell antiques.'

'I mean real sales. Stocks. Shares. The margins we operate on, a guy like you could make a good living.'

'I'll pass,' I said. I nodded at my business card which he'd put down on the table. 'If by any chance he gets in touch again, give me a call, yeah?'

30

THE FRIDAY NIGHT poker game was at the house of John Muller, an American who I'd met soon after arriving in Thailand. John was a Vietnam vet who'd been involved in the Phoenix programme, winning the hearts and minds of the Viet Cong and occasionally throwing them out of helicopters. That's just rumour and conjecture, John doesn't talk much about what he did back then. He's been married to a Thai lady for more than thirty years and runs a security company that looks after big hotels and VIP clients in Thailand and Cambodia.

John and his wife live in Sukhumvit 101 in a house they bought just after they married. I went by taxi because a lot of alcohol is consumed on poker night.

A rottweiler on a chain snarled at me as I pressed the doorbell and ignored my attempts to win it over by making shushing noises. The dog hates me, but when I visit with Noy it's all sweetness and light.

The door opened and Muller grinned amiably. 'Brought your money with you, Bob?' he asked and gave me a bear hug that forced the breath out of me. I'm not a small guy but Muller is a couple of inches taller and good deal heavier. His hair and moustache are greying but he looks good for sixty-odd.

'I've gotta warn you, I'm feeling lucky tonight,' I said.

Muller laughed and slapped me on the back, then finally released me and I stumbled into the house. 'The wife's out with the girls so we've got free rein,' said Muller. 'And the pizzas are on the way.'

I went through to the sitting room where there was a large circular table covered in green baize.

Somsak was there, dressed casually but expensively in chinos and a pink Lacoste shirt. He raised his glass of brandy in salute. 'The late Bob Turtledove,' he said.

'We're in the middle of nowhere,' I said. 'And the traffic was terrible.'

Muller handed me an opened bottle of Phuket Beer and waved me to an empty chair. I sat down and took out a wad of banknotes.

Sitting opposite me was a Brit, a real estate agent by the name of Tim Maplethorpe who always seemed to be smiling, probably because more often than not he left the game as a winner. When he wasn't selling apartments to wealthy foreigners he was usually honing his poker skills on line. He grinned as he played with his stacks. 'Thought you'd chickened out,' he said. He was wearing a green polo shirt with the name of his company on the back.

Muller took my money and gave me chips.

Sitting next to Maplethorpe was Annan, a muscular trainer who worked at a popular gym on Soi Ekkamai. Annan was a friend of Tim's and had helped him lose more than thirty pounds over the past two years by setting up a vigorous exercise regime and making sure that he stuck to it. Now he wants to do the same for me but I've never been a fan of gyms.

Annan's pile of chips was about half as big as Tim's but I was pretty sure that the position would be reversed by the end of the game. Not that Annan would be worried. His father owned one of the biggest taxi companies in Bangkok and his mother was a well-known TV presenter who everyone assumed would run for political office within a year or two. Annan was quite definitely hi-so.

Annan grinned and pointed at my waistline. 'You need to lose a few kilos, Khun Bob,' he said.

I took off my jacket and held it up. 'That should do it,' I said. 'Gotta be a kilo or two there.' I twisted around and hung the jacket on the back of my chair.

'I'll spot you in the gym, no charge,' said Annan.

'I prefer tennis,' I said. 'I always feel like a hamster on a wheel when I'm on a treadmill.'

Sitting on the other side of Annan was Andy Yates, a stockbroker in his early forties who had been in Asia for almost twenty years. He raised his bottle of Corona in salute and went back to arranging his chips.

The doorbell rang and Muller went to answer it. He returned a few minutes later with three large pizzas.

Annan grinned as I helped myself to a slice. 'I haven't eaten all day,' I said.

'Your body is a temple,' he said.

'I'm not sure that's true,' I said. 'I like to think of it as more of an amusement park.'

Muller sat down and began to shuffle the cards. 'Texas Hold 'Em, same as always,' he said. 'Rebuys for the first hour.'

We all nodded. We'd been playing Texas Hold 'Em for almost a year. We'd tried other variations of poker but we'd all agreed that Hold 'Em was the best.

Muller dealt us all a card each so see who would be the first to deal. Maplethorpe got an ace and he punched the air triumphantly.

I settled back in my chair, munched on my slice of pizza, and waited for Maplethorpe to deal.

When we first started playing poker on a Friday night, we'd tried bringing in a rule that no one could talk about business. Or politics.

Or religion. But as that excluded pretty much everything we wanted to talk about the rule was quickly scrapped and now anything was fair game. Muller moaned about the hassles of doing business in Cambodia, Maplethorpe complained about the state of the Bangkok property market and Annan bitched about his new boss at the gym.

We were about halfway through the game when Muller asked me if I was up to anything interesting. I told them about Jon Junior and the lack of progress I was making in finding the missing Mormon. 'I keep trying his phone and the cellphone he called but they're both off,' I said.

'Which phone company?' asked Muller.

I shrugged. 'No idea,' I said. 'Why?'

'If it's AIS I've a guy who can get me call details and GPS position.'

Somsak wagged a disapproving finger at Muller. 'Now John, you know that's illegal,' he said.

'It's a grey area,' said Muller. Somsak continued to wag his finger and eventually Muller threw up his hands in surrender. 'Yes, okay, strictly speaking I suppose it might be less grey and more illegal.'

Somsak grinned and drained his glass. He slid it across the baize to Muller. 'Fill me up with your excellent brandy and we'll say no more about it,' he said.

Muller went to get a refill for Somsak and beers for everyone else. 'Let me know the numbers and I'll get my guy to check them out on Monday,' he said.

'You're a star, John.' I sipped my drink. 'At least I know he wasn't caught up in the Kube fire. That's what his parents were most scared of, I think.'

'How's the Kube investigation going?' Annan asked Somsak.

'Slowly,' he said.

'Will they be charging anybody?' asked Maplethorpe, voicing

the question that was on the tip of my tongue.

'I'm not sure,' said Somsak.

'It was terrible,' said Annan. 'Two of the girls from the gym died there. Is it right that they locked the emergency exits?'

Somsak nodded. 'That's true, yes.'

'Whoever did that should be locked up and the key thrown away,' said Maplethorpe.

'Unfortunately it's not my decision,' said Somsak. 'Who gets charged and with what is down to the Public Prosecutor.'

'The lovely Miss Jintana,' I said.

'Exactly,' said Somsak, picking up the deck and shuffling it. 'The problem is, Khun Jintana might not be the safest pair of hands for such a decision.'

'Why's that?' I asked.

'I told you that her parents live in Chiang Mai?'

'Her father's an MP there, you said. I remember.'

'Well, her family have just registered a large chunk of land by the river, land that used to be owned by a family who just happen to be close friends with one of the owners of the nightclub.'

'No way,' I said. 'How much land?'

'Twenty rai,' said Somsak, studying his cards. 'Very picturesque by all accounts.'

A rai is a Thai measurement of area, equivalent to one thousand six hundred square metres. Twenty rai is a lot of land. And land around Chiang Mai isn't cheap. Jintana's father was an MP so he wouldn't be short of money, but it seemed to be one hell of a coincidence that he acquired the land just as his daughter started investigating the nightclub fire.

'Will you be looking at it?' I asked.

'The land?' Somsak shrugged. 'It's not my jurisdiction.'

'Amazing Thailand,' said Muller.

'Exactly,' said Somsak.

'It's not fair,' said Maplethorpe. 'A lot of kids died in that blaze. Someone should be held accountable.'

'I agree,' said Somsak. 'And I think that will probably happen, with or without Khun Jintana's assistance.'

'How come?' I asked.

'Some very important people lost their children in the fire,' said Somsak. 'An Army general for one. Several businessmen with links to local mafia. I think that no matter what Khun Jintana does, justice will be done.'

'You're talking about vigilantes,' said Muller.

Somsak began to deal the cards. 'I'm not talking about anything,' he said. He nodded at Yates. 'Ante up, Andy,' he said.

The last hand of the night was a close call. I had an ace and king of hearts and the ace of clubs flopped and the king of spades came on the river so I was looking at two pairs but there were three clubs on the table including the king and Somsak started blinking. It's the perfect tell, whenever Somsak has a good hand he blinks and he didn't start blinking until the third club dropped.

I folded my two pair and Maplethorpe threw down his hand. I'm pretty sure that he's also spotted Somsak's tell. Anyway, Somsak took the pot but I could have lost a lot more. I walked away from the game down about ten thousand baht, which is about par for the course.

I don't play poker for the money.

Obviously.

31

DAO-NOK ANTIQUES is open on a Saturday but generally I take the weekend off and let Ying hold the fort. Noy wanted to go shopping in Siam Paragon and who was I to argue? Siam Paragon is one of the biggest shopping centres in Asia, packed with all the top designer stores and home to the biggest aquarium in South East Asia. I'd arrived in Bangkok just after they'd knocked down the Siam Intercontinental Hotel to make way for Siam Paragon, and I'd seen the development grow from a huge hole in the ground to a massive twenty-one acre complex containing four hundred thousand square metres of retail space.

Shopping with my wife is fun, not the least because I get to see her wearing lots of different outfits and she always asks me what I think.

To be honest, I'm not the best person to ask because I think she looks beautiful whatever she's wearing.

We spent the morning wandering around the shops and then we had lunch at Fuji, her favourite Japanese restaurant.

As we left the restaurant I saw a face that I recognised.

Petrov Shevtsova.

He was wearing black Armani jeans and a tight-fitting white shirt and impenetrable sunglasses. Holding his left arm was a tall, pretty blonde wearing a white miniskirt and impossibly high stiletto heels. They were looking into the window of a jewellers.

I steered Noy in the other direction.

We'd driven to Paragon in my Humvee. Driving in Bangkok is generally unpleasant and dangerous and the Humvee is the only car that I feel safe in. I figure if it's good enough for US troops in Iraq and Afghanistan then it's good enough for me to drive down Sukhumvit Road.

The basic problem is that Thai drivers have very little respect for the rules of the road, of for the law in general. Drink-driving is illegal but in the evening probably over half the drivers on the road are over the limit. Truck drivers and bus drivers work long hours and think nothing of taking amphetamines to keep themselves going. Most Thai drivers simply ignore zebra crossings, even if there are people walking on them, and a red traffic light is generally regarded as advisory rather than a signal to stop. They weave in and out of traffic and rarely allow another motorist to pull in front of them, and just because a driver indicates that he's going to turn left doesn't necessarily mean that the car will actually go in that direction.

Added together, these factors result in a death rate on the country's roads which is many times that of Western nations. Maybe it's because they're Buddhists and believe in reincarnation, but whatever the reason I only ever get behind the wheel when it's my Humvee.

As we headed towards it, I heard my name being called. I looked around. It was the Russian.

'Who's that?' asked Noy.

I gave her the car keys. 'Friend of mine,' I said. 'You go ahead.'

'Is everything okay, honey?'

'I'll tell you later. It's no big deal.'

As Noy went over to the Humvee I turned to face Petrov. He left the blonde girl and walked towards me like a heavyweight heading for the ring.

My heart was racing but I smiled as if I didn't have a care in the world.

Jai yen.

Cool heart.

'I thought it was you,' said Petrov.

'Yeah, just doing some shopping.'

He gestured at Noy who was looking our way as she climbed into the car. 'I didn't know you were married.'

I didn't know what to say to that so I just shrugged.

'Nice car,' said Petrov. 'Thought about getting a Hummer myself.'

'They're safe, that's why I like them,' I said. 'Anyway, good to see you.'

I started to walk away but he gripped me by the shoulder, the fingers of his left hand digging into the flesh like talons. 'You bought it in Thailand, did you?'

'There's a showroom in Petchburi Road,' I said.

'I know there is,' said the Russian. 'How does an English teacher manage to afford a car like this?' he asked.

I smiled and didn't answer.

'Why did you disappear?' asked Petrov, lowering his voice to a deep growl. 'One lesson and then you were gone.'

The blonde girl was tapping her foot, a look of bored disdain on her face.

'I got a better offer,' I said. 'I did phone to let the office know.'

'No one told me,' said Petrov.

'Yeah, it just came up. An offer I couldn't refuse.'

Petrov nodded, his face a black mask, his eyes his eyes hidden behind the dark lenses. 'That's what the mafia do, isn't it?' he said. 'Make you an offer you can't refuse.' He made a gun from his right hand and pointed it at my face. 'Bang,' he said quietly, then he laughed and released his grip on my shoulder. He gestured at the Hummer with his chin. 'Drive carefully,' he said. 'Bangkok can be a dangerous place.'

I watched him walk over to rejoin the blonde girl and then the two of them walked over to a red Porsche.

I climbed into the driving seat of the Hummer and switched on the engine.

'Who was that, honey?' asked Noy.

'A Russian,' I said.

'Good friend of yours?'

'Not really.'

'He likes the car, doesn't he?' she said, squinting into the wing mirror.

'Yeah, he was asking where I got it from.'

'He's taking a photograph of it, with his cellphone.'

I looked in the driving mirror. She was right.

I didn't think he was interested in the Hummer, though.

It was a picture of the registration plate that he wanted.

That wasn't good.

That wasn't good at all.

32

ON SUNDAY NOY went to the Hyatt Hotel to sample its legendary buffet with a gaggle of her girlfriends. The Hyatt's Sunday buffet is best enjoyed over three or four hours followed by a three-day fast. The food is spectacular, from great sushi and oysters to a full Sunday roast, an array of Thai dishes from across the country, and a dessert spread that has me putting on weight just looking at it.

It was girls only so I had the afternoon to myself. I decided to swing by Tukkata's house in Sukhumvit Soi 39. I didn't take my car because a black Humvee is pretty distinctive so I caught a taxi in Soi Thonglor instead.

I had it drop me a hundred yards from the house and I walked slowly down the road. It was in the high thirties so I took off my jacket and rolled up my sleeves but even so I'd still worked up a sweat by the time I'd reached the house.

Several food stalls had set up on the opposite side of the road, wheeled trolleys next to a few battered metal tables and plastic stools. The middle stall was selling somtam. I'm a big fan of the dish which is a speciality of the Isarn people, a fiery concoction of shredded unripened papaya mixed with chilli, sugar, garlic, shrimp paste, lime and fish sauce. It's an acquired taste, but I'd been in Thailand long enough that there were times that I'd get a craving for the dish, ideally with chunks of barbecued chicken and sticky rice.

The Thais in the middle of the country make a sweeter and milder version and throw a handful of crushed peanuts into the mix, but the lady pounding the papaya with a stone mortar and pestle looked as if she was from Surin and she was making hers Isarn-style with padaek, brined land crabs found in ricefields and canals.

She grinned with blackened teeth when I ordered a plate and asked me if I wanted it spicy. 'Of course,' I said, and laughed. 'Somtam isn't somtam if it doesn't make me cry.'

She waved me to a table with her pestle. Her husband came over and asked me what I wanted to drink. They didn't have Phuket Beer so I asked for a Singha and he brought me one with a glass filled with chipped ice.

I drank from the bottle. Ice is generally okay in Thailand provided it's come out of a machine. Shaved or chipped ice has probably been hacked off a large block with a dirty knife and is a pretty efficient way of contracting hepatitis.

When the woman brought over my plate of somtam I asked her about the house opposite. 'They are a good family,' she said. 'They bought the house ten years ago and we were already here. My husband and I asked if they were happy for our business to be on the street and they said it wasn't a problem.' She laughed. 'Sometimes the husband comes here to eat. He says I make better somtam than his wife.'

'They must be rich to have such a big house,' I said.

She nodded sagely. 'Very rich,' she said. 'He has a big Mercedes and she has an Audi.'

'And a daughter, right?'

'A daughter and two sons,' she said, nodding. 'All the children are so polite. When they were very small they used to wave when they went to school.'

Another customer arrived and she went over to serve him. I ate the somtam, washing it down with beer. Her husband came back over when my plate was empty and I ordered another helping. And another Singha.

When the woman came over with my second plate, I asked her if she knew what the husband did for a living.

'He has many businesses,' she said. 'He has a property company and a computer company and an import-export business.'

'It must be good to be so rich,' I said.

'It is more important to be happy, and to be healthy,' she said.

Which is true.

Very true.

I tried not to think about cancer. And death.

She went back to her stall and started pounding papaya again.

I finished my second helping of somtam and the beer and I went over to pay the woman. I took a five hundred baht note from my wallet and handed it over with the photograph of Jon Junior. 'Did you ever see a farang boy visiting?

She looked at the money, then at the photograph, and smiled.

She understood.

She looked at the photograph carefully, then called over her husband and showed it to him. He wrinkled his nose and shook his head.

She gave me back the photograph and slipped the five hundred baht into the canvas bag hanging from her belt. 'We've never seen the farang,' she said. 'We've never seen any farang go into the house.'

I put the photograph in my pocket and thanked her. 'Your somtam is delicious,' I said. 'The best in Bangkok.'

'The best in Thailand,' she said, and I had to agree with her.

And that was when Mrs Santhanavit drove up in her large Audi.

33

I ALWAYS USED to think that it was Rabbi Burns the famous Jewish philosopher who said that the best laid plans of mice and men often go astray, and it wasn't until I was in my thirties that I discovered that it was really the Scottish poet Robbie Burns.

Who knew?

But the point was, I suppose, that it doesn't matter how you plan things, the unexpected can always happen. The trick is how you handle the unexpected. I had about thirty seconds to decide what do once I realised that the middle-aged woman at the wheel of the silver-grey Audi 8 was turning into the Santhanavit house and beeping her horn so that whoever was inside would open the gate for her.

An old lady in a stained denim dress dragged the wheeled gate back, using her shoulder to push it. Mrs Santhanavit tapped her fingers impatiently against the steering wheel until there was a gap large enough to drive through and she eased the Audi forward.

The old woman wiped her forehead with the sleeve of her dress and began to drag the gate closed. I jogged across the road and slipped through, ignoring her protests.

Mrs Santhanavit was climbing out of her car when I jogged up the driveway, a large Louis Vuitton bag on her arm.

'Mrs Santhanavit?'

She frowned at me through a pair of Dolce and Gabbana glasses. I stopped jogging. 'My name is Bob Turtledove,' I said, 'I'm from the Betta English Language School.'

Which, if you think about it, was strictly speaking true.

I decided against speaking to her in Thai and to play the slightly-stupid English teacher.

'I was wondering what had happened to Tukkata.'

'Tukkata?' she repeated. She leaned inside the car and pulled out half a dozen Siam Paragon bags.

'Your daughter hasn't been to the school, I wondered if I could talk to her.'

She closed the car door. 'Tukkata?' she repeated.

'Yes, Tukkata.'

'She's not here,' she said. She was heavyset with short-thick legs wearing a multi-coloured silk shirt and white trousers and white flat shoes, with a heavy gold bracelet on her right wrist and a gold Cartier watch on her left.

The old lady had stopped closing the gate and stood where she was, watching me and probably wondering whether or not she should call the police.

'Do you know where she is, Mrs Santhanavit?'

She shook her head and began to walk towards the house. I followed her, but then the front door opened and a stocky man in a starched white shirt and dark trousers glared at me. 'Who are you?' he shouted. 'What are you doing here?'

He was about fifty, his hair was greying at the temples and thinning at the back. He had a wristwatch that matched his wife's and around his neck was a gold necklace as thick as my thumb from which hung a large Buddhist medallion that was the size of a coaster.

He spoke to his wife in rapid Thai, telling her to go into the house. He sounded like a man who was used to being obeyed.

He walked past her and came up to me. He was about six inches shorter than me and he had to crane his neck to glare up at me. 'Get off my property!' he barked.

'Mr Santhanavit, I'm from the language school, I just wanted to check that Tukkata was okay,' I said. 'We haven't seen her for a while.'

'She's fine,' he said. 'I want you to go.' He pointed at the gate. 'Go now or I will call the police.'

'Can I speak to her?'

'Why do you want to speak to her?' he said.

'To see if there's a problem.'

'There's no problem,' he said. 'She's sick. In her room. Go now.'

I looked over at the house. A curtain moved in one of the ground floor windows. It was probably Mrs Santhanavit. I looked up at the bedroom windows. All the curtains were open. I didn't believe him. I didn't believe that his daughter was sick and I didn't believe that she was in her bedroom.

I believed Mrs Santhanavit when she said she wasn't there.

Which meant that Mr Santhanavit was lying.

Interesting.

I nodded and smiled and turned around and walked back through the gate. The old lady smiled and began dragging it shut behind me.

34

NOY WASN'T HOME when I got back. I wasn't surprised. Sunday buffet was often followed by Sunday shopping and if they were really enjoying themselves it would be topped off with Sunday drinks. I went through to my study and switched on my computer, then fetched myself a bottle of Phuket Beer from the kitchen.

I swung my feet up onto the desk which is something I only do when Noy isn't around because like most Thais she has a thing about feet. It's bad manners to point with your feet and even worse to put your feet on the furniture, but I figure that when I'm alone in the apartment I'm king of the castle so if I want to put my feet up, I will. I pulled my MacBook on to my lap and logged on to my email account.

Most were work related but there were half a dozen questions about Thailand from guys on their way for the first time and more than twenty possible sighting of Jon Junior.

That was the problem with asking for help on the Internet – every man and his dog was keen to help but when all they had to go on was a couple of photographs there were bound to be false leads.

Seven readers of the Stickman site had contacted him to say that they'd seen Jon Junior. One was in Laos and he said he'd seen Jon Junior at a temple, another had spotted him in Burmese market, and another said he'd seen him in Orchard Towers in Singapore, known throughout Asia as the Four Floors of Whores, buying drinks for a couple of ladyboys. As I knew that Jon Junior was in Thailand, they could all be discounted. One Stickman reader said that he'd seen him on Kho Samui, an island in the south of Thailand. Another said he'd been asleep on a bus heading for Korat, another that he'd been eating at a seafood restaurant in Pattaya, and yet another that he had been on a hiking tour visiting hilltribes around Chiang Mai.

The four sightings in Thailand were all valid possibilities but none of the readers provided any information that would help me to follow them up.

I went through the rest of the responses – six were overseas and I could ignore them straight away, especially the one that said Jon Junior had been spotted playing blackjack in a Las Vegas casino. The rest included Udon Thani, Surin, Kho Samui, Phuket, Kho Chang, and three in Pattaya. Again the readers hadn't provided any information that would positively identify Jon Junior, though the one in Kho Samui and one of the guys in Pattaya had said that they were called Jon, and the one in Surin was wearing a New York Yankees baseball cap and had an American accent.

I drank my beer and wondered what I should do next because while I had managed to establish that Jon Junior hadn't been caught up in the fire at the Kube I was still no closer to finding out where he was.

I logged out of my email address and onto Jon Junior's account but there was nothing but junk mail.

His parents had said that he wasn't using his credit card which meant that he was in hiding or that he was physically unable to use his card, which pretty much implied that he was dead because if someone had stolen the card they'd have used it and if he'd lost it he would have got a replacement by now.

I took out my cellphone and called his number but it when

straight through to the Thai recording, and I called the number that the receptionist in Soi 22 had given me but that was switched off.

I put the laptop back on the desk and took a long drink from my bottle. I wasn't getting anywhere finding Jon Junior. The only real clue I had was that a girl he might or might not have known also appeared to be missing. I was running out of options.

The front door opened and I heard Noy calling me.

'I'm in the study!' I called, swinging my feet off the desk. I'm only king of the castle so long as she's off the premises.

She pushed open the door, looking lovely in a black and white dress that was probably Karen Millen, one of her favourite designers. 'Working?' she said.

'Still looking for that missing Mormon.'

'No luck?'

I shook my head. 'How were the girls?'

She grinned. 'Girlish,' she said. 'They wanted to go to Q-Bar but I bailed out.'

'I'm glad you did. I missed you.'

'You say the sweetest things.'

She slid onto my lap and kissed me, on the lips.

'Are you okay?' she asked.

'Sure,' I said.

'You look tired.'

'I'm fine.'

Except for the cancer.

If it was cancer.

Now would be a good time to tell her.

'Are you worried about something?'

'Why do you say that?'

She rubbed my temples with her fingertips. 'Because you're doing that frowning thing you always do when there's something worrying you.'

Noy was my wife.

I loved her.

And she loved me.

I smiled and took a deep breath, and lied.

'Just a bit of a headache.'

I'd tell her later. When she didn't look so darn sexy.

I hugged her.

I told her that I loved her.

And we went to bed.

I didn't think about cancer until I woke up.

35

I WAS IN THE shop bright and early Monday morning, dealing with orders that had come in through the website over the weekend. I had put some small bronze bowls from Laos onto eBay and they'd all sold. They were nice pieces but hard to date. They were either a hundred years old or clever fakes, and frankly even an expert would be hard pushed to tell the difference. I just described them as old Laotian bowls and let the photographs speak for themselves.

A buyer in New York had taken three, one had gone to a buyer in Paris, another to a woman in Italy and a regular customer in London had bought one and sent me an email asking if I could sell him another dozen at the same price. It was a good weekend's work considering that I hadn't lifted a finger. I loved ecommerce but I also liked meeting customers face to face.

Usually, that is.

Sometimes there were visitors to the shop that I really didn't care for.

The little bell on the door tinkled as it opened and Ying already had her welcoming smile in place as she looked up from the box she was sealing.

Two men walked in and at first glance I knew that they weren't customers. They were big men, well over six feet, both wearing tight Versace jeans and black leather jackets and with thick gold chains around their necks. One had shaved his head, revealing an ugly scar above his left ear, and the other had slicked his hair back with gel so that it glistened under the shop's fluorescent lights.

'Are you Bob Turtledove?' said Shaved Head, jutting his chin forward.

'Who wants to know?' I said, trying to sound less apprehensive than I felt.

'Mr Shevtsova wants to talk to you,' said Gelled Hair.

'So Mr Shevtsova can call me,' I said.

'Now,' said Gelled Hair, pulling back his jacket to show me the handle of a Glock pistol nestled in a nylon holster. He did it cleverly so that Ying couldn't see the weapon. 'Don't make me ask you again.'

'Is something wrong, Khun Bob?" asked Ying.

'Everything's fine,' I said, even though it wasn't. 'I'm just going out with these gentlemen to see an old friend. His name's Petrov Shevtsova. Mr Shevtsova is a Russian who runs the Betta English Language School in Sukhumvit Soi 22.'

Ying looked at me quizzically, wondering why I was giving her so much information, but I could tell from Gelled Hair's annoyed stare that he knew why. If anything should happen to me, Ying would know where to send the police. I smiled at him and gestured at the door. 'Let's not keep Petrov waiting, shall we?' I said.

I expected the two heavies to take me to the language school in Soi 22 but instead we headed for the expressway and north towards Don Muang, which had served as the city's international airport until Suvarnabhumi had opened in 2006.

They had walked me from the shop and straight to a large Mercedes. The driver was smaller than the two heavies, with close-cropped hair and a goatee beard. Shaved Head sat in the front passenger seat and Gelled Hair sat in the back with me. He didn't take out his gun.

He didn't have to.

They didn't push me down to the floor or put a bag over my head, which was a plus.

And the driver asked me if there was any particular channel I wanted to listen to on the radio, which was nice of him. I said I was fine with whatever he wanted.

We left the expressway at the turn-off before the airport and drove through farmland until we reached a walled estate with two uniformed guards manning a barrier at the entrance. They raised the barrier as soon as they saw the Mercedes and we sped through.

There were just five modern houses on the estate, massive homes three stories high with swimming pools and tennis courts. The Mercedes pulled up in front of one of the houses and parked between a black Bentley and a red Porsche. Gelled Hair opened the door and climbed out and then waved for me to follow him.

He and Shaved Head took me around to the back of the house where Petrov was sitting on a lounger at the deep end of a massive oval pool. Sitting next to him was the blonde girl I'd seen with him at Paragon. She was wearing a tiny black bikini and black Chanel sunglasses and rubbing suncream over her long legs.

Petrov was wearing a miniscule pair of red Speedo swimming trunks that left little to the imagination and Oakley sunglasses. His chest was matted with thick black hair and he had a wicked scar across his stomach, as thick as a finger, and what looked like an old bullet wound at the top of his left thigh.

There was a bottle of Cristal champagne in an ice bucket by his side and he poured some into a glass as I walked up, flanked by his two heavies. He drank from the glass then put it on the table next to his lounger. 'So you're not a teacher,' he said.

'I gave it my best shot.' I smiled as if I didn't have a care in the world but my mind was racing. Sweat was starting to pool between my shoulder blades. The sun was fierce and there was no shade by the pool.

'What's your game, Turtledove?'

I smiled again. 'Tennis, but I like watching football. American football, I mean. Not soccer. I'm a big fan of the New Orleans Saints.'

The Russian frowned. I guess he didn't have much of a sense of humour. 'Why did you come to my school?' he asked.

He obviously knew that I wasn't a teacher, so there was no point in continuing with the charade. 'Okay, I'm sorry I lied to you. I'm sorry that I claimed to be something I wasn't. But I was looking for someone and your people had already lied to me.'

His frown deepened. 'My people? What people?'

'I phoned your school, they said they'd never heard of Jonathon Clare. But I was pretty sure that he'd worked for you as a teacher.' I shrugged. 'I figured the only way I could be sure was to check the school out for myself.'

'This Jonathon Clare, why is he so important?'

'He isn't,' I said. 'He's just a kid whose gone missing. His parents are worried about him.'

The Russian nodded slowly. 'And have you found him?'

'Not yet.'

He reached for his glass and drank his champagne before continuing. 'Why didn't you just ask me? Why go through that charade of pretending to be a teacher?'

'That's a good question,' I said.

'And I'd like an answer,' said Petrov. 'Because if I don't get an answer from you that I like, something very bad is going to happen to you.'

Gelled Hair said something to Petrov in rapid Russian and Petrov sneered at me. 'You think I care that your staff know where I am?' He waved a hand dismissively. 'It's even easier to kill someone here than it is in Russia. If I say the word...' He snapped his fingers. 'It would be done, just like that.'

'I'm sure it would be,' I said. 'But it seems like a bit of an overreaction. And let's face it, you didn't even pay me so you got an hour's work out of me for nothing.'

Petrov's eyes hardened. 'You think this is funny?'

I stopped smiling. No, I didn't think it was funny. But I'd been threatened by men with guns several times in my life and in my experience it's not the guys who make threats that you have to worry about. The real danger comes from the ones who just point the gun and pull the trigger.

Not that I was going to explain that to Petrov, just in case he decided to prove me wrong.

'Like I said, it seems an overreaction. But if I'd asked you about him, would you have told me anything?'

'Why should I?'

'Exactly,' I said. 'I really didn't have any choice, did I?'

'My school is my business, you had no right to stick your nose in.'

'I don't care about your school, I only wanted to know that he's okay. Do you know why he left?'

Petrov looked at me but didn't say anything.

'Did he leave because of you?' I asked, which was pushing my luck but I'd already convinced myself that his men weren't going to shoot me.

'Why do you ask me that?' he said.

'He did a visa run to Cambodia and told someone that he wasn't happy at the school. I was told he was complaining all the time.'

'Teachers always complain,' he said. 'I tell them, if they want more money, get another job. English teachers earn shit money. It's a shit job. Anyway, they're not in Thailand because they want to teach, they're here for the girls.' He pointed a finger at my face. 'Do you know how many times I have to sack teachers because they're sleeping with a student? Once a month, my friend. Once a month.'

'Jon Clare isn't like that,' I said. 'He's a good kid.'

'They're all good kids until they get to Thailand,' said Petrov. 'Then they walk into a go-go bar and it's all over.'

'Did he ask you for more money?'

The Russian nodded. 'Sure. I told him that I paid what I paid. There's no shortage of teachers in Bangkok, I replaced him the day he left.'

'And I don't suppose he said where he was going?'

'He just didn't turn up one day.'

'And why do your office staff say that he never worked there? Why is there no file on him?'

Petrov rubbed his chin. 'You sell antiques, right?'

'That's my day job,' I said. 'But I help people when they need it.'

'You were a cop, right?'

'Why do you say that?'

'Because you've got a cop's eyes.'

I nodded. He wasn't the first person to have told me that. 'I used to be, yeah.'

'In the States?'

'New Orleans.'

'Yeah, well you're not in New Orleans now.'

The blonde girl stood up, stretched, and dived into the pool. She began to swim lengths in a lazy crawl.

'You didn't answer my question,' I said. 'Why is there no file on

Jon Junior at the school?'

'Because he was a complainer and I thought he might make trouble for me.'

'You think that's what he was going to do?

Petrov shrugged. 'He was a moaner. A complainer. I wouldn't put it past him to try to get me in trouble with the authorities so I removed all his details. That way if anyone came knocking I could just say that he'd never worked there.'

'And did anyone come knocking?'

Petrov shook his head. 'Not so far,' he said. He pushed his sunglasses up onto the top of his head. 'Why did you want to know how much tax I paid?' he asked.

'What?' I said, even though I'd heard him perfectly.

'You went to the tax office with some cock and bull story about looking for a school for your daughter. But we both you don't have any children, don't we?'

I looked at him but didn't say anything.

He was right, I didn't have any children. Not anymore.

He'd been checking up on me, and I didn't like that.

I didn't like it one bit.

'A friend's daughter,' I said. 'I was looking for a school for the daughter of a friend.'

'I want you to understand something, Bob Turtledove. If I find out that you've been asking anyone else about my business, anyone at all, I'll have you killed.' He looked at me with unfeeling pale blue eyes and I could tell that he wasn't making an idle threat. He meant it.

'A contract killer in Bangkok costs less than fifty thousand baht, even when it's a farang being killed. You cause me any more problems, and I'll have it done. Do you understand?'

I nodded.

Yeah, I understood.

'Is that what happened to Jon Junior?' I said quietly.

His eyes hardened. 'What?'

'You heard me.'

'You think I had him killed?'

'You just threatened me with a hitman. Maybe you did more than threaten him.'

Petrov laughed. 'He was a kid. Why would I kill a kid?'

'Maybe he found out something he shouldn't have. Maybe he was annoying you. Maybe he made a pass at your wife. How the hell do I know what makes you tick. That's why I'm asking you, did you kill Jon Junior or have him killed?'

'You're a sick bastard, Turtledove.'

'Yeah? Maybe I am, and maybe I'm not. But Jon Junior is missing and you seem to think it's clever to threaten to kill people, so I'm just putting two and two together.'

'I didn't kill him,' said Petrov. 'He wasn't that important. He couldn't do anything to hurt me. He wanted more money, I said there wasn't any, he said he'd get another job, I told him to go for it.'

I nodded slowly. 'There's something you should know, Petrov.'

He jutted his chin up. 'What?'

'I don't threaten easy,' I said. 'I know people often say things in the heat of the moment that they don't mean, but if you ever try to hurt me or my family, I won't bother with a hitman. You're right, life is cheap in Thailand, but I fight my own battles and you won't be the first man I've killed.'

I looked at him long enough for him to know that I was serious, then I smiled and left.

Did I mean what I'd said?

Damn right, I did.

36

THE NIGHT BEFORE I was due to go in for the colonoscopy, I told Noy what was happening. I had to. As part of the procedure I had to drink eight pints of a solution to clean out my intestines and there was no way I could do that in secret. I wasn't supposed to eat dinner so when she asked me what I wanted to eat, I told her that I had to go back to the Bumrungrad and what they were planning to do to me.

She wasn't happy. But then neither was I.

I told her that it was only a precaution, that I had no symptoms, just a blood test that suggested that there might, just might, be a problem.

I didn't say anything about a red flag.

Or cancer.

But I could see from the look on her face that she was scared.

'Really, it's nothing,' I said. 'It's just a precaution. Hundreds of thousands of people have it done every year and more often than not there's nothing there.'

'Tomorrow?' she said. 'You're doing this tomorrow?'

'Tomorrow morning.'

'Bob, why are you telling me this now? How long have you known?'

'There's nothing to know,' I said. 'It's just a test. An examination. It's no big deal.'

'You should have told me before,' she said. She wasn't angry. She was hurt. I tried to hold her but she took a step back which was more painful than if she'd slapped me across the face.

'Honey, I didn't want you to worry.'

'Ignorance is bliss? I'm your wife, Bob. You shouldn't shut me out, not at a time like this.'

'Honey, it's a test. A routine test.'

'For cancer.'

I tried not to wince at the sound of the word, but I didn't do a very good job.

'That's what colonoscopies are for, aren't they? They look for cancer?'

The word made me wince just as much the second time she said it.

I stepped towards her and this time she let me hold her. 'I don't have cancer,' I said. 'I swear.'

'So why are they giving you a colonoscopy?' She held me tightly and for the first time I was really scared, not because of what might lie in my intestines but because I'd hurt her.

'They did a blood test that showed up a marker that sometimes, just sometimes, indicates a problem. But I've no symptoms, no blood, no pain, no nothing. I'm as regular as clockwork, honey.'

She sniffed. 'That's nice to know,' she said.

'I'm serious,' I said. 'If it wasn't for the silly marker thing, we wouldn't even be having this conversation. The doctor who's doing the procedure is one of the best in the country. She was trained in the States and she said that even if there was a problem, they'd probably be able to nip it in the bud there and then.'

'It's a woman doctor?'

'Don't go all sexist on me, honey. She's very highly regarded.'

Noy giggled. 'A woman is going to put a camera up your ...' She giggled again.

'Thank you,' I said. 'Thank you very much.'

'Oh my Buddha,' she said.

'She said the camera she uses has a laser attachment that can zap anything that looks like it might be a problem,' I said. 'But she said exactly what I've told you, more often than not the marker tends to be a false positive.'

She stopped hugging me and looked at me, her eyes sparkling with amusement. 'You should have told me before,' she said.

'I know, and I'm sorry.'

'I'm coming with you, tomorrow,' she said.

'You don't have to.'

'I want to. ' She smiled. 'I want to meet the woman who is going to shove a camera up my husband's...' She started giggling again.

37

I GOT TO THE hospital at just before nine o'clock in the morning. I persuaded Noy not to go with me because I didn't want to make a big thing of it. It was a simple procedure, in and out and then home. If she had come with me it would have been something bigger, something more important, and I didn't want to feel that it was anything other than a check-up.

Noy understood. Bless her. She kissed me on the cheek and wished me luck and I went downstairs and caught a taxi.

I was shown to a changing room where I took of my clothes put on a pale blue hospital robe. I was shown through to another room where a pretty nurse who looked about fifteen years old sat me down in a chair and put a needle into a vein in my left arm and held it in place with a strip of sticking plaster. There were two other patients there, a Thai man in his seventies and an obese Arab who kept wiping his face with a large white handkerchief.

Dr Ma-lee arrived fifteen minutes after I'd been prepped. She was wearing surgical scrubs and her long hair was tucked back in a net. She checked the needle and asked me how the cleansing had gone.

Ah yes, the cleansing.

I'd gone onto the internet to check out what was in store for me and pretty much everything I'd read suggested that the preparation was a lot more uncomfortable than the procedure. I had to drink the eight pints of solution that the hospital had given me, then wait until the eight pints had passed through me, taking pretty much everything with it.

It was not pleasant.

Not pleasant at all.

The first intestinal rumblings began about six hours after I'd finished the last drop and I spent a further two hours in the bathroom.

But I just smiled and nodded and told Dr Ma-lee that the cleansing had gone just fine.

She explained the procedure again and asked me if I had any concerns.

Any concerns?

Well, yes, actually. I was concerned that there might be a tumour the size of a grapefruit in my gut and that I'd be dead by the end of the year because, please God, I didn't want to die.

'No, I'm good,' I said, and smiled confidently.

'It's going to be fine, Khun Bob,' she said, and patted the arm that didn't have a needle in it.

I guess my smile wasn't as confident as I thought.

She went away and five minutes later two female orderlies in pale green scrubs came in pushing a gurney. They asked me to lie down and they wheeled me down a corridor into an operating room. Dr Ma-lee was there. She'd put on a cap that matched her scrubs and was wearing surgical gloves. She asked me to lie on my side and then she attached a hypodermic to the needle in my arm and I felt a coldness spread along it and across my chest and then I felt warm and safe and happy, so happy that I actually giggled.

I felt a draught as a nurse loosened my robe and I was still giggling as she inserted the camera and it began its twenty-two-foot voyage of discovery.

38

I WASN'T LAUGHING when I was wheeled into the recovery room, but I wasn't feeling any pain, either. I'd been conscious for the whole procedure, and for most of the time had been able to watch the camera's progress in and out of my digestive tract. Even I could see that my colon was in good shape, smooth and pink and glossy. I had the colon of a twenty-five-year old, Dr Ma-lee said at one point.

I rolled onto my back and stared up at the ceiling and sighed. It was over. And I was pretty sure that everything was okay. Now I just wanted to go home.

After about fifteen minutes, Dr Ma-lee came to see me. She'd taken off her hairnet but she was still wearing her scrubs. She gave me a beaming smile. 'No problems at all,' she said.

'That's a relief,' I said.

And it was.

'I'd recommend that you have another colonoscopy in five years,' she said.

'I'll put it in my diary,' I said.

'Get yourself checked every five years and I can pretty much guarantee that you'll never have a major problem with your colon,' she said. 'Once you get to your age, five-year checks are a life-saver.' She placed a DVD on the table next to my gurney. 'Here's a copy of the recording we made.'

'Thanks, doc,' I said. 'Can I go home now?'

'Isn't your wife coming to get you?'

'I don't want her to see me in hospital,' I said.

'Very macho,' she said.

'She doesn't like hospitals much,' I said.

And to be honest, neither do I.

'Just be careful,' she said. 'You might find you're a bit unsteady on your feet for a while.' She flashed me another beaming smile and left me to it.

I actually didn't feel too bad.

I sat up and swung my legs over the side of the bed, took a deep breath and stood up.

I was fine.

I was fit, I was healthy, I was going to live for ever.

By the time I'd changed into my clothes I felt even better.

I left the hospital and climbed into a taxi and told the driver where I wanted to go. Home.

He drove away from the hospital and turned right onto Sukhumvit Soi 3. I looked at the DVD that the doctor had given me and wondered what I was supposed to do with it? Did people actually watch them? Did they sit down with a cup of coffee or a beer and revisit the journey through their intestines? Did they invite their friends and family around? I figured the best place for it was the trash can.

I heard the roar of a motorcycle engine and looked out of the window.

There was a gun pointing at me.

A big gun.

A revolver.

A Smith & Wesson Model 637 Chiefs Special Airweight revolver, snubnose stainless-steel barrel, aluminium alloy frame, exposed hammer, black rubber grips, .38 calibre.

It's funny how your mind focuses on the little things when you're about to die.

The Model 637 only has five shots but the .38 is a big bullet so five is all you need, especially when your target is sitting in a taxi just three feet from you.

It's a snubnose so it's easy to conceal. And it weighs less than a pound so it's easy to carry. Under any other circumstances I'd have said that it's a nice gun.

The man holding it was dark-skinned and wearing a red and white bandana across the bottom of his face. He was sitting on the back of a small motorcycle, a 110cc black Honda Click. The driver was wearing a full-face helmet with a black visor and he was revving the engine impatiently as he waited for the pillion passenger to pull the trigger.

The shooter was holding the gun with his right hand and holding on to the driver's shoulder with his left. The Model 637 packs a punch and I don't think even I would try to fire it one-handed if I had the choice.

It kicked as it fired and the window exploded into a thousand cubes and the bullet smacked against the side of my head.

Time seemed to stop.

I could feel a searing pain, just above my right ear.

I could hear a bus sounding its horn.

I could see the hatred in the shooter's eyes which I really didn't understand because he must have been a hired gun so it shouldn't have been personal.

I could smell the cordite.

My ears were ringing from the explosion but I could hear the driver shouting 'again, again!' in Thai as he revved the Honda.

I could feel cubes of glass cascading down the front of my shirt.

I could hear the taxi driver screaming in panic.

I could feel blood trickling down my cheek.

I could see the shooter's finger tightening on the trigger for the second shot.

I could hear the pounding horn of a bus, louder now.

I could see the red flecks of blood on the headrest of the front passenger seat. My blood.

I felt the DVD slip from my fingers and clatter onto the floor of the taxi.

And that's when the cream and blue Bangkok Mass Transit Authority bus smashed into the back of the bike and sent it and the two men on it hurtling down the street.

I guess that's when I lost consciousness.

39

'MR TURTLEDOVE? Can you hear me Mr Turtledove?' It was a man's voice. Speaking English but with a Thai accent. Then he spoke in Thai to someone else. 'He's still unconscious.'

'No, I'm all right,' I said, but the words came out all wrong as if I'd forgotten how to work my tongue.

'Mr Turtledove?'

I felt a pressure on my eyelid and then it was forced open and a bright light made me wince. I groaned and blinked and then I opened my eyes to see a young doctor looking down at me. 'Where am I?' I asked, and this time my tongue seemed to have regained the knack of forming words.

'Bumrungrad Hospital,' he said. 'The emergency room.'

That was good news.

At least I wasn't dead.

I guess if you're going to be shot anywhere, the best place would be outside one of Asia's best hospitals.

'How do you feel, Mr Turtledove?'

'My head hurts. And my throat is dry.'

The doctor asked a nurse to get me some water and a few seconds later a straw was slipped between my lips and I sipped gratefully.

'Do you have any other pain anywhere else?' asked the doctor.

The nurse took the water away. 'No,' I said. 'No pain. How many times was I shot?'

'Just once,' said the doctor. 'The bullet glanced across your temple. You were lucky.'

'I don't feel lucky,' I said.

The doctor took my right hand. 'Squeeze, please,' he said.

I did as I was told.

'Good,' said the doctor. He put down my right hand and picked up my left. 'And again, please.' I squeezed again.

'That's good, Mr Turtledove. Very good.'

There was a metallic whirring sound and the bed began to tilt up. I was in a private room with an LCD television on the wall and a sofa for visitors. I guess they'd found the insurance card in my wallet.

'There was some bleeding, obviously, but it was superficial. I'd like you to come back in a couple of days to change the dressing, but other than that you'll be fine.'

'My head really hurts,' I said.

'We'll prescribe painkillers, but we did a scan while you were unconscious and there's no sign of damage to the skull or the brain,' he said. 'You're good to go.' He signed a form on a clipboard and handed it to the nurse, wished me a good afternoon and left.

I asked a nurse to bring me my cellphone and I tapped out Noy's number.

'Where are you?' she asked.

'Hospital,' I said.

'I thought you were done by eleven,' she said.

'That was the plan,' I said.

'How did it go?'

'Good news, bad news,' I said.

'Oh my Buddha, they didn't cut off your manhood, did they?'

'No, honey, I'm still in one piece.'

'So what's the good news?'

'My colon is fine. No cysts, tumours or anything untoward. Clean bill of health.'

'That's great, honey. So what's the bad news?'

'I've been shot.'

40

Noy came to pick me up at the hospital and drove me back to our apartment in Soi Thonglor, after we'd paid the hospital bill, of course. You get great treatment at the Bumrungrad, but it comes at a price.

She didn't ask me any questions in the car, but once I was on the sofa with a cup of coffee in my hand, they came thick and fast.

Who had shot me?

Why had they shot me?

What had happened to the man who'd shot me?

Was he working for someone else?

The problem was, most of the questions I couldn't answer even if I'd wanted to. It looked like a professional job, which means the hitman had been bought and paid for. But who would want me dead?

Petrov, the Russian, maybe.

Thongchai or one of the Kube investors.

Tukkata's father, maybe. He hadn't been happy about me going around to his house.

But I didn't think that me asking questions merited any of them putting a price on my head.

Maybe it was one of the other cases I'd worked on over the years.

Hell, it could even be a case of mistaken identity. I wouldn't have been the only middle-aged farang leaving the Bumrungrad and Thai hitmen aren't generally known for being smart.

'I don't know, honey, really I don't know.'

'Is it one of your cases, do you think?'

'It's either that or someone on eBay thinks they got a raw deal.'

She folded her arms and gave me a withering look. 'This isn't funny, Bob.'

'I know, honey. I'm just trying to lighten the moment.'

'Someone tried to kill you.'

'I know that honey.' I touched the plaster carefully. 'I think that's pretty obvious, isn't it?'

'And they might try again.'

'I don't think so,' I said. 'They were hit by a bus.'

She frowned. 'What are you talking about?'

'A bus ploughed into the bike. I'm guessing they're in much worse condition than me, and I'm pretty sure they won't have had health insurance so they won't be getting the Bumrungrad treatment.' I sipped my coffee. 'I'll go and see Somsak tomorrow. He'll know what's going on.'

My mobile rang. I fished it out of my pocket and squinted at the screen. 'Speak of the devil,' I said.

41

SOMSAK WAS SITTING behind his desk when the secretary showed me into his office. He stood up and shook my hand then showed me to a hard-backed wooden chair. 'How's the head?' he asked sympathetically. It had been two days since I'd been shot, two days that I'd spent at home being fussed over by Noy. Which, truth be told, I actually quite enjoyed.

My hand went instinctively up to the dressing on my temple. 'It's fine. Just a headache.'

'You were lucky.'

'You must be using some definition of lucky that I'm not familiar with,' I said. 'Where I come from, a four-leaf clover is lucky. Getting shot in the head definitely ranks up there with black cats and broken mirrors.'

Somsak frowned and I quickly explained about black cats crossing paths and shattered mirrors bringing seven years of bad luck.

'I meant you were lucky to be alive,' he said patiently.

It was my own fault for using sarcasm. Somsak was as straight as a dye and while he had a good enough sense of humour where anything involving slapstick was involved, irony and sarcasm were generally lost on him.

'I am,' I said.

'That bus driver saved your life,' he said. 'If he hadn't been high on amphetamines he probably wouldn't have hit the motorcycle and the guy would have got off another shot.'

'They dead?'

'The driver is but the shooter's in hospital.'

'Talking?'

'Life support. Fifty-fifty.'

I sighed. 'Think he'll talk?'

'If he doesn't die, he'll probably talk. Depends who hired him.'

'You'll cut him a deal?'

'If he pleads guilty and cooperates then any sentence is automatically halved, Khun Bob. You know that.'

'I'd lock him away for ever,' I said.

'It's more important to know who wanted you dead because whoever paid for the hit might want to pay again. And don't worry, he will go to prison and Thai prisons are not holiday camps.'

He was right. Fifty men per cell, sleeping on concrete floors, a couple of bowls of rice a day and an open sewer for a toilet.

'And he's in a worse state than you are,' said Somsak. 'He's lost his spleen and his left leg is never going to heal properly.'

I shrugged. Somsak was right. There was no point in bearing grudges. He'd tried to kill me, he'd failed, and he was the one on life support. I should be counting my blessings.

'Let me know what he says, yeah?'

'Of course.

'I wouldn't have though this case would have been in your jurisdiction,' I said. 'Don't the Lumpini cops deal with Soi 3.'

'Indeed they do, but I thought you might like things handled by a friend. Especially in view of what we found in the taxi.'

He smiled. It was a mischievous smile. Like he knew something that I didn't. Something that amused him.

'What?'

His smile widened and he leaned over and took a DVD case out of one of his desk drawers. He tossed it to me and I caught it. 'You've got a strange taste in movies, Khun Bob.'

I groaned. It was the Bumrungrad DVD of my colonoscopy that I'd dropped in the taxi. 'You've seen it?'

'We've all seen it. You paid good money for that?'

I sighed mournfully.

'I've seen better pornography on sale at Pantip Plaza,' he said.

'It's a colonoscopy.'

'Really?'

'They put a camera through your intestines.'

'The things you farangs do for fun.' He chuckled.

'It wasn't fun,' I said.

'That's your colon?'

'All twenty-two feet of it.'

'And you're carrying around a video of the procedure?'

I sighed. I explained that I'd just left Bumrungrad Hospital when the hitman had taken his shot. And that the colonoscopy had been clear.

'See,' he said. 'It really was your lucky day.' He lit a cigarette and blew smoke up into the air. 'What about your missing American? Did he ever turn up?'

I shook my head. 'All dead ends,' I said. 'I keep trying his phone and email but his phone is off and he doesn't seem to be logging on to get his emails. My only hope now is to get him next time he does a visa run.'

'You don't think something has happened to him?'

'Somsak, I just don't know. It looks as if he left his place in Soi 22 of his own free will, and I think he might be with a girl.'

'And what about what happened to you? Do you think there's a connection?'

'What, you think Jon Junior wanted to have me killed?'

Somsak blew a perfect smoke ring. 'I wondered if perhaps someone you had spoken to...'

'It's possible,' I said.

'Do you want to give me a list?'

I nodded. 'Okay,' I said. 'I can do that.'

Somsak grinned. 'I probably won't need it, I'm pretty sure that the hitman is going to talk. They usually do.'

42

SOMSAK PHONED ME the following evening, just as I was just sitting down to eat with Noy. She'd cooked prawns with ginger, chicken wrapped in banana leaves and a red duck curry that was one of my favourite dishes, so I had half a mind to let the answering machine pick it up.

Noy nodded at me to take the call as she put a bowl of boiled rice onto the table. 'They'll only keep calling,' she said. 'And I want you to myself tonight, to celebrate the bandage coming off.' I'd been to the Bumrungrad in the afternoon and the doctor had taken off the dressing and said that all was well and that from now on the wound would just heal naturally. I had stopped taking painkillers and the headache had gone, so Noy had bought a very good bottle of champagne and was insisting on an early night, which I figured was the least I could do under the circumstances.

I took the phone out on to the terrace. 'You'll never guess who wanted you dead,' said Somsak.

'I bet I do.'

'I bet you don't.'

'This is a silly game, Somsak,' I said.

'I know, but you'll never guess, not in a million years. The hitman is singing like a canary.'

'So tell me.'

'And spoil my fun?'

I sighed. 'The Pope.'

'Why would the Pope want you dead?'

'He wouldn't. Unless he'd heard that I was pro-Choice.'

'Pro-Choice? What does that mean?'

'Nothing, Somsak. I was joking about the Pope.'

'A serious guess, then,' said Somsak. 'Who do you think paid for the hitman?'

I sighed again. 'You said I wouldn't be able to guess.'

'Try.'

I sighed. 'It was Petrov Shevtsova,' I said.

The Russian. He wanted me dead because I'd uncovered his money-laundering scheme.

'No.'

That surprised me. But then again maybe if Petrov had wanted me dead he'd probably have shot me himself. He seemed the type.

'Who was it then?'

'Guess again.'

'Somsak, please ...'

Somsak chuckled. I don't think I'd given him so much pleasure since he took ten thousand baht off me with a straight flush that I hadn't seen coming.

'One more guess.'

'Santhanavit.'

Tukkata's father. I'd told Somsak that maybe he'd wanted me dead because he didn't want me chasing after his daughter. It was a bit drastic but Thais often overreacted where family were concerned.

'No. Not him. But you're getting warmer.'

'Warmer? You mean Mrs Santhanavit?'

'No, not the wife.'

'Tell me, Somsak, or I'll pay someone to shoot you.'

'It was Big Red,' he said.

He didn't say 'Big Red' exactly. He said it in Thai. Daeng Yai. But it didn't matter what the language was, I was still none the wiser.

Big Red?

Who the hell was Big Red?

'He runs a magazine company. Glossy trade magazines.'

I shrugged. I wasn't a big reader of glossy trade magazines. Noy was but I doubt that Big Red was going around putting out contracts on men just because their wives were buying his products.

'He has a big BMW,' said Somsak. 'A Seven series.'

'A red one?' I said hopefully. I didn't know anyone who drove a BMW, big or small.

'A black one. With tinted windows.'

Realisation dawned.

I'd seen Kai getting into a big black BMW with tinted windows. And there had been a big man sitting in the back. A big man in a suit.

'Now you know who I'm talking about?' asked Somsak.

'He picked up one of the girls at Tukkata's school,' I said. 'She was underage. I didn't get a good look at him.'

I rubbed the back of my neck. This still wasn't making sense.

'I didn't even speak to him. Why the hell would he want me killed?'

'You spoke to the girl. He probably thought that you were asking about him.'

'That's a bit of an overreaction, don't you think?'

'You don't know Big Red.'

'Put me out of my misery, Somsak,' I said. 'Why does he want me dead?'

'He's married to the daughter of a very senior army general,' said Somsak. 'In fact, Big Red's company had been bankrolled by his wife since day one. But Mrs Big Red isn't the most attractive of women, putting it mildly. So he's obviously been looking elsewhere for rest and relaxation as the Americans put it.'

'He was sleeping with Kai?'

'I don't think there was much sleeping going on. And I don't think he was confining his activities to the one girl. Our enquiries suggest that Big Red was paying half a dozen schoolgirls for sex. Kai seems to be his favourite. In fact, he'd promised to set her up as a mia noi when she reached eighteen.'

Mia noi.

Minor wife.

Permanent mistress with benefits, like a house and a car.

'How old is Big Red?' I asked.

'Fifty-seven.'

Forty-two years older than Kai. The Thais have a saying for it. Old cows prefer to eat young grass.

I could see why he might want to get rid of anyone who threatened to disrupt his cosy little arrangement. I doubt that the general's daughter would react well to the news that her husband had set up a girl forty years his junior as a full-time mistress. He had probably seen me give my number to Kai. Once he had my number it would have been easy to track me down.

'So what happens now?' I asked.

'We put together a case against Big Red. The shooter is already talking and we have a statement from the girl.'

'I hope they throw away the key.'

'I think he'll be more worried about what his wife will do to him.'

Somsak was probably right. The traditional retribution for wronged Thai wives was to wait until the errant husband was asleep and to cut off his member. What happened then depended on how angry the woman was.

She might wrap it in ice and phone for an ambulance.

She might throw it to the ducks.

She might put it in the kitchen blender.

She might tie it to a helium-filled balloon and wave goodbye to it as it headed for the clouds.

I figured the general's daughter would be pretty angry.

'So the great Bangkok Bob couldn't solve the mystery of the hired killer,' said Somsak. 'You didn't even know who wanted you dead.'

'I think I'm a pretty good judge of character, generally,' I said.

'Are you sure about that?' said the policeman.

'I'm not usually wrong.'

Somsak chuckled. 'Let me tell you something, Khun Bob. But first you must promise never to tell anyone else.'

'Cross my heart and hope to die.'

'When we play poker ...'

'Yes?'

'Sometimes when I have a pair of jacks or better, I blink.'

I smiled. 'I know that.'

'And sometimes, when I don't have anything, I also blink.'

Right then.

You live and learn.

43

SHE WAS WALKING with two other girls, laughing animatedly and waving around her BlackBerry. All three were in school uniform but carrying brand-name bags and wearing expensive high heels. She'd never seen me in the Hummer so she jumped when I wound down the window and said hello. 'It's all right, Kai,' I said. 'I just need to talk.'

'I've already talked to the police,' she said. Her two friends were looking at her, tugging nervously at the straps of their designer bags.

'I just need to clear some things up,' I said. 'I promise you, you're not in trouble.' I got out of the car and locked the door. 'Let me buy you some noodles,' I said, nodding at the noodle stalls on the pavement. 'Or a Coke. Your friends, too. I won't be long, I promise.' She looked reluctant and I couldn't be too forceful because at the end of the day she was a schoolgirl and I was three times her age and some. 'Please, Kai,' I said. I put my hand up to the wound on my temple. 'You see this? A man tried to kill me, you owe me a few minutes of your time, at least.'

'Who shot you?'

'Didn't the police tell you? Big Red paid someone to kill me.' I smiled. 'He wasn't a very good shot.'

'Am I in trouble?'

I shook my head. 'Of course not,' I said. 'But I just want to ask you a few things. Please.' I waved at the nearest noodle stall and she walked towards it.

One of the girls asked what she was doing and Kai told them to wait.

I sat down opposite her on a wooden stall and ordered two Cokes.

'So the police came to talk to you? At school?'

She shook her head. 'At home. My parents are really mad at me. The police told them everything. Big Red's driver told the police about me, and about his other girls.'

'I'm sorry.'

'It's okay. The police say we're not going to be in trouble. Not with them, anyway. My parents have grounded me for three months.'

'Did you tell Big Red about me?'

She nodded. 'He wanted to know who you were and why you were talking to me.'

An old man shuffled over with two bottles of Coke and two glasses filled with shaved ice. 'And you gave him my number?' She bit down on her lower lip and nodded. She was scared. 'Kai, it's okay. I'm not upset.' It didn't take much to get the name and the address of the owner of a mobile phone in Thailand, a few thousand baht at most.

'I'm sorry you were hurt.'

I smiled. 'It's a scratch,' I said. 'I'm fine now. And you didn't do anything. It was Big Red.'

'He gave me money. He helped me.'

'He's a grown man and you're a kid, Kai. You're fifteen years old.'

'I know, but he didn't force me to do anything.' She held up her Gucci bag. 'He bought me this. And my phone. He buys me anything I want.'

'That doesn't make it right, Kai.'

She bit down on her lower lip again. She was close to tears. I couldn't work out if she was upset because of what Big Red had done or because I had been shot at or because she knew she had lost her sugar daddy.

I figured it was probably the latter.

'The first time you went with him, where was that?' I asked.

She frowned, not understanding the question.

'How did you meet him?' I asked. 'The first time?'

Her face brightened. 'The internet.'

'The internet?'

'There's a website you can go to meet people.'

'Like Facebook?'

She shook her head. 'It's a chat room,' she said. 'You can talk to people and if you like them you give them your phone number.'

'A chat room for men to meet girls?'

She nodded.

'Young girls, Kai?'

'Mainly young girls,' she said. 'The men usually want to know how old you are and what school you go to.'

'And the girls have sex?'

She shook her head. 'No, not always. Sometimes the men just want to talk while they touch themselves. Or sometimes they just want to touch.' She giggled. 'There's one Japanese man who just wants to buy the underwear you're wearing. He pays five thousand baht, just for your panties.'

'He's welcome to my boxer shorts,' I said, and she laughed. 'How did you find out about the website?' I asked.

'Everyone was talking about it at school. One of my friends had a new BlackBerry and I asked her how she'd paid for it and she said that she'd met a man in the chat room and he'd given it to her. She showed me what to do and I tried it.'

'And you weren't shy? Or scared?'

She shrugged carelessly. 'I didn't care. I just wanted a BlackBerry.'

'And where did you go with him?'

'The first time we met at the Penthouse Hotel in Soi 3. It's one of those hotels where they pull a curtain around the car and you go straight into the room. The first time we just talked. But the second time he wanted me to...' She shrugged.

'He wanted sex with you?'

She nodded.

'And you were okay with that?'

She nodded again. 'He gave me five thousand baht the first time. And he said he'd buy me a BlackBerry. And an electronic dictionary that I needed.'

'And he did?'

'He bought me lots of things,' she said. 'Clothes. Handbags. A Sony computer.'

'And didn't your parents ask where all this stuff was coming from?'

She shook her head.

'But the money? They must have known that you had money? Didn't they want to know where it came from?'

'My dad gave me pocket money.'

I ran a hand through my hair. Sometimes kids confused the hell out of me. 'If you had pocket money from your father, why did you sell yourself?'

She shook her head. 'I wasn't selling myself,' she said. 'It wasn't like that. Men gave me money and I made them happy.' She looked me in the eyes. 'What's wrong with that?'

I didn't know what to say to her.

'Better to earn something myself than to take it from my father,' she said.

'I suppose so,' I said. I didn't agree with her for one second but I doubted that she would listen to anything I had to say.

She looked at her watch. It was a Rolex and I knew without asking how she'd earned it. 'I have to go,' she said.

'Just one more thing,' I said. 'Tukkata. Did she do the same thing? Did she visit the same website? Did she go with men for money?'

Kai laughed out loud and then covered her mouth with her hand. 'No,' she said. 'Tukkata would never do that.'

'Why did she run away, Kai?'

She tensed and I could tell that she was about to lie to me.

'I know she ran away, Kai. I know she left her family. Why, Kai? Why did she run away?'

Kai shook her head.

'You told her what you did, didn't you? You told her that you went with men for money?'

She nodded. 'I showed her the chat room but she said I was crazy.'

'Did you ask her to do it?'

She nodded enthusiastically. 'I told her it was an easy way to get money but she said she couldn't do it.'

'So why did she run away?'

A look of guilt flashed across her face and I knew that there was something she wasn't telling me.

'I need to know that she's all right,' I said.

'She's fine,' said Kai.

'How do you know? Did she tell you that she was running away?'

She looked down, avoiding my gaze. 'Yes,' she said.

'With Khun Jon?'

'I think so, yes. She didn't say his name but she said she was going with a friend.'

I sighed.

Finally, I was getting to the truth.

'Where did she go, Kai?'

'I don't know.' She looked at her watch again.

'What was she running away from? From Big Red?'

She shook her head. 'No. Not him.'

'Who then? Who was she afraid of? Who was she running from?'

And then I knew.

Before she opened her mouth to speak, I knew.

'Her father,' I said, and it was a statement, not a question.

She jerked as if she'd been stung, and then looked at me quizzically. 'How did you know?'

'What happened, Kai? You can tell me.'

'I have to go,' she said.

'Tell me what happened.'

She closed her eyes as if she was wishing that I would disappear. 'I didn't know it was him, not at first,' she said.

'You met him in the chat room?'

She nodded, then slowly opened her eyes. 'We chatted online and then he called me and we talked. He seemed really nice and he said he'd give me five thousand baht for just one hour so I said that I'd meet him. He booked a room in the Landmark Hotel and told me to meet him there. He wanted me to wear my school uniform. Most of the men do. The lights were off and it was quite dark and he wanted to make love quickly and it was only afterwards when he was showering that I realised who he was. I'd seen him at the school sports day with his wife and Tukkata. And I'd seen him at the English school sometimes, dropping her off.'

'Did he know that you knew his daughter?'

She shook her head. 'He asked me what year I was in, that's all.'

'So he knew you were fifteen?'

'He liked it. He said he liked me because I was young. He asked me to call him Daddy while he was making love to me.'

I felt my stomach lurch.

She got up to go but I put my hand on her shoulder and she looked at me, suddenly scared, and I pulled my hand away and apologised.

'You told Tukkata?' I asked. 'You told her that you'd seen her father?'

She nodded. 'At first she didn't believe me but her father had asked for my phone number and he kept sending me text messages. I showed her and then she knew that I was telling the truth.'

'Do you still have the messages on your phone?'

She nodded cautiously.

'Can I see them?'

She took out her phone and called up her messages, then handed it to me. I read them and my stomach lurched again. Messages from a middle-aged man to an underage schoolgirl. Telling her what he wanted to do with her.

'Did she talk to her father about this?'

'I don't think so.'

'And how soon after she saw the messages did she leave?'

'A couple of days.' She held out her hand. 'Can I have my phone back, please?'

I scrolled back through the text messages. I stopped when I saw one from Tukkata. I opened the message.

'I'm okay,' it said. 'Don't worry.'

The message had been sent three days ago. I looked at the number. It was the number that Jon Junior had called.

'Please, can I have my phone back,' she said.

I gave it to her.

'I have to go,' she said. She stood up and hurried away.

I watched her walk away with her friends.

Now I understood everything.

But I was still no closer to finding Jon Junior.

As I walked over to the Hummer my phone rang. It was John Muller, apologising for not calling me back sooner.

'Where are you, Bob?' asked Muller. 'Word on the grapevine is that you were shot by a jealous husband.'

'I'm hanging around outside a school,' I said. 'Which is what got me shot in the first place.'

'Are you serious?'

I climbed into the Hummer and closed the door. It was already swelteringly hot even though the air-con had only been off for ten minutes or so. I switched on the engine. 'Fairly serious, but I'm okay.'

'You need anything, let me know,' he said, and he sounded like he meant it. 'I'm calling about the two numbers you wanted checking. It took my contact longer than usual.'

'Better late than never,' I said.

'One of them was a DTAC number so that was a non-starter. The other was an AIS number but it's been switched off for almost two weeks now and no calls have been made from it. But three days ago it was on long enough to send an SMS.'

'Did the message by any chance say "I'm okay, don't worry" and please don't ask me if I'm psychic.'

'That's it exactly. The phone was on for less than two minutes.'

'And please tell me that you have the phone's location?'

'Koh Samui,' said Muller.

Interesting.

44

KOH SAMUI USED to be one of my favourite islands, and when Noy and I were first married we used to go down several times a year, just to watch the waves crash on the sand and eat seafood and breathe in the fresh air. It's got what Bangkok hasn't – white sandy beaches, coral reefs and coconut palms. But it's become much more commercialised recently, with faceless hotels spoiling the coastline and foreign firms building overpriced villas with no infrastructure to support them. The fact that foreigners can't own land in Thailand hasn't stopped the villas selling, and now there are parts of the island where the only Thais you see are the maids and poolboys. It's now the second-most popular tourist destination in the country, following Phuket, but it has become a violent place too, with foreigners getting raped and robbed on a regular basis and estate agents hiring hitmen to sort out contractual problems. The full moon parties have become world famous for drug-fuelled raves that go on for days at a time, with many a bemused foreigner being busted by undercover cops. It's been at least five years since Noy and I visited and when I told her that I was going there to look for Jon Junior she told me to be careful and didn't offer to come with me.

The easiest way to get to Koh Samui is by plane with a flight time of an hour, give or take. The island's airport is cute, with thatched buildings and palm trees, and the customs check for those arriving on international flights is minimal to say the least. It's the third-biggest island in Thailand, fifteen miles long and thirteen miles wide, and most of the hotels and huts are clustered around the beaches. John Muller had been able to identify the cellphone transmitter that Tukkata's phone had logged on to when she'd switched it on, so I had a pretty good idea where to start looking. Mae nam, on the north side of the island.

Mae means mother and nam means water and together mae nam means river. There's a seven kilometre beach with pure white sand, shielded by a line of coconut palms. Lots of small resorts and restaurants and bars catering for tourists. I caught the first flight from Bangkok and had a taxi drop me at the east end of the beach and figured that I could walk the full length in three hours, and if I had to I'd walk back. If I didn't find them during the day then my plan was to book into one of the resorts for the night and to try again the following day.

I wandered into a restaurant called Mr Pu's and showed a waitress Jon Junior's photograph. She frowned and shook her head. I sat down and ordered a coffee and a bottle of water, figuring that I ought to get my fluid levels up before I started walking down a sun-drenched beach with temperatures in the mid-forties. I'd brought a New Orleans Saints baseball cap with me and some factor thirty sunblock because the Thai sun can be devastating to Western skin. I rubbed the sunblock over my face and hands as I waited for my coffee. A couple of Italian girls came in wearing string bikinis and I showed them the photograph but they both shook their heads.

I drank my coffee and half the bottle of water and then paid my bill and took the bottle outside. The sea was blue and the sky was cloudless and I could feel the hot sand through my shoes as I headed for the water. I walked along the wet sand, heading west. It was one o'clock in the afternoon, just about the hottest time of the day, but there were plenty of people lying on the beach, roasting like pigs on a spit as if they'd never heard of UV damage and skin cancer.

I'm with the Thais when it comes to sunbathing. They don't do it, and most of the time they cover themselves up on the beach, and even swim in t-shirts and jeans.

Most of the girls on the beach were farang, so I didn't have to get too close, and most of the men with Thai girls were in the forties or older, so again I could give them a wide berth. What I was looking for – a young American and a Thai student – was a rarity on Koh Samui.

An hour into my walk along the beach I'd already finished my bottle of water and I was heading for a bar to replenish my supply when my cellphone rang. It was Somsak. 'What's that I can hear?' he asked.

'The sea,' I said.

'Where are you?'

'Koh Samui.'

'Vacation?'

'Work,' I said. 'I'm hoping that Jon Junior is here.'

'Jon Junior?'

'The missing Mormon.'

'Good luck with that,' he said. 'Now I've got good news, bad news for you.'

I was hearing that a lot lately.

'The good news is that the guy who shot you is pleading guilty.'

'And the bad news?'

'He's not naming Big Red as the paymaster.'

'What?'

'Now he's claiming that Big Red's driver paid him to shoot you.'

'Oh, come on ...' I stood looking out over the sea. On the horizon were four fishing boats, heading east.

'I know, I know. But that's what he's saying.'

'So he'll plead guilty to what, attempted murder?'

'Assault perhaps. He's claiming that he didn't intend to kill you.'

'He shot me, Somsak.'

'Yes, but he didn't kill you. For which we are all grateful. I wouldn't be anywhere near as understanding if you were dead, my friend.'

'So assault, then. Ten years?'

'Six if there was a trial, but it will be halved if he pleads guilty.'

Three years, then. For trying to kill me.

And with the king's birthday coming up, maybe halved again.

Eighteen months.

'And Big Red's driver?'

'Another guilty plea. He'll admit that he paid the guy to shoot you but will say that it was just as a warning.'

'Wonderful,' I said. 'Two years?'

'Hopefully,' said Somsak.

'And Big Red carries on as normal. Paying schoolgirls for sex and sending motorcycle assassins to deal with anyone who crosses him.'

'Amazing Thailand,' said Somsak.

'Indeed,' I said. 'Sometimes life isn't fair, is it?'

'It isn't,' agreed Somsak. 'We just have to deal with it as best we can. But we will do something about Big Red and the schoolgirls. Vice is watching him.'

'Do you think they'll make a case against him?'

'Big Red isn't as rich or well connected as he thinks. A lot of cops send their kids to that school and they'll want something done. You know that things have a way of working out in Thailand. Just give it time.'

'And what about Tukkata's father?'

'Vice is monitoring him when he goes online. He's grooming a number of girls and next time he goes to meet one he'll be picked up.'

'And then what? A slap on the wrist? On an appeal for a donation?'

'One step at a time, Khun Bob.'

'I suppose so.'

'At least no one died,' said Somsak.

'That's true.'

'I've some more news for you,' he said.

'My cup runneth over.'

'Remember the owner of the Kube, the figurehead? Thongchai?'

'I remember.'

'He's dead.'

'Dead?'

'He was found in a house out near the airport. Heart attack.'

'Heart attack?'

'Yeah, same as Ronnie Marsh, the manager.'

'Coincidence?' I said.

'Amazing Thailand,' he said. 'Poker next week?'

'Definitely.'

So that was that. Case closed. Still, as Somsak had said, at least I wasn't dead.

I put my cellphone back into my pocket and headed inland. I found a small bar, little more than a wooden shack with a few roughly-hewn wooden tables and benches in front of, shielded with large beach umbrellas advertising Phuket Beer, which I took as a good sign.

I sat down and before I'd even taken off my baseball cap a pretty girl with skin the colour of mahogany and her hair tied back in a ponytail handed me a cold towel that send shivers down by spine when I wiped the back of my neck.

I ordered a Phuket Beer and it was as chilled as the towel. I overtipped her and showed her Jon Junior's photograph.

'Have you seen my friend?' I said. 'His name's Jon, I think he's staying near here with his girlfriend.'

She smiled and nodded. 'He was here yesterday.'

My jaw dropped and I thought I'd misheard her.

'With Tukkata,' she added. 'Pretty girl from Bangkok.'

I handed her another hundred baht note and thanked her. 'Do you know where they're staying?" I asked.

She pointed along the beach, to the west. 'One of the bungalows down there,' she said. 'I don't know which one.'

She went off to serve another customer, her ponytail twitching from side to side as she walked. I smiled to myself and raised my bottle in salute to no one in particular.

I love it when a plan comes together.

I finished my beer and then went back to the beach. It was almost three o'clock. I took off my shoes and socks and walked barefoot along the wet sand. Ahead of me was a resort of cheap bungalows, maybe a dozen, with sharply sloping roofs and small terraces shielded from the sun by coconut palms.

I could see a couple lying on rattan loungers under a large white beach umbrella. A farang boy and a Thai girl. As I walked towards them the boy sat up and began applying sunblock to his arms. Then the girl sat up, took the sunblock from him and began to rub it over his back and shoulders.

My heart began to race. I couldn't see the boy's face but I was sure it was Jon Junior. And the young Thai girl rubbing sunblock into his shoulders could only be Tukkata.

45

TUKKATA SAW ME first and she whispered something to Jon Junior. He looked around and stood up, his arms at his side as if he wasn't sure if he should attack me or run off down the beach. I put my hand up in greeting. 'It's okay,' I said, 'I come in peace.'

'Who are you?'

'My name's Bob Turtledove,' I said, taking off my baseball cap. 'Your parents wanted me to find you.'

'My parents? Why?' He was wearing sunglasses and he pushed them up onto the top of his head.

'Because they haven't heard from you in weeks,' I said. 'They're worried about you.'

'I told them I'd be in Thailand for a while.'

'Your phone's off and you've stopped using your email account.'

He waved at hand at the beach. 'There's no wi-fi here,' he said.

'And the phone?'

'What do you want, Mr Turtledove?'

Tukkata slid off her sunlounger and put her arms around Jon Junior. 'What's happening?' she asked him. She was wearing a yellow t-shirt and a long white wraparound skirt.

'It's okay, teerak, he's a friend of my parents.'

Teerak.

It means darling.

He smiled at her. 'Tukkata, can you wait for me in the hut?'

'I want to stay with you,' she said, resting her cheek against his arm.

'Let me talk to him on my own,' he said. He patted her on the hip. 'It's okay. We're just going to talk.'

'I'm not going back,' she said. 'I'm not going back to Bangkok.'

'I know,' said Jon Junior. 'I just need to explain things to Mr Turtledove.'

Tukkata hugged Jon Junior and then kissed him on the cheek. She was close to tears.

'It's going to be all right, teerak,' he said. 'I swear.'

She nodded, picked up her towel and padded across the sand towards their hut in the shade of a clump of coconut palms.

'She's a lovely girl,' I said.

'The best,' he said.

He sat down in his sunlounger and I dropped into the one that Tukkata has just vacated. 'Your parents are worried, Jon,' I said. 'Frantic.'

'I guess so.'

'Why didn't you call them? Or write to them?'

'I've been busy.' He looked out over the sea.

'You're sitting on a beach,' I said.

'Like I said, with no internet connection and I've no idea where the nearest post office is.'

'You've got a phone.'

He looked across at me. 'We can't use the phone because then her father will find us. No phones, no credit cards. We have to stay off the grid.'

'And how long can you live like that?' I asked.

He gestured at the beach hut. 'We can stay there for as long as we want.'

'What are you doing for money?'

'I've got cash. Tukkata has some. She had some gold jewellery that she sold in Bangkok. The hut's cheap and we eat local food. A couple of hundred baht a day is all we need.' He ran a hand through his sun-bleached hair and frowned. 'How did you find us?'

'Tukkata sent a text message, three days ago.'

'Who to?"

'Her friend, Kai.'

Jon Junior sighed. 'I told her to leave the phone off. If you found us, her father can, too. We'll have to move.'

'That's your plan?' I said. 'To keep running?'

Her shook his head. 'She's eighteen next week,' he said. 'Then her family can't do anything.'

'To be honest, I don't think her father is looking for you.'

'Why do you say that?'

'When I talked to him he seemed more worried about how much I knew then whether or not I knew where you were. Seems to me that he's not telling anyone that Tukkata is missing.'

'She's his daughter.'

'Yes, but she's the daughter who knows his dirty little secret. I think the last thing he wants just now is a confrontation with her.'

Jon Junior nodded thoughtfully. 'What about you, Mr Turtledove? What do you do now that you've found me?"

'I'm working for your parents, not for Tukkata's father. And to be honest all your parents want to know is that you're safe.'

'They want me back home, working for my father.'

'That's understandable,' I said.

'I want to stay in Thailand,' he said.

'A lot of people do,' I said. 'But you have to think it through. It's not the easiest place to live and work when you're a foreigner.'

'You seem to be doing all right,' he said.

I laughed. 'I've got a Thai wife who makes my life a whole lot easier,' he said.

'That's what I'm planning, Mr Turtledove. Tukkata and I, we're going to get married.'

'That's what Tukkata wants?'

'It's what we both want.'

'Jon, you're twenty-one and Tukkata is just seventeen.'

'Eighteen next week. Mr Turtledove, I'm four years older than her. When I'll be a hundred she'll be ninety-six.' He grinned. 'Who's going to care about four years then?' He waved a hand around the beach. 'Since I came to Thailand I've seen sixty-year-old men walking around with girls in their twenties, girls young enough to be their grand-daughters. Is that what I should do, Mr Turtledove? Follow their example?'

It was funny but every time he called me 'Mr Turtledove' I felt about a hundred years old.

'Because applying that philosophy, the girl of my dreams isn't going to be born for another twenty years.'

'I do understand what you're saying, Jon, But you're very young to be thinking about getting married, and Tukkata's even younger.'

'You've met my parents, Mr Turtledove?'

'Yes. They came to my office.'

'Well, next time you talk to them, why don't you ask them how old they were when they got married?'

'Ah,' I said, catching his drift.

He nodded. 'That's right,' he said. 'Younger than me. Quite a bit younger as it happens. So I don't think they'll be casting the first stone on that score.' He leaned forward. 'You know that Mormons don't marry for life, they marry for eternity?'

'I had heard that,' I said.

'For eternity, Mr Turtledove. It's not something that you enter into lightly. You have to make sure that you have made the right choice. And I know that Tukkata is the girl I want to spend eternity with. Do you understand that?'

I nodded slowly.

Actually, I did.

Because that's exactly how I felt about Noy.

'I understand,' I said.

'So now what?' he asked.

I shrugged. 'You're an adult, you make your own choices. And like you said, as of next week Tukkata's an adult too.'

'What would you do, Mr Turtledove? About her father?'

I sighed. It was a good question.

'You could try talking to him. Or she could. Or Tukkata could talk to her mother.'

'It would destroy her family if her mother found out. Kai was underage. He could go to prison.'

'I'm not sure if that would happen,' I said. 'I've met Kai, she's hardly a victim in this.'

'She's just a kid,' said Jon Junior. 'Tukkata's father committed statutory rape.'

'Well, strictly speaking Tukkata's under age too.'

Jon Junior frowned. 'What do you mean?'

I nodded at the beach hut. 'The two of you are sleeping together, right?'

His jaw dropped. 'What, you think...?' He shook his head. 'I haven't laid a finger on her. I swear to God.'

'Okay,' I said.

'I mean it, Mr Turtledove. Yes, we stay in the hut together and we hold each other but that's as far as it goes and we won't be doing anything else until we're married. I'm a virgin and so is Tukkata and that's the way we'll be on the day we exchange our views before God.'

I guess that's the great thing about being young.

You've got your whole life ahead of you.

Jon Junior was a good kid and I figured he'd be all right.

I stood up. 'I'm going back to Bangkok,' he said.

'You won't tell anyone where we are?'

'It's none of my business,' I said. I took my phone out of my pocket. I had already stored Mr Clare's number in Utah and I called it. I didn't know what time it was in Salt Lake City and I figured that the Clares wouldn't care once they found out who was calling. The phone began to ring out and I handed it to Jon Junior. 'But you need to talk to your parents.'

'What do I tell them?'

'The truth,' I said. 'Generally that works. Your parents are good people, Jon, They'll stand by you.'

He nodded and took the phone from me.

46

THERE WAS AN intellectual argument going on when I walked into Fatso's. Relentless was claiming that he'd met a girl called Komon Fukme working for the Bangkok Bank. Bruce and Alan were claiming that he was making it up.

Big Ron was holding court in his massive chair. Kom was a fairly common prefix for girl's names he said, and Fuk, a type of vegetable, was often used in surnames. Komon Fukme wasn't as far-fetched as it sounded.

Bruce wouldn't have it and kept shaking his head and muttering 'no way'. I eased myself onto the stool next to Big Ron's. One of the Fatso's girls was already opening a bottle of Phuket Beer for me.

Relentless raised the stakes and said that he'd once shared a taxi with a girl called Sukmy Boobies and Alan threw a handful of peanuts at him.

I leaned over and slowly rang the bell three times. The Fatso's girls cheered and began pouring drinks for everyone.

Big Ron grinned and pointed a finger at me. 'I knew it,' he said triumphantly.

'I should have listened to you,' I said.

'A girl?'

'Oh yes.'

'And a beach?'

'Indeed.'

'Who's the daddy?' shouted Big Ron.

'You are,' I said. 'You're the daddy.'

Big Ron tilted his head back and howled at the ceiling like a wolf in heat.

Oh well. You live and learn.

If you're lucky.

Read more by
Stephen Leather

CONFESSIONS OF A BANGKOK PRIVATE EYE

STEPHEN LEATHER
& WARREN OLSON

Two-timing bargirls, suspicious spouses and lesbian lovers—it was all in a day's work for real Bangkok Private Eye Warren Olson.

For more than a decade, New Zealander Warren Olson walked the mean streets of the Big Mango. Fluent in Thai and Khmer, he was able to go where other Private Eyes feared to tread.

His clients included Westerners who had lost their hearts—and life savings—to money-hungry bargirls. But he had more than his fair share of Thai clients, too, including a sweet old lady who was ripped off by a Christian conman and a Thai girl blackmailed by a former lover.

Twenty-three of Olson's most unusual, but true, cases are retold by bestselling author Stephen Leather.

'*Confessions of a Bangkok Private Eye* should be read by males considering visiting these shores. It would save them a lot of grief. This book hits the nail on the head.'
Bangkok Post, Thailand

THE CASE OF THE

DOUBLE-CROSSED DUTCHMAN

There are a whole host of things I love about living in Thailand: the gorgeous women, the climate, the food, the beaches. But right at the top of the list of things I hate is being pursued at high speed by two motorcyclists with gun-toting pillion passengers. The guys out to put a bullet in my head weren't flashing the smiles that Thailand is famous for—they were glaring at me with murder in their eyes. I swerved over to the right, trying to clip the rear wheel of the bike nearest to me but he moved away easily. The pillion passenger was caught off balance and he grabbed the waist of the driver. I took a quick look over my left shoulder. The second pillion passenger had his gun aimed at my head. I slammed on the brakes and the bike roared by, the passenger's hair whipping in the wind.

I cursed, spitting out pretty much all the swear words I knew. I was in deep, deep shit, and it had all been the fault of my brand new digital camera.

The case had started easily enough. I'd received a phone call from a Dutch detective agency in Amsterdam that I'd done business with a few times. They were good payers and good payers are like hens teeth in the private-eye business. They were acting for a well-known Dutch businessmen who'd married a girl from Bangkok five years earlier. The businessmen had started taking his wife to a local Thai restaurant and was worried that she might have started a relationship with a young waiter. The Dutch detectives had put the wife under surveillance but so far hadn't caught her misbehaving, but now the wife was planning to fly to Thailand for Songkran, the Thai new year. It's the traditional time for Thai families to get together, and the businessman was too busy adding to his millions to go with her. A red flag was raised when the Dutch detectives discovered that the Thai waiter had booked onto the same flight to Bangkok. It could have been a coincidence, of course, but the Dutch guys wanted me to mount a surveillance operation once they'd arrived in Bangkok.

The girl's parents lived in Chiang Mai, in the north of Thailand, so the first thing I did was to check if she had booked an onward flight from Bangkok. She hadn't, but she might be planning to buy the ticket once she'd arrived, or even travel up by train or bus. I asked for a description of the jewellery and watch she usually wore, because photographs were often surprisingly unhelpful for identifying people and there would be several dozen young and pretty girls, all with black hair and brown eyes, getting off the KLM 747 from Amsterdam. The information, along with her passport number and a copy of her Thai ID card, came over with her pictures, plus a photograph of the waiter, and a sizeable retainer was transferred into my account with Bangkok Bank.

She was due to arrive at Don Muang at eleven o'clock in the morning in two days' time. The problem was, I had no idea what she was going to do once she'd arrived. I bought Business Class tickets on the three flights that were due to leave for Chiang Mai after her flight had arrived, just in case she decided to head up north straight away. But if she took a car into Bangkok, I had a problem. I'd have to be in the terminal to check that she arrived, but that would mean parking my car in the multistorey. If she hopped into a cab I'd lose her before I got back to my vehicle. If she was picked up by a friend then the friend would have parked in the multistorey and by the time I'd identified their car it would be too late to get to my own vehicle. I couldn't use motorcycles to follow her because motorcycles aren't allowed on the country's expressways, and the route from the airport to the city was all expressway. I didn't have the money to start paying half a dozen guys to stake out the airport to cover every eventuality so I decided to nab a taxi driver at the airport and offered him 2,000 baht for a four-hour hire. He practically bit my hand off and I gave him 500 baht up front and told him to wait outside the terminal for me. He had a mobile phone so that if the girl headed to the car park I could follow her and then call the taxi to pick me up. If she hired a cab then I was ahead of the game, I just had to get into my taxi and follow her. And if she walked over to the domestic terminal and bought a ticket to Chiang Mai, all I'd have to do would be to get on the flight with her. I was feeling pretty pleased with myself as I sipped a cup of coffee in the arrivals area.

The terminal was packed, as hundreds of thousands of Thais rushed home in time for the New Year celebrations. There were lots of tourists too, who think it's fun to douse each other with water as a way of celebrating Thai New Year. Frankly, after ten years of having water thrown in my face every April, I celebrate the festival by staying at home and ordering pizza and beer over the phone. But that's just me.

The flight landed bang on time and it took them just over an hour to pass through Customs and Immigration. I spotted the girl among a group of Thais. She was pushing a trolley piled high with suitcases and bulging nylon bags, presumably gifts for her family. The waiter was a few paces behind her, pushing his own trolley. Nothing suspicious about that, they would have been sure to have met on the plane even if they hadn't been planning to travel together. The photographs that the Dutch agency sent didn't do the girl justice. She had waist-length hair, high cheekbones, and was model-pretty with curves in all the right places. She was tall for a Thai, five-seven or thereabouts, and she was wearing a short denim skirt that showed off a gorgeous pair of legs.

There were four people waiting to greet the girl, two were a few years younger than her and they quickly waied her, pressing their hands together and placing the tips of the fingers against their chins. Showing respect. That tends to be how Thais greet each other, even after long absences. No great show of emotion, no hugs or kisses. A nice, respectful wai. The girl first waied the two older members of the group, then returned the wai to the girl and boy who had waied her. Then she introduced them to the waiter. He waied them all, then they pushed their trolleys towards the car park. That answered two questions right there. She wasn't flying to Chiang Mai and she was definitely travelling with the waiter.

I kept my distance but the terminal was so crowded that I doubted they would have spotted me even if they'd looked my way. They walked to the car park and started putting the bags into the back of a Toyota van. I made a note of the registration number and hurried back to the waiting taxi.

I was feeling even more pleased with myself as the van pulled out of the multistorey car park. I told the taxi driver to follow the van and settled back in my seat. All we had to do was keep the van in sight on the expressway and make sure that we took the same exit. The fact that I was tailing the van in a Bangkok taxi meant that there was virtually no way they'd spot me. Taxis account for about ten per cent of the cars on the roads at any time.

The van started to pull away from us and I told the driver to step on it. He nodded enthusiastically but we didn't go any faster. I told him again, this time in Khmer, but that didn't seem to sink in so I repeated myself in the Isaan dialect that many taxi drivers speak. He nodded again but the van continued to disappear into the distance. I peered into the footwell. The accelerator was flat against the floor. I groaned. The engine was juddering like a heart-attack victim and we hadn't even broken sixty kilometres an hour. The driver grinned and gripped the steering wheel so tightly that his knuckles started to turn white.

We lost the van before we reached the first turn off so I told the driver to take me back to my office. I gave him half the fee we had agreed on but he threw a temper tantrum and started waving his mobile phone at me and threatened to call his friends. Most taxi drivers have at least a crowbar or baseball bat in their vehicles, and guns aren't unknown, and one of their favourite pastimes is roughing up troublesome farangs, as they call us foreigners, so I gave him the full 2,000 baht. The Dutchman would be covering my expenses anyway so it was no big deal.

I phoned the Dutch agency and spun them a story about knowing the general area where the subject was, but that I wanted a recent phone bill from the client to see if there were any Bangkok numbers that the girl had called before arriving in Thailand. An hour later and a phone bill was faxed through to me. I was in luck—there were four numbers with Bangkok's 02 prefix. I fed the numbers into a reverse directory I use and the computer gave me the addresses. Three were offices and one was an apartment in the Bangna area of the city. I drove out to Bangna in a rental car and sat outside the apartment block for the rest of the day.

The apartment was in a small side road and it was difficult to get a view of the main entrance without sticking out like a sore thumb so I parked the car and went and sat in a small chicken restaurant opposite the block. I ordered some kow man gai, steamed chicken and rice with a tangy sauce and a bowl of watery soup. There was a British soccer game on the television set in the corner and after muttering 'Man U *channa nanon* (Manchester United are sure to win) I was pretty much ignored by the half dozen male customers sitting at a Formica table drinking Singha beer. After about an hour I saw the waiter walking towards the apartment block. Bingo. He went inside.

I phoned my contact in the Dutch agency and explained that the waiter was definitely staying with the girl and there was no indication that they were heading up to Chiang Mai. My contact was pleased, but said that his client wanted a photograph of the girl and the waiter together.

I had a brand new digital camera in the boot of the car, so I parked as close to the apartment block as I could and sat with the camera on my lap. It had a telephoto lens and the salesman had assured me that it was state-of-the-art. Being digital, I could use my computer to email the pictures without having to wait for film to be processed. I as starting to feel pretty pleased with myself again. I had found where they were staying, there was only one way in and out, all I needed was a photograph and the fee was in the bag.

Time passed. It got dark. I had a couple of bottles of water in the car and I drank them both. Midnight passed. I was thinking about abandoning the surveillance for the night, figuring that perhaps the girl and the waiter were having too much fun to go out, when I saw movement in the lobby. I wound the window down and got the camera ready. It was the waiter. He held the door open and the girl walked out. 'Yes,' I hissed triumphantly. I brought up the camera lens and took a couple of quick shots. Just then there was a double flash of lightning. It looked as if my luck was changing for the worse—the weather had been fine all day and now that I had them in my sights a tropical storm was starting. I fired off another two quick shots and lightning flashed again.

Click. Flash. Click. Flash.

Then it hit me. My state-of-the-art digital camera with its onboard smarter-than-a-human-being computer had decided that as it was dark I should be using the flash. What the bloody thing hadn't realised was that the last thing a private detective on a stakeout needs is a flash going off, computer-controlled or otherwise. The girl and the waiter looked in my direction and hurried along the road away from the car.

I cursed and fumbled with the camera, trying to find the control that turned off the flash.

Something smacked against the bonnet of the car and I looked up to see a muscle-bound Thai man glaring at me. He had a thick gold chain around his neck and a wicked scar across his left cheek that cut through a crop of old acne scars. He thumped on the bonnet again.

'*Tham arai*?" he screamed, which means 'I'm sorry old chap but what exactly are you doing?' or words to that effect.

I put the camera on the passenger seat and hit the central locking switch. The thuds of the locks clicking into place antagonised the man even more and he slapped the windscreen. A second man, just as heavily built, ran over and began pulling at the passenger door handle.

I looked around. Two more men were walking purposefully out of the restaurant and one of them was swinging a large machete. I didn't know what I'd done to upset them but they didn't look like the sort of guys who were going to respond to reason. I had the engine running to keep the aircon cold so I put the car into gear and moved forward, slowly enough to give the guy with the scar a chance to get out of the way. A foreigner running over a Thai would end only one way and sleeping on the floor of a Thai prison wasn't how I was planning to spend my retirement.

I pushed harder on the accelerator. The guy kept hold of the passenger side door handle and jogged to keep up. I cursed. I didn't want to drag him down the road, but I was equally unhappy at the prospect of the guy with the machete doing a remodelling job on the rental car.

Machete Guy shouted something and started to run. I stopped worrying about the man on the passenger side and pushed the accelerator to the floor. The wheels screeched on the tarmac and the car leapt forward. I roared down the road, snatching a quick look in the rear-view mirror. The four men were standing on the pavement, screaming at me. I grinned and took the first right turn, onto a major road. I was just starting to relax when I saw the motorbikes.

As they got closer I recognised one of the drivers—it was Machete Guy. I had no idea what I'd done to upset the guys, but figured they had obviously been up to something iffy and thought that I'd been taking photographs of them. Drugs maybe, or gambling. There might have been an underage brothel above the restaurant for all I knew. In an ideal world I'd have just explained that I had been taking pictures of an unfaithful wife, but Bangkok wasn't an ideal world and it was probably too late for any explanation.

There was a fair bit of traffic around and I had to slow down. The motorcycles quickly gained on me. Machete Guy's pillion passenger brandished a pistol and motioned for me to pull over to the side of the road. Yeah, right. I shook my head, braked hard, and pulled a left, cutting across a bus and feeling the rear end fishtail as I floored the accelerator again. I knew there was no way I was going to be able to outrun the bikes in the city. It would only be a matter of time before I hit traffic or a red light.

I could feel sweat trickling down my neck. Life is cheap in Bangkok. That's not a cliché, it's an economic truth. The going rate for a professional hit is 20,000 baht for a Thai, 50,000 if it's a farang. But amateurs were also happy to use bullets to solve a quarrel because most murderers end up serving seven years at most, and that was in the unlikely event of them being caught. All of this was running through my mind as I drove through the streets at high speed. Along with wondering why I hadn't chosen another profession, why I'd moved to the Land of Smiles in the first place, and why I hadn't read the manual for the camera before taking it on the job.

The best I could hope for was to run across a police patrol car but even that was no guarantee that I'd be safe. For all I knew, the four guys in hot pursuit could well be off-duty cops.

The second bike drew up on my passenger side and the pillion passenger waved a large automatic at me. I swung the car to the right. I had a really, really bad feeling about the way this was going to play out. They were getting madder and madder and all it would take would be one shot to a tyre and it would all be over.

Suddenly I saw a sign for the Pattaya Expressway and realised that it was my best hope: bikes aren't allowed on the expressway and even if they ignored the law and followed me I'd be able to get the car up to full speed and with them being two up on small bikes they wouldn't be able to keep up with me.

I kept on going straight, accelerated, then as the ramp approached I slammed on the brakes and pulled the car hard to the left, just missing the concrete dividing wall that separated the ramp from the road. The bikes continued to roar down the road then I saw the brake lights go red as they realised what had happened. I sped towards the line of toll booths, pulling my wallet out of my pocket and flicking through the notes. The toll was forty baht but I flung a red 100-baht note at the toll booth attendant and yelled at her to keep the change as I sped on through.

As I accelerated down the expressway I kept looking in the rear view mirror but there was no sign of my pursuers, and after twenty minutes barrelling along at more than 140 kilometres an hour I started to relax. I left the expressway at the third exit, then parked up and had a bowl of noodles and pork and a bottle of Chang beer at a roadside vendor to calm my nerves. My hands stopped shaking by the time I'd put the third bottle away.

I waited a couple of hours before driving back to the city, and I caught a few hours sleep after emailing a full report to the Dutch agency along with the photographs I'd taken.

I was woken by the phone ringing. It was one of the Dutch operatives—the client had booked himself on the next flight to Bangkok and he wanted to confront his wife, ideally while she was in bed with her lover. I've never understood that, but it's happened time and time again. It's not enough for the wronged guy to know that his wife has been unfaithful, he wants to rub her face in the fact that he knows. If it was me, I'd just up and leave. Okay, I'd clear out the bank accounts first and maybe take a razor blade to all her clothes, but I wouldn't bother with a confrontation. That's just me, though, and in this business the client is always right. Even when he's wrong.

I got up and showered, then returned the rental car. The guy who ran the rental company was an old friend and he agreed to swap my paperwork with that of an American tourist who'd just flown back to Seattle so I was covered just in case the bike guys had taken my registration number.

The Dutch agency had told me to take good care of the client so I booked a Mercedes and driver and got to Don Muang Airport an hour before the flight was due, holding a piece of card with his name on it as I sipped my black coffee. The man who walked over to me and introduced himself was just about the fattest guy I had ever set eyes on. He wasn't big. He wasn't even huge. He was obese and must have weighed at least 400 pounds straight out of the shower. He was in his early forties, with slicked back hair and half a dozen chins. He was wearing a light blue suit that was stretched like a sail in a high wind; I figured he must be at least five times the weight of the his wife and I couldn't imagine how they went about having sex. We shook hands. His was the size of a small shovel but the fingers were soft, like underdone pork sausages. He had no luggage and hadn't shaved on the plane, but he said he wanted to head straight out to the apartment. I sat upfront as we drove out to Bangna. The client didn't say anything and only grunted at my attempts to start a conversation so after a while I just let him sit there in silence.

It isn't unusual for a pretty young Thai girl to marry an older guy. Like girls all over the Third World they want someone to take care of them and their families and there's no doubt that a few thousand dollars in the bank can help add to a man's attractiveness to the opposite sex. But there was no way on earth that the match between the lovely girl we were going to see and the blimp I had in the back of the Mercedes was a marriage made in heaven. He must have known that. Every time he caught a glimpse of the two of them in a mirror it must have hit home that he was simply too big for her. If it had been me, I'd have just been grateful for the fact that I was allowed to sleep with a woman as beautiful as her, and if the downside meant that she had the occasional fling with a man nearer her own age, well then I'd just put that down to the price I had to pay. The Dutch guys hadn't managed to catch her being unfaithful in Amsterdam, which meant that she was probably only fooling around in Thailand. I wanted to tell the client that he'd be better off turning a blind eye to the occasional indiscretion and that the best thing he could do would be to go straight back to Holland, but I kept quiet.

I had the driver park around the corner from the apartment block, and pulled on a pair of shades and a Singha beer baseball cap before I got out of the car. The client was obviously used to sitting in the back of expensive vehicles because he didn't make a move to open his door himself, he just sat staring straight ahead until I opened it for him. He wheezed as he hauled himself out of the car, and I swear the suspension sighed with relief. 'I burn easily,' I said, explaining away the cap and sunglasses, but the real reason was that I didn't want to risk being recognised if Machete Man and his gun-wielding buddies were back in the restaurant. They weren't, and I relaxed a little when I saw that the restaurant was closed.

A receptionist buzzed us into the apartment block and a purple 500-baht note got us the room number. We rode up in the lift in silence to the fourth floor. I looked around to see if there was a weight limit for the lift, and I kept having visions of the cables snapping and us both plummeting to our deaths.

There were a couple of dozen rooms on either side of a long corridor. We walked slowly along to the room. I waited at the side of the door as the client knocked, twice.

The door opened. The girl was there wearing a white T-shirt and blue denim shorts. She stared at him sleepily, then her jaw dropped as she realised who it was.

'Darling …' she said, but then the words dried up and her mouth open and closed silently.

'Don't "darling" me, you whore!' hissed the client, and he pushed the door open. It was a studio apartment and the waiter was lying on the double bed, wrapped in a towel. The waiter leapt to his feet as the big guy strode into the room and rushed out, his bare feet slapping on the tiled floor as he bolted down the corridor.

I stayed where I was. The client had left the door open so I could hear everything that was being said. The girl began pleading that there'd been a mistake, that the waiter was just a friend, that she was only staying in the room until she could get a flight to Chiang Mai. The client let her beg and plead, then silenced her with an outburst of expletives that suggested he'd had an army career in his younger, and probably thinner, days.

'You were a whore when I met you, and you're a whore now!' he shouted once he'd finished swearing. 'I gave you everything. I gave you the clothes on your back, the watch on your wrist. I gave you money for your parents, I paid for your brothers to go to school. Anything you needed, anything you wanted, I gave to you. And you do this to me? You fuck around behind my back.'

She started to cry.

'You're dead to me, you bitch!' he shouted. 'When I get back home I'm destroying everything of yours. Every dress, every handbag, every shoe; everything I ever gave you, I'm burning. Every photograph of you, I'm destroying. You're dead to me. I'm divorcing you and you won't get a penny. The best lawyers in the country work for me, and if I get my way you'll lose your Dutch citizenship.'

There was a dull thud and I took a quick look into he room just in case she's beaten him over the head with a blunt object but she was the one on the floor, slumped down next to the bed, her hands over her face, sobbing her heart out.

He waddled over to a dressing table and grabbed her handbag. He pulled out a Dutch passport and ripped it into several places, went over to the toilet and flushed away the pieces. Then he threw the handbag into the toilet for good measure.

'Please, darling ...' sobbed the girl.

The client sneered at her and walked out of the room, his ham-sized hands clenched into fists. I followed him back to the lift. I saw the waiter in the stairwell, anxiously looking in our direction, his hands clutching the towel around his waist. I waved for him to keep out of the way.

The lift doors opened and we rode down. 'Bitch,' said the client, venomously. His face was bathed in sweat and there were damp patches under the arms of his jacket.

I said nothing. I could see his point, but I figured that of the two of them, he'd lost the most. She'd lost a sugar daddy, but then she wouldn't have to satisfy the sexual urges of a man big enough to crush her if he rolled over in his sleep. And a girl as pretty as her wouldn't have to look too hard to find another husband. He'd lost a beautiful young gold-digger but now he'd have to sleep with nothing more than his right hand for company. Swings and roundabouts? I didn't think so. If ever there was a Pyrhic victory, this was it.

We walked out of the block and over to the Mercedes. 'I don't need you any more,' he wheezed. 'I can take care of myself at the airport. Thank you. For everything.' He handed me a fistful of euros which I guessed was my cab fare home.

I opened the rear door of the Mercedes and he hauled himself slowly into the back. The suspension groaned in protest. I closed the door behind him and the car moved away from the kerb. I got one last look at the client as the car drove off. There were tears streaming down his fleshy cheeks.

PRIVATE DANCER

STEPHEN LEATHER

Pete, a young travel writer, wanders into a Bangkok bar and meets the love of his life. Pete thinks that Joy is the girl of his dreams: young, stunningly pretty, and one of the top-earning go-go dancers in Nana Plaza.

What follows is a roller-coaster ride of sex, drugs, lies and murder, as Pete discovers that his very own private dancer is not all that she claims to be. And that far from being the girl of his dreams, Joy is his own personal nightmare.

'The best book regarding relationships with bargirls that you can ever read. This should be compulsory reading for all first-timers to Thailand'
Pattaya Mail, Thailand

'A gripping, highly readable thriller that cleverly intertwines the stories of the main two protagonists—bargirl and naked pole dancer Joy and her British, travel guide writing customer/lover Pete'
The Asian Review of Books, Hong Kong

'Because of all of its local wisdom, *Private Dancer* ought to be made available to every tourist at port of entry'
The Bangkok Post, Thailand

#1 bestseller in Thailand!

PETE

She's dead. Joy's dead. Joy's dead and I killed her. I can't believe it. I killed her and now I don't know what I'm going to do. I don't know what I'm going to do without her and I don't know what's going to happen to me when they find out she's dead. They'll know it's my fault. I trashed the room, my fingerprints are going to be everywhere. The manager of the building saw me storm out. The guy in the room, he'll remember me, too. Her friends knew that we were always arguing, and they know where I live.

The taxi driver keeps looking at me in his mirror. He can see how upset I am. I have to keep calm, but it's difficult. I want to scream at him, to tell him to put his foot down and drive faster but we're sitting at a red light so we aren't going anywhere for a while. Ahead of us is an elephant, swinging its trunk at a guy carrying a basket of bananas. A group of tourists give the guy money and he hands them fruit so that they can feed the elephant.

'Chang,' says the driver. Thai for elephant. I pretend not to understand and keep looking out of the window. A typical Bangkok street scene, the pavements lined with food hawkers and stalls piled high with cheap clothing, the air thick with fumes from motorcycles and buses. I see it but I don't see it. All I can think about is Joy.

It's as if time around me has stopped. Stopped dead. I'm breathing and thinking but everything has frozen. She's dead and it's my fault. They'll see my name tattooed on her shoulder and they'll see my name carved into her wrist and they'll know that it's all my fault. I'm not worried about what the police will do. Or her family. There's nothing they can do that can make me feel any worse than I do right now as I sit frozen in time at a red traffic light, watching overweight tourists feeding bananas to an elephant with a chain around its neck.

I know with a horrible certainty that I can't go on living without her. My life ends with her death because I can't live with the guilt. Joy's dead and I killed her so that means that I have to die, too.

BRUCE

I always knew it was going to end badly. Joy was a sweet thing and whether or not she'd been lying to Pete, she didn't deserve to die, not like that. Sure, she was a bargirl, but she was forced into it, she'd never have chosen the life for herself, and I know she wanted Pete to take her away from the bars. I was in shock when I heard what happened. Now I don't know what's going to happen to Pete. It's like he's on autopilot, heading into oblivion. I've got a bad feeling about it, but it's out of my hands. He's going to have to come to terms with what he's done, her death's going to be on his conscience for the rest of his life. To be honest, I don't know how he's going to be able to live with himself.

BIG RON

Joy's dead, huh? Can't say I was surprised when Bruce told me. Do I care? Do I fuck. I'm not going to shed any tears about a dead slapper. It's not exactly a long-term career, is it, when all's said and done, what with the drugs and the risks they take. Slappers are dying all the time. Overdoses, suicides, motorcycle accidents. And the way Joy fucked Pete over, I'm surprised he didn't top her months ago. She was a lying hooker and she deserved whatever she got, that's what I say. As for Pete, I don't know what'll happen to him. If he's smart he'll get on the next plane out of Bangkok.

PETE

I don't know if it was love at first sight, but it was pretty damn close. She had the longest hair I'd ever seen, jet black and almost down to her waist. She smiled all the time and had soft brown eyes that made my heart melt, long legs that just wouldn't quit and a figure to die for. She was stark naked except for a pair of black leather ankle boots with small chrome chains on the side. I think it was the boots that did it for me.

I didn't know her name, and I couldn't talk to her because she was already occupied with a fat, balding guy with a mobile phone who kept fondling her breasts and bouncing her up and down on his knee. She was a dancer at the Zombie Bar, one of more than a hundred go-go dancers, and between her twenty-minute dancing shifts she had to hustle drinks from customers. I kept trying to catch her eye, but she was too busy with the bald guy and after an hour or so she changed into jeans and a T-shirt and left with him. They looked obscene together, he must have been twenty stone and old enough to be her father.

I was with Nigel, a guy I'd met in Fatso's Bar, down the road from the go-go bars of Nana Plaza. Nigel was a good-looking guy with a shock of black unruly hair and a movie-star smile and a pirate's eye-patch. First time I met him I thought he was wearing it as a joke and I kept teasing him about it, but then it turns out that he lost an eye when he was a teenager. Stupid accident, he says, climbing through a barbed-wire fence on his parents farm. He's got a false eye but he still wears the eye-patch. Reckons it gives him an air of mystery, he says. Makes him look like a prat, if you ask me.

It was Nigel's idea to go to Zombie. It was one of the hottest bars in Bangkok, he said. It was my first time, I'd only been in Bangkok for two days, and I hadn't known what to expect. It was an eye-opener. Two raised dance floors, each with more than a dozen beautiful girls dancing around silver poles. Most of them naked. Around the edge of the bars were small tables, and waitresses in white blouses and black skirts scurried around taking orders and serving drinks.

'She's beautiful, isn't she?' I said to Nigel as the girl walked by holding the bald guy's hand.

'They're all beautiful,' he said, winking at a girl on the stage.

'No, that one's special,' I said. 'And I don't just mean the boots.'

Nigel drank his Singha beer from the bottle and wiped his mouth with the back of his hand. 'Pete, let me give you a bit of advice. From the horse's mouth. They're all hookers. Every one of them. Pay their barfines, take them to a short-time hotel, screw your brains out, then pay them. But whatever you do, don't get involved. Trust me, it's not worth it.'

I watched the girl and her customer disappear through the curtain that covered the exit to the plaza.

I asked Nigel how it worked, how you got to go out with one of the girls. He explained how the barfine system worked. You paid the money to the bar—it varied between four hundred baht and six hundred baht depending on which bar you were in, and the girl was then free to leave with you. What you did was pretty much up to you, but usually a customer would take the girl to one of the numerous short-time hotels within walking distance of the plaza. How much you paid the girl depended on what she did and how generous you were, it could be as little as five hundred baht, as much as two thousand baht, more if you wanted to spend the whole night with her.

Nigel waved at the two stages, crammed with girls. 'Go on, pick one,' he said.

I shook my head. There was no one there I wanted.